D0921779

679
BIE
V 2

VANCOUVER SHORT STORIES

Vancouver Museums & Planetarium Ass'n. Gift Shop

VANCOUVER
SHORT STORIES

EDITED BY CAROLE GERSON

UNIVERSITY OF BRITISH COLUMBIA PRESS
VANCOUVER 1985

Vancouver Short Stories

© The University of British Columbia Press, 1985

The publication of this book has been made possible with the help of grants from the Vancouver Centennial Commission and the Canada Council.

Canadian Cataloguing in Publication Data

Main entry under title:

Vancouver short stories

ISBN 0-7748-0228-6

1. Short stories, Canadian (English)* 2. Canadian fiction (English)—20th century.* 3. Vancouver (B.C.) —Fiction. I. Gerson, Carole.
PS8323.V3V36 1985   C813'.01'083271133
PR9197.32.V36 1985   C85-091229-6

Printed in Canada

ISBN 0-7748-0228-6

For Daniel and Rebekah

Acknowledgements

We wish to thank the following authors for permission to reprint their stories: George Bowering, Wayson Choy, Frances Duncan, Cynthia Flood, Joy Kogawa, Sky Lee, Dorothy Livesay, William McConnell, Alice Munro, Kevin Roberts, Audrey Thomas, and Gabriel Szohner. Mrs. Cherry Whitaker kindly gave permission to reprint Bertrand Sinclair's story.

We would also like to thank Clarke, Irwin & Co. for permission to reprint Emily Carr's story, Lester & Orpen Dennys Publishers for use of the selection from Joy Kogawa's *Obasan*, Literistic Ltd. and Margerie Bonner Lowry for Malcolm Lowry's story, McClelland & Stewart for the stories by George Bowering and M.A. Grainger, and the University of British Columbia Library for the Ethel Wilson story. It was not possible to locate descendants of Francis Owen or Jean Burton.

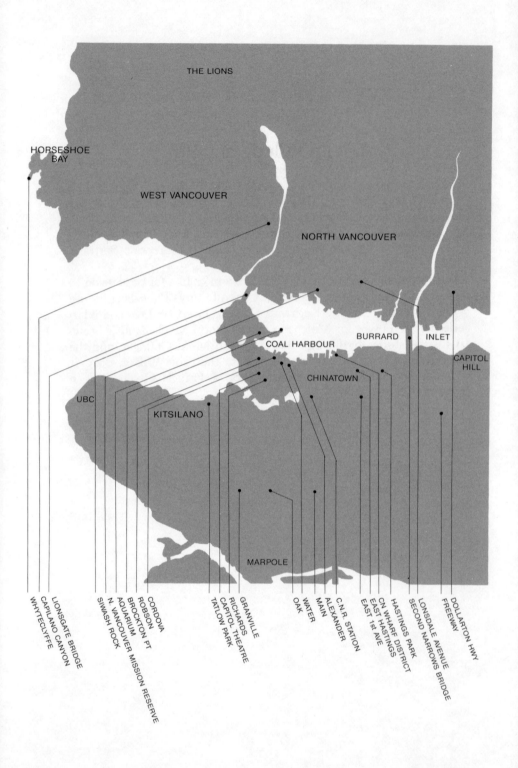

THE LIONS

HORSESHOE
BAY

WEST VANCOUVER

NORTH VANCOUVER

BURRARD   INLET

COAL HARBOUR

CAPITOL
HILL

CHINATOWN

UBC

KITSILANO

MARPOLE

WHYTECLYFFE
CAPILANO CANYON
LIONSGATE BRIDGE
SIWASH ROCK
N. VANCOUVER MISSION RESERVE
AQUARIUM
BROCKTON PT
ROBSON
CORDOVA
TATLOW PARK
CAPITOL THEATRE
RICHARDS
GRANVILLE
OAK
WATER
MAIN
ALEXANDER
C.N.R. STATION
EAST 1st AVE
EAST HASTINGS
CN WHARF DISTRICT
HASTINGS PARK
LONSDALE AVENUE
SECOND NARROWS BRIDGE
FREEWAY
DOLLARTON HWY

CONTENTS

INTRODUCTION

The first writing in English about the place now known as Vancouver appeared in 1792, when Captain George Vancouver recorded in his journal the naming of Point Grey, Point Atkinson, and Burrard Inlet (his original word was "canal") after friends and associates in the Royal Navy. The first appearance of the city of Vancouver in fiction may well be in Sara Jeannette Duncan's travel novel, A Social Departure (1890), which describes Vancouver two years after it was incorporated in 1886. In this book, a demure young Englishwoman who is accustomed to municipalities "with at least three centuries of blue mould upon them" pronounces the young metropolis "an infant prodigy."[1] So delighted is she with its boomtown vitality that during her brief visit she sheds her customary restraint, joins in the favourite local pastime of real estate speculation, and departs with a handsome profit.

During Vancouver's adolescence, cultural matters were not a priority. One of the city's first literary landmarks was Pauline Johnson's Legends of Vancouver (1911), a slim volume of Indian stories written down by the popular part-Mohawk poet shortly after she moved here. Two of these legends, which endow the landscape with mythic associations, appear in this collection of short stories set in Vancouver. The early 1900s are also represented by Martin Allerdale Grainger's "In Vancouver," a realistic description of loggers' activities on Cordova Street, and Francis Owen's "The Prophetess," an intriguing account of the great Vancouver fire of 1886, which razed the fledgling city just two months after it received its charter. Interesting as they may be, these early pieces represent only sporadic moments of inspiration. Grainger wrote just one creative work relating to Vancouver; Pauline Johnson's reputation had already been made before she retired here; and Owen's entire literary output apparently consists of this single story.

Between the wars, Vancouver began to assert its validity as a location for literature. In 1919 and 1920 The British Columbia Monthly published Robert Watson's amusing series of sketches titled "The Canadianization of Sam MacPhail," and several years later Bertrand Sinclair and Jean Burton discovered that Vancouver's social and economic life offered interesting material for realistic fiction. Major events during the Depression and the Second World War were documented in poetry by Dorothy Livesay and in fiction by Irene Baird, whose powerful novel, *Waste Heritage* (1939), vividly recounts the plight of the unemployed and their occupation of the Vancouver Post Office. Towards the end of the 1930s a literary community emerged as writers began to meet in formal and informal gatherings and in association with Alan Crawley's important magazine, *Contemporary Verse,* which began publication in North Vancouver in 1940. Of the better known writers of this era, Dorothy Livesay, Malcolm Lowry, and William McConnell appear in *Vancouver Short Stories.* Irene Baird, unfortunately, did not write any pieces suitable for inclusion, nor did Earle Birney, who studied at the University of British Columbia during the 1920s and returned to live in Vancouver in 1948. In his novel, *Down the Long Table* (1955), his verse-play, *Trial of a City* (1952), and many short and longer poems like "Vancouver Lights" and "November Walk at False Creek Mouth," Birney substantially enhanced the literary identity of Vancouver as a complex city whose symbolic dimension is enriched by its proximity to the mountains and the sea. A later writer who is also omitted — with great editorial regret — is Margaret Laurence. An accomplished writer of short stories and the author of three fine novels with Vancouver settings, Laurence has nowhere married these two interests in a story about Vancouver.

Of all the writers who have contributed to this book, Ethel Wilson enjoyed the longest and perhaps most intimate association with Vancouver. Brought here in 1898 at the age of ten, she grew up with the city and transformed that experience into the genial fiction of *The Innocent Traveller* (1949). Her involvement in local cultural life began in the first decade of the century when she met Pauline Johnson and studied painting with Emily Carr (whose ability as an artist was matched by her literary talent, as demonstrated by "Sophie," included here). During the thirty years that Wilson devoted to serious writing, her tone of sophisticated irony never dampened her enthusiasm for the city's spectacular natural setting.

The greatest problem encountered in compiling a book of Vancouver short stories with an historical perspective is that for the first seventy-five years of Vancouver's existence there is too little material, and for the last twenty-five there is too much. By the mid-1960s, Vancouver had become a hive of literary activity. Through the magazines *Tish* (1961–69) and *Prism International* (founded in 1959) emerged many prominent figures of the literary avant-garde, while the scholarly quarterly, *Canadian Literature* (also founded in 1959), spurred academic interest in Canadian writing. In 1965, further stimulus was added by the establishment of Canada's first university Department (as distinct from a program) of Creative Writing at the University of British Columbia, and by the founding of Simon Fraser University. The latter's English Department, which has included poets, playwrights, and novelists, publishes the *West Coast Review*. Other enduring Vancouver area periodicals which have encouraged local writers include *The Canadian Fiction Magazine* (founded in 1971 and moved to Toronto in 1979) and *The Capilano Review* (founded in 1972). In recent years, with the growth of the women's movement, women writers have found support in the feminist periodicals *Room of One's Own* (founded in 1974) and *Makara* (1975–78), and in the West Coast Women and Words Society. So abundant has been the literary output of the Vancouver region that an anthology like *Vancouver Short Stories* can offer only a sampling of the fiction of the past two decades.

This book is not a collection of Vancouver authors, but of Vancouver short stories, chosen because they highlight facets of the city's social history and literary development. Their chronological arrangement according to the date of first publication (or, in the case of Sinclair and Lowry, presumed composition) provides an overview of Vancouver's past and present which is both colourful and selective. Among the city's more distinctive events and characteristics which appear in these particular stories are the great fire of 1886, Vancouver's role in the logging industry, Prohibition rum-running, the Great Depression, the internment of the Japanese, the Chinese community, and the hippie era.

These stories also illustrate some of the narrative approaches adopted by Vancouver writers over a span of eight decades. At the same time that Grainger produced his coolly realistic account of turn-of-the-century loggers, Francis Owen was casting a romantic eye over Vancouver's unforgettable first summer. Before Emily Carr developed a lean literary style reflecting the selective eye of the visual artist, Bertrand Sinclair united his ability to spin exciting adventure tales with his intimate knowledge of the local coastline. Modern writers have rejected the sentimentality of Pauline Johnson in favour of the ironic tone suggested by Jean Burton in the 1920s. In the hands of some authors, like George Bowering and Kevin Roberts, the style becomes almost elliptical, requiring careful attention from the reader. Other writers concentrate on evoking mood and character, frequently bringing the reader into intimate contact with the personal, inner experiences of specific individuals. Each of these modes speaks to a particular audience, and contributes to our view of the city.

What, then, do these stories tell us about Vancouver? To begin with, they illustrate Robert Kroetsch's dictum that "The fiction makes us real." Kroetsch explained that "We haven't got an identity until somebody tells our story,"[2] to which Rudy Wiebe recently added,

"The true writer writes her people, her place, into existence."[3] For we have a deeper understanding of where we live and how we live there when our artists have created a vision with which we can identify. Just as the Group of Seven has shaped the way we see the Laurentian Shield and Emily Carr has given us recognizable images of the West Coast, our fiction writers present insightful versions of our social landscape. Margaret Atwood has said that

A piece of art, as well as being a creation to be enjoyed, can also be . . . a mirror. The reader looks at the mirror and sees not the writer but himself; and behind his own image in the foreground, a reflection of the world he lives in. If a country or a culture lacks such mirrors, it has no way of knowing what it looks like; it must travel blind.[4]

The same holds true for a city; its identity is created by and reflected in its art and literature, and until its citizens know these works, they lack authentic knowledge of themselves and the place they inhabit.

One of the first things we learn from Vancouver writers is that the city is inseparable from its setting, whose mountains and ocean suggest a potential expansion of the human spirit beyond the petty materialism of common urban life. Most of the stories in this book propose that people living here cannot fail to be affected by their proximity to the Coast Range and the sea, a combination especially enjoyed by Ethel Wilson's Mrs. Gormley when she stops the taxi for "ten cents' worth of view." As her eyes sweep the horizon, she briefly revels in "nearly all the glory of the world and no despair." Unlike most large cities, Vancouver has not yet lost the possibility of harmony with its natural environment, a harmony evoked in Wilson's panoramic vista, or in Harry Eldridge's involvement with his backyard birds in Cynthia Flood's story, or in the lifelong connection between William McConnell's unnamed man and his neighbourhood park. It is felt just as strongly on the North Shore, where Frances Duncan recreates the intense physical and emotional sensations of a child's contact with the forest and the sea, and where Malcolm Lowry's symbolically named Sigbjørn Wilderness, while ranting at the spoliation of the terrain by developers, can still find "a kind of hope" in "the cool silver rainy twilight of the forest."

In relation to the Native Indians, however, Vancouver appears less benign, and is depicted as an imposition on the land. "Woe to the vile invaders! Woe to the unholy city!" intones Francis Owen's Indian prophetess, interpreting the fire of 1886 as retribution upon the defilers of the Indians' environment. More poignant is Emily Carr's account of her Indian friend, Sophie Frank, and her family of "little cemetery

mounds," victims of the white man's tuberculosis and general indifference.

Her people's negative experience of the city is shared by other characters in these stories, especially newcomers. The postcard version of
Vancouver – skyline, shoreline, park and garden – is denied by Gabriel
Szohner's displaced artist, whose brief encounter with an abused street
child only serves to confirm his sense of alienation. Jean Burton's story
of a similarly victimized young woman also presents Vancouver as a
big city where exploitation and destruction await the innocent. In Dorothy Livesay's anecdote of the Depression, the bleakness of the city,
which provides no refuge for the destitute, underscores the futility of
their struggle; while Kevin Robert introduces us to the crude night
world of barroom brawls and drug deals through the eyes of a young
Australian visitor.

As some of these stories demonstrate, the complexity of the city's
amalgam of economic and ethnic enclaves can intensify problems of
domestic life. Both Sky Lee and Alice Munro detail the effects of
phases of Vancouver's social history upon specific families. The tone of
Munro's narrative, uttered by a working-class woman whose brother
joins an arcane Kitsilano sect, is amusing; that of Sky Lee's story of
inter-generational conflict within a Chinese family is more serious. A
Vancouver childhood may be warm and delightful if spent in Wayson
Choy's secure Chinese community or at Frances Duncan's Dollarton
shack, but not for a child who suffers the traumatic upheaval caused by
the unjust internment of all Japanese-Canadians in 1942. Joy Kogawa's
depiction of young Nomi's bewilderment translates the abstract sense
of threat and alienation that frequently characterizes literary depic-
tions of the city into the actual displacement of citizens who are
ejected from their rightful homes.

While many of the stories in this book draw upon specific aspects of
this city's social history, the Vancouver setting of others illustrates
that sexual and social relations can be as thorny here as anywhere else.
Writers like William McConnell, Ethel Wilson, Audrey Thomas, and
George Bowering express their characters' conflicts and concerns in
the context of specific local images. Their choices may puzzle newcomers to the city, who may not recognize McConnell's setting as Tatlow Park in Kitsilano, Bowering's as the University of British Columbia, or Thomas's as the Vancouver Aquarium with its now-deceased
star performer, Skana the killer whale. And they might not appreciate
the way a story like Cynthia Flood's, which contains few actual place
names, captures the texture of everyday Vancouver life. To assist the
reader with a taste for geography, a map identifying the locales of the
stories has been included. xv

The occasion of this book is the one hundredth anniversary of the in-corporation of the City of Vancouver. Hence its publication is a cele-bration of the past, but even more, it is a gesture towards the future. Poised almost on the edge of the continent, Vancouver has tradition-ally been a destination for the westward-bound idealist or escapist, as well as for the adventurer who shares the sentiment expressed by Sara Jeannette Duncan in 1890 that "There is a satisfaction difficult to parallel in getting as far as you can go."[5] The city has now matured; it is no longer seen as the end of the line but as Canada's entrance to the new economic zone of the Pacific Rim. And it retains the optimism that thrilled Ethel Wilson's irrepressible Topaz Edgeworth at the turn of the century when the city's new slogan—"In nineteen ten, Vancou-ver then, Will have one hundred thousand men"—promoted her to exclaim, "...fancy that, one hundred thousand men! I wonder if that includes women and children! *There's* a slogan for you!"[6]

If, as many artists have said, the impulse to create art arises from a desire to repudiate mortality, then perhaps the act of writing in and about a place like Vancouver is doubly an act of faith in the future—the future of this particular place, and the future of our troubled planet.

Few books represent solely the work of one person, and a collection like this one depends upon the contributions of many. I would like to express my gratitude to all those whose advice and insights have aided in the preparation of this book. Linda Hale, Bill New, Anne Yandle, Laurenda Daniells, Victor Hopwood, Carole Itter, Margaret Wadding-ton, Anne Marriott, Marya Hardman, William McConnell, and Kathy Mezei are some of the many generous individuals who took the time to answer my queries and share their knowledge. I am also indebted to my editor, Jane Fredeman, who guided this project from an embryonic proposal to a fully-developed book, and to Martin, my domestic assistant and general consultant. Above all, I must thank the writers themselves, to whom this book is a tribute.

Notes

1. Sara Jeannette Duncan, *A Social Departure. How Orthodocia and I Went Around the World By Ourselves* (London: Chatto, 1890), p. 51.

2. Robert Kroetsch, "A Conversation with Margaret Laurence," in *creation,* ed. Robert Kroetsch (Toronto: new press, 1970), p. 63.

3. Rudy Wiebe, "On Death and Writing," *Canadian Literature,* No. 100 (Spring, 1984), p. 358.

4. Margaret Atwood, *Survival: A Thematic Guide to Canadian Literature* (Toronto: Anansi, 1972), pp. 15–16.

5. Duncan, p. 51.

6. Ethel Wilson, *The Innocent Traveller* (Toronto: Macmillan, 1959), p. 126.

Note on the Text

For most of the stories, the copytext has been the first version to appear in book form, usually in a collection of short stories by the author. Some of the pieces which appeared only in periodicals have received silent editorial correction, and Jean Burton's story has been shortened by two paragraphs. The stories by Frances Duncan and Joy Kogawa include emendations supplied by the authors.

THE PROPHETESS

FRANCIS OWEN

My friend Weston and I were among the first to hear the call of the Golden West and to trust our future in the hands of the guardian spirit. Those were the days of the pioneer, the real pioneer, not the settler of today who is rushed at the speed of thirty miles an hour through the rocky solitude of the Superior District, on over the bound-less prairies, "the gardens of the desert," and then again through the serried rolls of snow-capped mountains, by the brink of yawning chasms, beneath frowning bluffs and over winding rivers to the wave-washed shore of the Pacific Coast. Travelling is a pleasure now-a-days—no long, weary walks, no jolting over stony roads, no camping among the lonely mountains with the cries of coyotes and hungry wolves ringing in your ears.

At the time of which I speak the C.P.R. was in the process of con-struction and, in spite of almost insurmountable difficulties, had hewed its way through countless walls of rock, until finally, arrived at Port Moody, it only remained to lay the foundations of its Western Ter-minal, Vancouver, the present Queen City of the West, but which then had only a few thousand inhabitants—daring adventurers who had braved the perils of an unknown land to carry the standard of Western civilization to the barren regions of the Pacific Coast. The bulk of the city clustered around Cordova and Water streets, stretch-ing out on one side toward Hastings' saw-mill and on the other as far as any speculator wished to go, which was not very far. Back of this sec-tion to False Creek, where now stand hundreds of smiling homes and pretty lawns, was bush and brush, a tangled mess of fallen trees that crossed each other in hopeless intricacy, partially charred and check-ered by fires, which had raged and laid low the monarchs of the forest, but leaving a horde of smaller trees which looked like a sea of needles, with thin sharp points rising high in the air, and their weird, leafless branches protruding like thorns from their sides. Large gangs of work-

This story first appeared in Westward Ho! *magazine in 1907.*

men were employed by the C.P.R. clearing this land and making ready for the laying of a roadbed to the water front.

Weston and I had been attracted by the high wages offered by the Company to surveyors and we had followed the progress of the line nearly all the way through the mountains. At this particular time we were in Vancouver and were quartered in a three-story wooden structure on Alexander street, which we made our base of supplies for the extensive journeys we were often compelled to make. The weather had been hot and dry, scorching hot; we felt ourselves shrinking perceptibly every day, and our health began to be impaired. As we had been working steady for several months without a rest, Weston proposed one day that we go for a few weeks' shooting in the mountains, adding by way of further inducement that we might run across a good gold proposition in our ramblings. For three weeks we fished, hunted and prospected along the Fraser river, thoroughly enjoying the bracing mountain atmosphere and the beautiful scenery of the Canadian Alps. But the lonely life at last began to tell upon our spirits. Not a living soul but Indians had crossed our paths during all this time and we began to long for the joys of companionship.

It was on a Saturday night, I remember it as distinctly as if it were yesterday, and we had decided to go down the river the following day on our homeward journey. We had gone for a last excursion among the mountains about two miles away from our camp. The sun was just setting; a crimson glow suffused the sky; the twilight blushed; the silver gems of the snow-capped peaks became golden with the sunset flush; the rushing streams seemed to allay their headlong course to be caressed by the lingering sunbeams, which left a purple hue upon the dancing waters, turning them into streams of gold; the birds spread out their wings to catch the radiance of the setting sun and warbled their evening songs of happiness and peace.

We were standing beside a clump of stunted trees which had climbed as far up the mountain side as their small strength would allow and had been forced to stop half way, whence they could see below them the sturdy heads of their stronger brethren, and far above the dwarfed statures of smaller but more daring and hardier adventurers who had scaled the slope even to the snow-line, but there had stopped, repulsed by the cool reception of the aerial spirits. We stood gazing at the glory of the sunset, lost for the moment in the grandeur and nobility of the eternal, fascinated by the varied shades of color, and the succession of changes from silver through all the mutations of gold and crimson to a deep purple hue as if the blood of battling spirits had stained the sky. Suddenly an apparition darted from behind the trees, sprang upon a projecting rock, raised a skinny arm and pointed toward the setting sun. It was the form of a woman. Her face was wild and

2

haggard and her Indian features tanned still swarthier by exposure to the sun. Large coal-black masses of tangled hair fell over her naked shoulders. Her eyes were weird and roaming, and flashed at times like diamonds in the night. Her only covering was a garment of leaves intertwined so as to cover her emaciated form and angular body. Tall and commanding in appearance, she rose to her full height, threw back the matted locks from her wrinkled brow, and with one hand still indicating the sea of fire in the West, she slowly raised the other arm and with a look of inextinguishable hatred pointed in the direction of Vancouver. With extended arms and trembling body, in piercing tones that penetrated the very stones in the intensity of their passion, she hurled forth her denunciation: "Woe to the vile intruders! woe to the impious city! The fires of wrath shall descend upon their guilty heads. They shall flee before my anger, they shall hide and cower when I spurn them with my vengeance!"

"See these valleys and these mountains," continued the forboding spectre, comprising with one sweep of her extended arms the whole district around her, "they were the home of my people, the hunting ground of my tribe; the land of the red man. They lived and laughed; they basked in the sun; they hunted and they fished; they died in the land of their fathers. But the vile intruder came. He came with his internal devils that scared the fish from the rivers, that shivered the hills to fragments, that filled the mountain streams and hewed down our sacred trees. They drove us before them like sheep and we starved among the rocks."

She ceased, buried her face in her bony hands and wept bitterly. Then as if here grief inspired her with renewed hatred, "Look at me," she screamed. "look at my withered face, my skinny arms and emaciated form. Once I was fair, once I was beautiful, once I was loved. The idol of my people. I lived like a Queen. I was the Queen of the mountains, the mistress of the valleys; the fish came at my call and the birds obeyed my voice. That was before the white fiends came and disturbed our solitudes with their unholy noises and their fire devils. Woe to the vile invaders! Woe to the unholy city!"

With these last words, uttered in a perfect crescendo of emotion, she pointed once more to the ground, muttering to herself: "Three weeks! three weeks!" The ghostly phantom vanished behind the trees with a dismal howl.

As soon as we could recover from our astonishment we darted behind the bushes to see where she had gone, but there was no trace of the strange creature to be seen. She had vanished as quickly as she had come.

Silently we proceeded toward our camp, as the darkness was falling fast. Weston was the first to speak. "I wonder what she meant," he

3

said. "I don't think I am superstitious, but—I've heard of strange things happening sometimes."

"Oh, nonsense!" I replied, "she is only a poor, crazy Indian. There are lots of them around. Something has turned her brain."

"I suppose you're right," he said, but did not look satisfied.

When we reached our camp we lit a cheerful fire, had some supper and then sat down beside 'the blaze to enjoy a smoke. Under the soothing influence of my pipe and the ruddy glow of the fire, my thoughts went back to my distant home. Familiar scenes flashed through my mind; old friends and loved ones peered at me from the mazy wreaths of smoke. I was startled from my reverie by Weston's voice: "I say," he said, "haven't you heard that the Indians place a great deal of confidence in these wild women. They believe them to be inspired, to have the gift of prophecy, oracles in fact?"

"Still thinking of that," I replied impatiently. "I don't believe any of that rot. There never was anything in it and never will be. How can a poor, crazy woman know what's going to happen?"

"Well," said Weston slowly, "I'm not saying that she does know or that she can do anything, but you know that many people claim to have intimations of the future. 'Coming events cast their shadow before them' is an old saying, you know."

"Yes," I replied, "it is old, that's the trouble with it. It's too old."

"Perhaps," was all the answer he made.

I dismissed the matter from my mind and supposed he did the same, for he didn't mention it again. We turned in for the night, and slept the sleep of the mountain climber.

The next morning we packed up and started for town, glad to get back again, even though it meant hard work and long hours. We arrived at Vancouver without any further adventures and found everything in motion. All was hurry and bustle. The work of clearing the land had proceeded rapidly in our absence and scores of huge piles of logs and rubbish lay waiting for the match.

It was Saturday night again, just three weeks after our unearthly visitor of the mountains. I had noticed that Weston had been very quiet all that day, but the reason for it had never entered my head. I left him for the night about 10 o'clock in the evening and went to my room. I tried to sleep but could not; all sorts of things came crowding on my brain. I rolled over and over; I tried every possible expedient to induce the god of sleep to close my eyes, but it was of no avail. Finally I got up, and, knowing that Weston often sat up late at night reading, I crept softly down the hall to his room, opened the door and peeped in. There he was, sitting beside the table, his elbows resting on the edge, and his head supported by his hands. A book lay near him which he had evidently been reading. He did not hear me open the door.

4

"Hello!" I said.

He never moved. I approached him noiselessly and gently touched him on the shoulder.

"Good heavens," he cried, springing up with a terrified expression on his face.

"What's the matter," I asked.

"Oh, it's you!" he exclaimed. "I thought you were asleep."

"And I thought you were," I replied.

"What, what on earth is the matter with you?"

"The prophetess," he whispered hoarsely. "It is three weeks today. Did you not notice the sunset tonight? It was as red as blood. The sky seemed to be on fire. She was there. I saw her."

"Come! come! what nonsense!" I exclaimed. "Are you going to let a little thing like that keep you awake?"

"Why couldn't you sleep?" he asked, turning round sharply.

"I don't know, the heat perhaps."

"I do," he answered as he sat down and motioned me to do the same.

"I'll tell you what," he continued after a moment's silence. "I'm going to pack my few things tonight so that if anything should happen...."

"You're a fool," I snapped.

"Perhaps I am," he replied calmly. "I hope I am in this case, but I'd rather be a living fool than a dead sage."

"Why," I cried, "that blessed old Indian has forgotten the whole affair by this time!"

"After we came back to town," Weston rejoined, as he began to pack his things in a small trunk, "I made inquiries about the woman among the Indians. They were very reticent, but I finally learned that she had been a noted personage among the tribes of this district, but owing to an unfortunate alliance she had had with a white trapper who had treated her harshly and then deserted her, she has ever since dwelt alone among the mountains. Her mind became unhinged, and her people regard her with awe and veneration." He had by this time finished packing. "There," he said, "I hope you are right, but I couldn't sleep until I had done that."

I was awakened the next morning by a loud shouting on the street. Wondering what was the matter, I arose, looked at my watch and found to my surprise that it was 11 o'clock. I opened the window and looked out. A fearful sight met my eyes. People were hurrying and running in all directions with spades, shovels, axes and buckets. A huge roll of fire was advancing upon the little town, driven on by a strong west wind. An indefinable dread thrilled me. "The prophetess," unconsciously escaped my lips. I hurried out to the scene of the fire and found that the men had been ordered early in the morning to set fire to the large piles of rubbish. No one had thought there was any danger.

All at once a strong wind had arisen, had fanned the flames to fury and whirled them from one pile to another, closer and closer to the outlying houses. The wind increased and poured its vials of wrath upon the devouring flames, sending long fiery streams and serpentine coils hundreds of feet into the air, ever reaching forward toward the town as if eager to try its uncurbed strength upon the unprotected wooden structures that lay clustered in a heap. Dense volumes of burning smoke obscured the sun and fired the heavens. On swept the seething mass towards the city in eddies and whirls that looked like a sea of serpents twisting and twining their coils around each other. Frail houses disappeared in the twinkling of an eye. A fierce crackling, a cloud of smoke, and then the fiery demons passed on, leaving the charred ruins behind to mark their path. The frantic people fled from the houses in every direction, crazed with fear yet fascinated by the aweful spectacle of destruction.

The fire had eaten its way to the water front when suddenly the wind veered to the northeast and the whole cloud of fire started on its path of annihilation in a new direction. Down Alexander street it rushed, licking up the rows of houses as if they had been paper. I thought of my few possessions in my room, but it was too late to save them. I found Weston standing in speechless terror, pointing with trembling hand to the roof of the house.

"The prophetess," he finally gasped.

There was the wild woman of the mountains, with her long black hair streaming in the wind, her tall form reflecting the glow of the approaching flames, her weird eyes gleaming like burning balls, waving her long arms in wild gesticulation at the fire, her body swaying to and fro as if keeping time to the withering advance of the snake-like tongues of blood, and mute as her native mountains. Instinctively I started for the house to save the poor creature from a fearful death, but Weston seized my arm.

"Too late," he whispered hoarsely, and pointed to the rolling flames which were rushing upon the house in a perfect maelstrom. I looked again at the woman. Once more she had extended her long arms, one towards the west and the other toward the burning city.

"Woe to the vile invaders! Woe to the impious city!" she shrieked in a voice that was heard above the roar and crackling of the blaze, and then the sea of fire received her in its coils.

"The prophetess!" cried Weston, and fell to the ground in a death-like swoon.

IN VANCOUVER

MARTIN ALLERDALE GRAINGER

As you walk down Cordova Street in the city of Vancouver you notice a gradual change in the appearance of the shop windows. The shoe
stores, drug stores, clothing stores, phonograph stores cease to bother
you with their blinding light. You see fewer goods fit for a bank clerk or
a man in business; you leave "high tone" behind you.

You come to shops that show faller's axes, swamper's axes – single-
bitted, double-bitted; screw jacks and pump jacks, wedges, sledge-ham-
mers, and great seven-foot saws with enormous shark teeth, and huge
augers for boring boomsticks, looking like properties from a pantomime
workshop.

Leckie calls attention to his logging boots, whose bristling spikes are
guaranteed to stay in. Clarke exhibits his Wet Proof Peccary Hogskin
gloves, that will save your hands when you work with wire ropes.
Dungaree trousers are shown to be copper-riveted at places where a
man strains them in working. Then there are oilskins and blankets and
rough suits of frieze for winter wear, and woollen mitts.

Outside the shop windows, on the pavement in the street, there is a
change in the people too. You see few women. Men look into the windows; men drift up and down the street; men lounge in groups upon
the curb. Your eye is struck at once by the unusual proportion of big
men in the crowds, men that look powerful even in their town clothes.

Many of these fellows are faultlessly dressed: very new boots, new
black clothes of quality, superfine black shirt, black felt hat. A few
wear collars.

Others are in rumpled clothes that have been slept in; others, again,
in old suits and sweaters; here and there one in dungarees and working
boots. You are among loggers.

They are passing time, passing the hours of the day of their trip to
town. They chew tobacco, and chew and chew and expectorate, and
look across the street and watch any moving thing. At intervals they

This story was originally published as the first chapter of Grainger's *Woodsmen of the West* (1908).

will exchange remarks impassively; or stand grouped, hands in pockets, two or three men together in gentle, long-drawn-out conversations. They seem to feel the day is passing slowly; they have the air of ocean passengers who watch the lagging clock from mealtime to mealtime with weary effort. For comfort it seems they have divided the long day into reasonable short periods; at the end of each 'tis "time to comean-avadrink." You overhear the invitations as you pass.

Now, as you walk down street, you see how shops are giving place to saloons and restaurants, and the price of beer decorates each building's front. And you pass the blackboards of employment offices and read chalked thereon:

50 axemen wanted at Alberni
5 rigging slingers $4
buckers $3½, swampers $3.

And you look into the public rooms of hotels that are flush with the street as they were shop windows; and men sit there watching the passing crowd, chairs tipped back, and feet on window-frame, spittoons handy.

You hear a shout or two and noisy laughter, and walk awhile outside the curb, giving wide berth to a group of men scuffling with one another in alcohol-inspired play. They show activity.

Then your eye catches the name-board of a saloon, and you remember a paragraph in the morning's paper—

In a row last night at the Terminus Saloon several men...

and it occurs to you that the chucker-out of a loggers' saloon must be a man "highly qualified."

The *Cassiar* sails from the wharf across the railway yard Mondays and Thursdays 8 p.m. It's only a short step from the Gold House and the Terminus and the other hotels, and a big bunch of the boys generally comes down to see the boat off.

You attend a sort of social function. You make a pleasing break in the monotony of drifting up the street to the Terminus and down the street to the Eureka, and having a drink with the crowd in the Columbia bar, and standing drinks to the girls at number so-and-so Dupont Street—the monotony that makes up your holiday in Vancouver. Besides, if you are a *woodsman* you will see fellow aristocrats who are going north to jobs: you maintain your elaborate knowledge of what is going on in the woods and where every one is; and, further, you know that in many a hotel and logging-camp up the coast new arrivals from town will shortly be mentioning, casual-like: "Jimmy Jones was down to the wharf night before last. Been blowing-her-in in great shape has

8

Jimmy, round them saloons. Guess he'll be broke and hunting a job in about another week, the pace he's goin' now."

You have informed the *Morning Post*!

If logging is but the chief among your twenty trades and profes-sions—if you are just the ordinary western *logger*—still the north-going *Cassiar* has great interest for you. Even your friend Tennessee, who would hesitate whether to say telegraph operator or carpenter if you ask him his business suddenly—even he may want to keep watch over the way things are going in the logging world.

So you all hang around on the wharf and see who goes on board, and where they're going to, and what wages they hired on at. And perhaps you'll help a perfect stranger to get himself and two bottle of whisky (by way of baggage) up the gang plank; and help throw Mike M'Curdy into the cargo-room, and his blankets after him.

Then the *Cassiar* pulls out amid cheers and shouted messages, and you return up town to make a round of the bars, and you laugh once in a while to find some paralysed passenger whom friends had forgotten to put aboard. . . . And so to bed.

The first thing a fellow needs when he hits Vancouver is a clean-up: haircut, shave, and perhaps a bath. Then he'll want a new hat for sure. The suit of town clothes that, stuffed into the bottom of a canvas bag, has travelled around with him for weeks or months—sometimes wet-ted in rowboats, sometimes crumpled into a seat or pillow—the suit may be too shabby. So a fellow will feel the wad of bills in his pocket and decide whether it's worth getting a new suit or not.

The next thing is to fix on a stopping-place. Some men take a fifty-cent room in a rooming-house and feed in the restaurants. The great objection to that is the uncertainty of getting home at night. In boom times I have known men of a romantic disposition who took lodgings in those houses where champagne is kept on the premises and where there is a certain society. But that means frenzied finance, and this time you and I are not going to play the fool and blow in our little stake same as we did last visit to Vancouver.

So a fellow can't do better than go to a good, respectable hotel where he knows the proprietor and the bartenders, and where there are some decent men stopping. Then he knows he will be looked after when he is drunk; and getting drunk, he will not be distressed by spasms of anx-iety lest someone should go through his pockets and leave him broke. There are some shady characters in a town like Vancouver, and per-sons of the underworld.

Of course, the first two days in a town a man will get good-and-drunk. That is all right, as any doctor will tell you; that is good for a fellow after hard days and weeks of work in the woods.

But you and I are no drinking men, and we stop there and sober up. We sit round the stove in the hotel and read the newspapers, and discuss Roosevelt, and the Trusts, and Socialism, and Japanese immigration; and we tell yarns and talk logs. We sit at the window and watch the street. The hotel bar is in the next room, and we rise once in a while and take a party in to "haveadrink." The bartender is a good fellow, one of the boys: he puts up the drinks himself, and we feel the hospitality of it. We make a genial group. Conversation will be about loggers and logs, of course, but in light anecdotal vein, with loud bursts of laughter...

Now one or two of the friends you meet are on the bust; ceaselessly setting-up the drinks, insisting that everybody drink with them. I am not "drinking" myself: I take a cigar and fade away. But you stay; politeness and good fellowship demand that you should join each wave that goes up to the bar, and when good men are spending money you would be mean not to spend yours too...

Pretty soon you feel the sweet reasonableness of it all. A hardworking man should indemnify himself for past hardships. He owes it to himself to have a hobby of some kind. You indulge a hobby for whisky.

About this time it is well to hand over your roll of bills to Jimmy Ross, the proprietor. Then you don't have to bother with money any more: you just wave your hand each time to the bartender. *He* will keep track of what you spend...

Now you are fairly on the bust: friends all round you, good boys all. Some are hard up, and you tell Jimmy to give them five or ten dollars; and "Gimme ten or twenty," you'll say, "I want to take a look round the saloons"—which you do with a retinue.

The great point now is never to let yourself get sober. You'll feel awful sick if you do. By keeping good-and-drunk you keep joyous. "Look bad but feel good" is sound sentiment. Even suppose you were so drunk last night that Bob Doherty knocked the stuffing out of you in the Eureka bar, and you have a rankling feeling that your reputation as a fighting man has suffered somewhat—still, never mind, line up, boys; whisky for mine: let her whoop, and to hell with care! Yah-hurrup and smash the glass!!

If you are "acquainted" with Jimmy Ross—that is to say, if you have blown in one or two cheques before at his place, and if he knows you as a competent woodsman—Jimmy will just reach down in his pocket and lend you fives and tens after your own money is all gone. In this way you can keep on the bust a little longer, and ease off gradually—keeping pace with Jimmy's growing disinclination to lend. But sooner or later you've got to face the fact that the time has come to hunt another job.

There will be some boss loggers in town; you may have been drinking with them. Some of them perhaps will be sobering up and beginning
to remember the business that brought them to Vancouver, and to
think of their neglected camps up-coast.

Boss loggers generally want men; here are chances for you. Again,
Jimmy Ross may be acting as a sort of agent for some of the northern
logging-camps: if you're any good Jimmy may send you up to a camp.
Employment offices, of course, are below contempt – they are for men
strange to the country, incompetents, labourers, farm hands, and the
like.

You make inquiries round the saloons. In the Eureka someone introduces you to Wallace Campbell. He wants a riggin' slinger: you are a
riggin' slinger. Wallace eyes the bleary wreck you look. Long practice
tells him what sort of a man you probably are when you're in health.
He stands the drinks, hires you at four and a half, and that night you
find yourself, singing drunk, in the *Cassiar*'s saloon – on your way
north to work.

---

*MARTIN ALLERDALE GRAINGER (1874–1941) was born in Lon-
don, England, and spent much of his childhood in Australia. Restless after
an illustrious graduation from Cambridge in 1896, he sought adventure
first in the Canadian North and then in the Boer War, after which he
returned to British Columbia. His personal acquaintance with the brutal,
challenging life of the coastal hand-logger was recorded in his only book,*
Woodsmen of the West, *written in 1908 to raise the money he needed to
allow him to marry. In 1910 he began his career in the British Columbia
forest industry, writing most of the report that led to the establishment of
the B.C. Forest Service and becoming Chief Forester in 1917. In 1920 he
turned to private business. "In Vancouver" is the first chapter of* Woodsmen of the West.

THE TWO SISTERS

PAULINE JOHNSON

The Lions

You can see them as you look towards the north and the west, where the dream-hills swim into the sky amid their ever-drifting clouds of pearl and grey. They catch the earliest hint of sunrise, they hold the last colour of sunset. Twin mountains they are, lifting their twin peaks above the fairest city in all Canada, and known throughout the British Empire as "The Lions of Vancouver."

Sometimes the smoke of forest fires blurs them until they gleam like opals in a purple atmosphere, too beautiful for words to paint. Sometimes the slanting rains festoon scarves of mist about their crests, and the peaks fade into shadowy outlines, melting, melting, for ever melting into the distances. But for most days in the year the sun circles the twin glories with a sweep of gold. The moon washes them with a torrent of silver. Oftentimes, when the city is shrouded in rain, the sun yellows their snows to a deep orange; but through sun and shadow they stand immovable, smiling westward above the waters of the restless Pacific, eastward above the superb beauty of the Capilano Canyon. But the Indian tribes do not know these peaks as "The Lions." Even the chief whose feet have so recently wandered to the Happy Hunting Grounds never heard the name given them until I mentioned it to him one dreamy August day, as together we followed the trail leading to the canyon. He seemed so surprised at the name that I mentioned the reason it had been applied to them, asking him if he recalled the Landseer Lions in Trafalgar Square. Yes, he remembered those splendid sculptures, and his quick eye saw the resemblance instantly. It appeared to please him, and his fine face expressed the haunting memories of the far-away roar of Old London. But the "call of the blood" was stronger, and presently he referred to the Indian legend of those peaks—a legend that I have reason to believe is absolutely

These two stories first appeared in the Vancouver Province *in 1910 and were reprinted in Johnson's* Legends of Vancouver *in 1911.*

unknown to thousands of Pale-faces who look upon "The Lions" daily, without the love for them that is in the Indian heart, without knowledge of the secret of "The Two Sisters." The legend was intensely fascinating as it left his lips in the quaint broken English that is never so dulcet as when it slips from an Indian tongue. His inimitable gestures, strong, graceful, comprehensive, were like a perfectly chosen frame embracing a delicate painting, and his brooding eyes were as the light in which the picture hung. "Many thousands of years ago," he began, "there were no twin peaks like sentinels guarding the outposts of this sunset coast. They were placed there long after the first creation, when the Sagalie Tyee moulded the mountains, and patterned the mighty rivers where the salmon run, because of His love for His Indian children, and His wisdom for their necessities. In those times there were many and mighty Indian tribes along the Pacific – in the mountain ranges, at the shores and sources of the great Fraser River. Indian law ruled the land. Indian customs prevailed. Indian beliefs were regarded. Those were the legend-making ages when great things occurred to make the traditions we repeat to our children today. Perhaps the greatest of these traditions is the story of 'The Two Sisters,' for they are known to us as 'The Chief's Daughters,' and to them we owe the Great Peace in which we live, and have lived for many countless moons. There is an ancient custom amongst the coast tribes that, when our daughters step from childhood into the great world of womanhood, the occasion must be made one of extreme rejoicing. The being who possesses the possibility of some day mothering a man-child, a warrior, a brave, receives much consideration in most nations; but to us, the Sunset tribes, she is honoured above all people. The parents usually give a great potlatch, and a feast that lasts many days. The entire tribe and the surrounding tribes are bidden to this festival. More than that, sometimes when a great Tyee celebrates for his daughter, the tribes from far up the coast, from the distant north, from inland, from the island, from the Cariboo country, are gathered as guests to the feast. During these days of rejoicing the girl is placed in a high seat, an exalted position, for is she not marriageable? And does not marriage mean motherhood? And does not motherhood mean a vaster nation of brave sons and of gentle daughters, who, in their turn, will give us sons and daughters of their own?

"But it was many thousands of years ago that a great Tyee had two daughters that grew to womanhood at the same springtime, when the first great run of salmon thronged the rivers, and the ollallie bushes were heavy with blossoms. These two daughters were young, lovable, and oh! very beautiful. Their father, the great Tyee, prepared to make a feast such as the Coast had never seen. There were to be days and days of rejoicing, the people were to come for many leagues, were to   13 bring gifts to the girls and to receive gifts of great value from the chief, and hospitality was to reign as long as pleasuring feet could dance, and enjoying lips could laugh, and mouths partake of the excellence of the chief's fish, game, and ollallies.

"The only shadow on the joy of it all was war, for the tribe of the great Tyee was at war with the Upper Coast Indians, those who lived north, near what is named by the Pale-face as the port of Prince Ru-pert. Giant war-canoes slipped along the entire coast, war-parties pad-dled up and down, war-songs broke the silences of the nights, hatred, vengeance, strife, horror festered everywhere like sores on the surface of the earth. But the great Tyee, after warring for weeks, turned and laughed at the battle and the bloodshed, for he had been victor in every encounter, and he could well afford to leave the strife for a brief week and feast in his daughters' honour, nor permit any mere enemy to come between him and the traditions of his race and household. So he turned insultingly deaf ears to their war-cries; he ignored with ar-rogant indifference their paddle-dips that encroached within his own coast waters, and he prepared, as a great Tyee should, to royally entertain his tribesmen in honour of his daughters.

"But seven suns before the great feast, these two maidens came before him, hand clasped in hand.

"'Oh! our father,' they said, 'may we speak?'

"'Speak, my daughters, my girls with the eyes of April, the hearts of June'" (early spring and early summer would be the more accurate In-dian phrasing).

"'Some day, oh! our father, we may mother a man-child, who may grow to be just such a powerful Tyee as you are, and for this honour that may some day be ours we have come to crave a favour of you—you, Oh! our father.'

"'It is your privilege at this celebration to receive any favour your hearts may wish,' he replied graciously, placing his fingers beneath their girlish chins. 'The favour is yours before you ask it, my daugh-ters.'

"'Will you, for our sakes, invite the great northern hostile tribe—the tribe you war upon—to this, our feast?' they asked fearlessly.

"'To a peaceful feast, a feast in the honour of women?' he exclaimed incredulously.

"'So we would desire it,' they answered.

"'And so shall it be,' he declared. 'I can deny you nothing this day, and some time you may bear sons to bless this peace you have asked, and to bless their mother's sire for granting it.' Then he turned to all the young men of the tribe and commanded: 'Build fires at sunset on all the coast headlands—fires of welcome. Man your canoes and face the north, greet the enemy, and tell them that I, the Tyee of the Capilanos, ask—no, command—that they join me for a great feast in honour of my two daughters.' And when the northern tribe got this invitation they flocked down the coast to this feast of a Great Peace. They brought their women and their children; they brought game and fish, gold and white stone beads, baskets and carven ladles, and wonderful woven blankets to lay at the feet of their now acknowledged ruler, the great Tyee. And he, in turn, gave such a potlatch that nothing but tradition can vie with it. There were long, glad days of joyousness, long pleasurable nights of dancing and camp-fires, and vast quantities of food. The war-canoes were emptied of their deadly weapons and filled with the daily catch of salmon. The hostile war-songs ceased, and in their place were heard the soft shuffle of dancing feet, the singing voices of women, the play-games of the children of two powerful tribes which had been until now ancient enemies, for a great and lasting brotherhood was sealed between them—their war-songs were ended for ever.

"Then the Sagalie Tyee smiled on His Indian children: 'I will make these young-eyed maidens immortal,' He said. In the cup of His hands He lifted the chief's two daughters and set them for ever in a high place, for they had borne two offspring—Peace and Brotherhood—each of which is now a great Tyee ruling this land.

"And on the mountain crest the chief's daughters can be seen wrapped in the suns, the snows, the stars of all seasons, for they have stood in this high place for thousands of years, and will stand for thousands of years to come, guarding the peace of the Pacific Coast and the quiet of the Capilano Canyon."

This is the Indian legend of "The Lions of Vancouver" as I had it from one who will tell me no more the traditions of his people.

THE SIWASH ROCK

Unique, and so distinct from its surroundings as to suggest rather the handicraft of man than a whim of Nature, it looms up at the entrance to the Narrows, a symmetrical column of solid grey stone. There are no similar formations within the range of vision, or indeed within many a day's paddle up and down the coast. Amongst all the wonders, the natural beauties that encircle Vancouver, the marvels of mountains, shaped into crouching lions and brooding beavers, the yawning canyons, the stupendous forest firs and cedars, Siwash Rock stands as distinct, as individual, as if dropped from another sphere.

I saw it first in the slanting light of a redly setting August sun; the little tuft of green shrubbery that crests its summit was black against   15 the crimson of sea and sky, and its colossal base of grey stone gleamed like flaming polished granite.

My old tillicum lifted his paddle-blade to point towards it. "You know the story?" he asked. I shook my head (experience has taught me his love of silent replies, his moods of legend-telling). For a time we paddled slowly; the rock detached itself from its background of forest and shore, and it stood forth like a sentinel – erect, enduring, eternal.

"Do you think it stands straight – like a man?" he asked.

"Yes, like some noble-spirited, upright warrior," I replied.

"It is a man," he said, "and a warrior man, too; a man who fought for everything that was noble and upright."

"What do you regard as everything that is noble and upright, chief?" I asked, curious as to his ideas. I shall not forget the reply; it was but two words – astounding, amazing words. He said simply:

"Clean fatherhood."

Through my mind raced tumultuous recollections of numberless articles in yet numberless magazines, all dealing with the recent "fad" of motherhood, but I had to hear from the lip of a Squamish Indian chief the only treatise on the nobility of "clean fatherhood" that I have yet unearthed. And this treatise has been an Indian legend for centuries; and, lest they forget how all-important those two little words must ever be, Siwash Rock stands to remind them, set there by the Deity as a monument to one who kept his own life clean, that cleanliness might be the heritage of the generations to come.

It was "thousands of years ago" (all Indian legends begin in extremely remote times) that a handsome boy chief journeyed in his canoe to the upper coast for the shy little northern girl whom he brought home as his wife. Boy though he was, the young chief had proved himself to be an excellent warrior, a fearless hunter, and an upright, courageous man among men. His tribe loved him, his enemies respected him, and the base and mean and cowardly feared him.

The customs and traditions of his ancestors were a positive religion to him, the sayings and the advices of the old people were his creed. He was conservative in every rite and ritual of his race. He fought his tribal enemies like the savage that he was. He sang his war-songs, danced his war-dances, slew his foes, but the little girl-wife from the north he treated with the deference that he gave his own mother, for was she not to be the mother of his warrior son?

The year rolled round, weeks merged into months, winter into spring, and one glorious summer at daybreak he wakened to her voice calling him. She stood beside him, smiling.

"It will be to-day," she said proudly.

He sprang from his couch of wolf-skins and looked out upon the coming day: the promise of what it would bring him seemed breathing

16

through all his forest world. He took her very gently by the hand and led her through the tangle of wilderness down to the water's edge, where the beauty spot we moderns call Stanley Park bends about Prospect Point. "I must swim," he told her.

"I must swim, too," she smiled, with the perfect understanding of two beings who are mated. For, to them, the old Indian custom was law—the custom that the parents of a coming child must swim until their flesh is so clear and clean that a wild animal cannot scent their proximity. If the wild creatures of the forests have no fear of them, then, and only then, are they fit to become parents, and to scent a human is in itself a fearsome thing to all wild creatures.

So those two plunged into the waters of the Narrows as the grey dawn slipped up the eastern skies and all the forest awoke to the life of a new, glad day. Presently he took her ashore, and smilingly she crept away under the giant trees. "I must be alone," she said, "but come to me at sunrise: you will not find me alone then." He smiled also, and plunged back into the sea. He must swim, swim, swim through this hour when his fatherhood was coming upon him. It was the law that he must be clean, spotlessly clean, so that when his child looked out upon the world it would have the chance to live its own life clean. If he did not swim hour upon hour his child would come to an unclean father. He must give his child a chance in life; he must not hamper it by his own uncleanliness at its birth. It was the tribal law—the law of vicarious purity.

As he swam joyously to and fro, a canoe bearing four men headed up the Narrows. These men were giants in stature, and the stroke of their paddles made huge eddies that boiled like the seething tides.

"Out from our course!" they cried as his lithe, copper-coloured body arose and fell with his splendid stroke. He laughed at them, giants though they were, and answered that he could not cease his swimming at their demand.

"But you shall cease!" they commanded. "We are the men [agents] of the Sagalie Tyee [God], and we command you ashore out of our way!" (I find in all these Coast Indian legends that the Deity is represented by four men, usually paddling an immense canoe.)

He ceased swimming, and, lifting his head, defied them. "I shall not stop, nor yet go ashore," he declared, striking out once more to the middle of the channel.

"Do you dare disobey us," they cried—"we, the men of the Sagalie Tyee? We can turn you into a fish, or a tree, or a stone for this; do you dare disobey the Great Tyee?"

"I dare anything for the cleanliness and purity of my coming child. I dare even the Sagalie Tyee Himself, but my child must be born to a spotless life."

17

The four men were astounded. They consulted together, lighted their pipes, and sat in council. Never had they, the men of the Sagalie Tyee, been defied before. Now, for the sake of a little unborn child, they were ignored, disobeyed, almost despised. The lithe young copper-coloured body still disported itself in the cool waters; superstition held that should their canoe, or even their paddle-blades, touch a human being, their marvellous power would be lost. The handsome young chief swam directly in their course. They dared not run him down; if so, they would become as other men. While they yet counselled what to do, there floated from out the forest a faint, strange, compelling sound. They listened, and the young chief ceased his stroke as he listened also. The faint sound drifted out across the waters once more. It was the cry of a little, little child. Then one of the four men, he that steered the canoe, the strongest and tallest of them all, arose, and, standing erect, stretched out his arms towards the rising sun and chanted, not a curse on the young chief's disobedience, but a promise of everlasting days and freedom from death.

"Because you have defied all things that come in your path we promise this to you," he chanted: "you have defied what interferes with your child's chance for a clean life, you have lived as you wish your son to live, you have defied us when we would have stopped your swimming and hampered your child's future. You have placed that child's future before all things, and for this the Sagalie Tyee commands us to make you for ever a pattern for your tribe. You shall never die, but you shall stand through all the thousands of years to come, where all eyes can see you. You shall live, live, live as an indestructible monument to Clean Fatherhood."

The four men lifted their paddles and the handsome young chief swam inshore; as his feet touched the line where sea and land met he was transformed into stone.

Then the four men said, "His wife and child must ever be near him; they shall not die, but live also." And they, too, were turned into stone. If you penetrate the hollows in the woods near Siwash Rock you will find a large rock and a smaller one beside it. They are the shy little bride-wife from the north, with her hour-old baby beside her. And from the uttermost parts of the world vessels come daily throbbing and sailing up the Narrows. From far trans-Pacific ports, from the frozen North, from the lands of the Southern Cross, they pass and repass the living rock that was there before their hulls were shaped, that will be there when their very names are forgotten, when their crews and their captains have taken their long last voyage, when their merchandise has rotted, and their owners are known no more. But the tall, grey column of stone will still be there—a monument to one man's fidelity to a generation yet unborn—and will endure from everlasting to everlasting.

PAULINE JOHNSON (1861–1913) *was born on the Six Nation Reserve near Brantford, Ontario, the daughter of an English mother and a Mohawk father. Raised in a cultured, literary environment, she turned seriously to poetry after the death of her father. In the 1890s she adopted the gruelling life of the touring performer, becoming internationally famous for her public recitations in which she appeared alternately in Indian costume and formal evening dress. In 1909 she settled in Vancouver, where her acquaintance with the Squamish Chief, Joe Capilano, inspired her to write down the stories which were collected as* Legends of Vancouver (1911). *When she died in 1913, at the height of her fame, the day of her funeral was declared a day of civic mourning and by special dispensation her ashes were buried in Stanley Park. Her books include* The White Wampun (1895), Canadian Born (1903), Flint and Feather (1911), The Shaganappi (1913), *and* The Mocassin Maker (1913).

THE GOLDEN FLEECE

BERTRAND W. SINCLAIR

Sherrin's office windows look down on the Galata wharf and out across the Inlet to where the Capilano range stands like a Hadrian's Wall against the impetuous assault of the north wind. Sometimes when Sherrin grows tired of dealing with bills of lading, charters, shippers' complaints, all the endless minutiae of a coastwise shipping business, it is a relief to sit back and look out at that chain of mountains lifting across the harbor, running east and west for many miles, shading from green terraces behind the houses on the North Shore to misty-purple summits capped with snow where fluffs of clouds drifted lazily above deep, glacial abysses. He knew singing streams up there where trout lay in black pools, where grizzlies came down to fish in the salmon run, where grouse fluttered in the thickets. A pleasing outlook for a routine-weary man.

And when he has looked a long time at the Capilanos his gaze comes back to the nearer vista, a bird's eye view of vessels great and small. The lesser craft intrigue his fancy most. He knows something of them and the men that man them—tugs, halibut schooners, purse-seiners, stubby yachts and yachty powerboats. They serve, for profit or pleasure, a thousand miles of coastline, a myriad of islands, inaccessible save by the furrowed highway of the sea. A hardy lot. They make a brave showing under his office windows, with their varnished spars, brass that glints in the sun like buffed gold, beautifully curved deck-lines, coiled gear and complicated rigging which has a use that mystifies landsmen. Some of these craft lie in the stream like gulls with folded wings resting between flights. More are fast bow and stern against wharf, slip, landing. They rock gently in the wash from passing harbour craft, their masts describing a lessening arc until they fall still again.

Sherrin was looking down on this one November afternoon, a crisp, sunny day which had followed a week of rain. He was weary of ac-

This story, found in the Sinclair Papers at UBC, likely dates from the 1920s.

counts, of complaints, oppressed with a dumb sense of futility. He laid it to his digestion. He needed exercise! He would not admit to himself—last of all to himself—that it was no more than one of his periodic rebellions against being cramped and caged. It was an old thing, that wordless resentment—old, yet always new. He had suffered for many years without understanding why, from that peculiar chafing of the spirit. It was worst in the spring, when the maples around his house put out buds through the winter grime and burst into green foliage. He would sit for an hour at a time then in his office, staring at the Capilanos, at the gray-green harbor floor, and turn in his chair for a glimpse of the open Gulf across the low land that ran westward from Coal Harbor. Or it would grip him unaccountably when he fell into talk with a company skipper, one of those red-faced men in soiled blue uniforms whose mild awkwardness in the presence of their employers became sureness and certainty on the bridge of a vessel. Or again Sherrin would feel that depressing unrest when some unit of the mosquito fleet cleared for a voyage the purpose and destination of which reached him by the underground route that traverses the waterfront in Vancouver, where curious ventures are not unknown.

When such a one's stern closed with Brockton Point Sherrin's eyes ceased to see her, but his fancy followed her out the Narrows, beyond the Strait of San Juan, saw her wallow in seas that rolled from the Marquesas and beyond. Or he would go with her in the spirit up where the Aleutian Archipelago is strung like beads on a chain across the Sunday-Monday line. But his body remained in the office, in the plain room he had occupied for twenty years.

Sherrin was a loyal servant. He believed a man should do the work for which he drew a wage. It was impossible for him to realize the nature of this dimly sensed rebellion against order, routine, daily commonplaces. He had a comfortable home, a fund that approached competence laid by against old age, a girl in high school and a boy in the U.B.C. He was forty-seven. He had reaped the reward of faithful service and stood high in the regard of his company. He would be an office superintendent and draw four thousand a year as long as he cared to hold the place. His thin, light-brown hair would grow thinner and lighter till it became grey. He would die in the harness of industry. It was ordered and foreordained for him and for thousands of others such as himself; well-fed, well-clad, sober, frugal citizens who poured out of offices and banks and bond-houses, evening after evening for three hundred days in the year—fixtures, cogs in the commercial machine, most of them satisfied to be cogs so long as they got on. Sherrin was getting on. He had always got on.

But he had fought against vagrant impulses ever since he could remember. His utmost adventure had been marriage to a placid-tempered

21

woman; his worst luck a mild indigestion; his greatest disasters a sprained ankle and a broken thumb. His farthest journeyings were fishing trips across the Inlet.

That was in the flesh. He travelled far and did great deeds in the spirit—and was sometimes shamefacedly aware of himself as a day-dreamer, a careless adventurer in the broad realm of the imagination.

Perhaps that was why he looked so long and so abstractedly down on the masts and decks and pilothouses this bright, cold afternoon.

He knew them all, as a man knows his neighbors. The *Lady of Lyons,* schooner-rigged, sixty tons burden. *Her* hold had known many cargoes, from sealskins filched off the Pribiloffs to contraband liquors landed on the California coast. *The Gou Pyng,* ditto. Astern of these two lay the *Charioteer.* She was just back from Ensenada, Mexico, and when the wharfingers said she had carried a load of canned salmon they winked and smiled. And this side the slip, almost under Sherrin's window loomed a lean, graceful cruiser with two stout pole masts and a false funnel abaft her wheelhouse—false, because she was powered with gas and needed no stack, except for ornament. She was flush-decked. Except for the white boot-leg at her water-line she was painted a drab grey, relieved by bits of polished brass. Sherrin stared at her longest of all. He knew her of old, when she flew a yacht pennant, and looked with disdain on the grubby brotherhood of commerce. How would she fare now that she had joined the ranks of those who gather their bread upon the waters?

Sherrin had acquired a material as well as a sentimental interest in the *Tosca.*

While he sat looking down at her he heard his door open, heard footsteps, without turning his head. Clerks came and went during the day, laid papers on his desk. They were the automata of his surroundings. They never broke needlessly into his musings. A throat-clearing behind him made him turn at last.

"Hello, Pete?" he greeted. "I was just looking at your ship, and thinking about her next voyage."

The man came to the window. He, too, looked down at the *Tosca,* smiling faintly.

"Well," he said, "I got it all fixed. Connors, that broker on Cordova, put in two thousand, and another fellow I know took a flier with us. We'll clear with five hundred cases."

"When will you sail?"

"Oh, day after tomorrow. Probably about ten in the morning."

"Good luck, Pete," Sherrin said. "Hope you have a quiet passage."

"Well, we're bound to have weather," the man shrugged his shoulders. "No gettin' away from it this time of year. We'll be standin' on our ear half the time. But the *Tosca's* able enough."

"You think she is, eh?"

"Hell, yes," Pete May exclaimed. There was a trace of irritation in his low, even tone. Sherrin reflected that he had asked this question before. Probably others had done so. "If the *Lady of Lyons* and the *Mamook* and the rest of 'em can make it, it's a cinch the *Tosca* can."

Sherrin swung in his chair to take a more deliberate survey, an appraising look at his visitor. He saw a medium-sized man about thirty dressed in a blue serge suit, wearing a jersey instead of a shirt, a peaked cloth cap set jauntily on his head. Keen blue eyes looked out from either side of a thin, slightly-curved nose. A cropped mustache stuck straight out, like a dab of fine brown bristles from his upper lip. There were hundreds like Pete trafficking in and out of the port, seamen of the newer dispensation, who flirt with lee shores and jutting reefs, whose navigation is accomplished by chart and compass and sounding-lead, a litany of time and courses, who cope with fog and swift tide-races and narrow-necked harbors, who never know the safety of vast sea-room like their offshore brethren—yet somehow keep their vessels afloat and make their ports of call.

It was only history repeating itself, Sherrin reflected when Pete went down the stairs. He looked after the man and thought that Pete May and his fellows were truly the collateral descendents of those Anglo-Saxons whose luggers troubled the shores of England with tobacco from Virginia and cognac from France without tribute to the king's excise, in generations gone. Sherrin's mind dwelt further upon legislation and liquor—the two factors controlling the activities of a dozen vessels he could name; voyages fraught with peril, undertaken for profit.

Sixteen miles due south from Sherrin's office an imaginary line, the forty-ninth parallel of latitude, divided the legal from the illegal, the wet from the dry. Volstead south of the border. Its antithesis, the B.C. Moderation Act, on the north. British Columbia, the alcoholic oasis of North America, with internal traffic in bottled goods a government monopoly, and export trade in liquor a recognized commercial pursuit. A quart of authentic Scotch whisky purchasable lawfully in Vancouver for five dollars. Moonshine at treble the price in San Francisco. Mexico with no laws for or against. Was it any wonder that cargoes of Scotch and rye and cognac, billed in due order from Vancouver to Ensenada, Mexico, vanished en route? Or that only empty boxes were duly delivered to a complaisant agent in the Mexican port? How was it done? Sherrin did not know. Only the men who accomplished the feat could say. They did not tell. They only smiled. Their manifests and clearances were always in order—and they smiled and were prosperous. All the revenue cutters between Puget Sound and San Diego could not stop them—lawful merchantmen on the high seas. How did

23

they land that which became contraband only within the three-mile coastal limit? That was their secret. A great profit for a great risk – for they were not uniformly successful. Sometimes they jettisoned a costly cargo to save their liberty and their ship. Sometimes, they lost both. But not often. There were men in the trade – *they* didn't call it smuggling – who had dodged subs in the Channel and the North Sea, and hunted them, too, in sixty-five foot M.Ls.

Sherrin had no prejudices one way or the other. He was concerned with all this chiefly as a spectacle, not a moral issue. Until the *Tosca* entered the game he had been an interested onlooker. He knew about it, as a man whose daily business lies on the waterfront of a seaport must be dull indeed if he does not know all that goes on. And there was no secrecy about the "export" trade. It was open and legitimate. The secrecy and the illegality took form far away, off the coast of Oregon, California – just as long as a cargo of beads and cotton lawfully passing out of some European port became the instrument of rapine and slavery when it reached the Gold Coast. One man's meat...

No, until Pete May bought the *Tosca* and found himself without enough money to load her, Sherrin had never expected to find himself anything but an interested onlooker, touched by the dash and spirit of the game, but personally remote. Now he was in it – at least his money was. Not much; only five hundred dollars. From what motive, he could scarcely say. Certainly not mere profit. To double that sum would have been no great incentive to a man like Sherrin. But it was enough to link him close through the medium of a receptive fancy, to make him view from a highly personal angle this small vessel and her crew of four, who were to sail out into the Pacific in the stormiest season of the year.

Sherrin had taken a short cruise aboard the *Tosca* once while she was the property of a man he knew. She had passed into other hands. During the latter days of the war she had seen government service, sailing under the Blue Ensign, clothed in the majesty of the law, hunting draft evaders along a coast peculiarly adapted to hiding. She had outlived her usefulness to the authorities in that respect, and Pete May had bought her for a song. If she were sound and able enough to make three voyages Pete's song might become the warble of a prima donna.

Sherrin went aboard the *Tosca* the morning of her departure. He sat in a cabin duskily lighted by portholes and talked to Pete May. Two men of her crew tramped heavily overhead, lashing gear, making all fast. There was a clink of metal in her engine-room, a slow, asthmatic wheeze as someone barred over the big pistons.

"Good luck to you, Pete," Sherrin said and rose.

When he hung up his hat and coat and turned to the office window the *Tosca* was backing into the stream, white water boiling under her stern, her exhaust beating like the smooth roll of a trap drum.

The wharf foreman came in to consult Sherrin. He, too, glanced out the window.

"Them guys got more nerve than judgement," he grunted. "Goin' to sea in *that*."

"Isn't she fit?" Sherrin asked.

"Oh, fit enough, I guess," the foreman admitted. "But Lord, she'll do the shimmy all the way. Rough and tumble every hour of every watch. They'll have to tie themselves to their bunks when they lie down to sleep. She ain't big enough to go outside, this time of the year."

Sherrin discounted this a little. His man had served his time in square-riggers when he was young. To him, anything under five thousand tons was a cockle-shell. He went away at last, and Sherrin watched the *Tosca* vanish into the Narrows, outward bound. In ten hours she would be swinging high and low in the ground swell that marches from Honolulu to burst in foam on Cape Flattery and Umatilla Reef.

Weather always means something to a waterfront man. It immediately took on a special significance for Sherrin. When he sat down before the living-room fire that evening he turned first to that page of the *Province* where, at the head of the shipping gossip, could be found wireless reports from every western sea station, and a forecast for the ensuing thirty-six hours. Clear, cold, light winds. Steady barometer. Sherrin turned to the news columns with a touch of relief.

When he laid down the paper at last his wife sat opposite, reading a magazine, a plump, fair woman of forty-five. Sherrin junior was whistling upstairs. Barbara twisted her youthful lips over a French conjugation. The pleasant atmosphere of home—where the unexpected was unknown, where the Eighteenth Amendment was as remote as Timbuctoo, where the weather was only a matter of rubbers and umbrellas, where a spoiled roast was the ultimate disaster—those four walls within which risks, hardships, dangers and despair could never come.

Yet Sherrin sat by his fire in a dumb discontent. Was it a man's highest possible attainment, this complete insulation from the hot glow of struggle, from all chance and change? It was good. Yes. But was it good enough? He had a swift, disconcerting vision of himself trudging from the house to the office, from the office to the house, a ten-day vacation once a year. He had done it for twenty years. He would do it for another twenty. His children would grow up and marry and go their way. His wife would grow older and more plump and placid, nourishing herself intellectually on interminable tales in the women's journals. They would sit by the fire in winter, and in grass chairs on the porch in summer, and they would talk about the cost of living, and about saving, and what Mrs. Jones said to Mr. Smith.

Oh hell! And he was forty-seven—too old to change—too cunningly enmeshed in responsibilities and duties and timidities. A man couldn't have his cake and eat it too. Sherrin felt for one moment—a moment of ghastly surprise at himself—that he had hoarded his until it had grown stale.

Then he recalled himself from this wildness of thought, this most disturbing emotion, this unaccustomed yielding to amazing fancies. He recoiled from his own revelation of suppressed desires, wanton cravings for a bold, free fling at life, life in which an ordered domesticity had no place. To be free to flirt with Chance, even to the uttermost edges of the earth! Sherrin smiled at the fancy. Yes, considering all things, that was an absurd fancy.

He kissed his wife on the cheek. That excellent woman, immersed in an excellent tale, merely murmured "yes, dear" when he said he thought he would go to bed.

Sherrin went upstairs to their bedroom. The shade had not been drawn. He stood looking out a window that gave seaward over English Bay. In a wan, unclouded night he could see the Point Atkinson light flash like some great, intermittent electric spark, a glittering eye winking on a white pillar. The *Tosca* would be dipping her bows to the open sea, lift and fall, lift and fall. She would take her departure, her last landward bearing in the dark, by the flash of the Umatilla Lightship. At daybreak the men of that watch would look out on the sea. It might be furrowed by gray swells, or a tumbled green, flecked with bits of white. But to port and starboard, ahead and astern there would be the sea and the sea only. And they would roll and pitch, and be boarded by wave-crests until the *Tosca* was bitter with salt from guard-rail to masthead, for ninety-six hours on end before the land became a faint blue line over their bows again.

Sherrin went to bed with a little envy of them. When the warning gong turned him out of bed again he thought of Pete May. The *Tosca* had Gray's Harbor over her port quarter now. She was a speck, ringed about by a watery horizon. Eight o'clock. One bell in the morning watch. There they were, while he, Sherrin, thoughtfully cracked his matutinal egg.

One day passed and another and a third. Upon the fourth the weather forecast took an ominous turn: Heavy southeast gales general along Pacific coast. Center of maximum velocity off California coast. Mariners warned.

Sherrin raised a window the better to peer out at the sky before he went to bed. The heralds of the storm were abroad. Smoke stood away from the chimneys in dusty pennants. High in the silvery night wisps of cloud streaked across the bright stars. The first breath of the wind already troubled the Gulf. He could hear the swell muttering on the beach at English Bay.

He walked to his office in the morning with the tails of his coat snapping about his legs. He watched the ripples run across the sheltered
harbor, saw the firs in Stanley Park bend their plumed heads to the
wind, heard the long tin roof of the wharf shed creak and rattle. He
saw a yacht part her mooring chain and scud, bare-poled, up the harbor, until she was captured by a pursuing launch. He could see the
storm signals flicker like dragon's teeth on the halyards at Brockton
Point. No yachtsman's gale that, but a proper blow. And the center of
maximum velocity was off the California coast. The *Tosca* should now
have those southern shores abeam. The Golden Gate, Santa Barbara,
San Diego, somewhere over her port rail, below the gray curve of the
sea. What did she face in that center of maximum velocity? How did
she fare?

Unanswerable questions. Sherrin forced his mind to his work, the
routine of correspondence, casual orders. He pacified an angry shipper
who stormed his quarters with a wordy tale of crated pigs unshipped
at the wrong landing. He dictated letters, checked reports, functioned
ideally as the lever controlling a mass of intricate machinery, of which
all the parts, animate and mechanical, operated to produce corporate
dividends. Ordered effort, modern vessels, skill, courage, loyalty, all
directed to the same ultimate purpose as took the *Tosca* down along
the south coast—into the center of maximum velocity.

By dark Sherrin had a more vivid comprehension of what was implied in that set phrase of the forecasters. He wondered if there might
be two centers of maximum velocity, or if the height of a great storm
was beyond the metal grasp of all save those caught in its grip.
Wireless informed him of a company vessel blown out of her track in
Queen Charlotte Sound, of another, old and slow, unable to buck the
gale in Johnstone Strait. A day boat, serving points seventy miles
along the Gulf, came in late, her forward cabin windows smashed by
boarding seas. And these were in semi-protected waters.

"What will it be like outside, off the Cape?" Sherrin asked the captain, as he looked over the broken windows, over all the forward structure gleaming with dried salt.

The man shrugged his shoulders.

"Rough stuff, I guess," he made laconic answer.

At noon next day Sherrin answered a telephone call.

"This is Connors, the broker," a voice said. "You had a little in the
Tosca, didn't you?"

"A little," Sherrin admitted. "Not much. Why? What about her?
Heard anything?"

"Yep. Got a wire from Ensenada," the man's tone was suddenly jubi-
lant. "Reads: 'Discharged cargo O.K. (get that, Sherrin? O.K!) Clear
to-morrow, weather permitting, in ballast for Vancouver. Signed,
May.' Good stroke of business, that, Sherrin."

27

Sherrin experienced a queer, unexpected relief.

"I'm glad they made it," he said into the mouthpiece. "It's been dirty weather. I've been wondering about them. Pretty small boat for offshore work."

"Didn't notice the weather. Needn't worry about them guys, anyway. *They* know their business, I guess. Well, so-long."

He hung up and leaned back in his chair. Against odds of sea and revenue cutters the *Tosca* had done it. The profit secured had little weight with Sherrin. Not because he despised profit. But the deed it-self counted. Against such odds. Fourteen hundred miles of open sea—in a craft scarcely larger than an admiral's pinnace. Cool nerve, skillful navigation, patient endurance—prime qualities in any cause. Sherrin envied them, as the tamed, cloistered man must always envy the man of action.

He put up against the office wall a small-scale chart of the Pacific coast. When the Tosca was due to leave Ensenada he pricked off with a pin her first day's run. Thereafter at noon each day the pin-prick moved northward by five-inch steps, so many nautical miles per twenty-four hours, as a master checks his position by dead reckoning. And he marked the weather morning, noon, and night as shrewdly as if he stood in the *Tosca's* wheelhouse conning the glass and the sea and the sky like any careful seaman.

When the pin-pricks had traced a dotted line north to that bleak coast between Cape Flattery and Gray's Harbor the glass fell, the storm signals fluttered on Brockton Point once more, the weather fore-cast gave terse warning: For following thirty-six hours heavy N.W. gales with sleet or snow.

Could the *Tosca* double the Umatilla Reef and drive to shelter up the Strait of San Juan before the storm struck her? Sherrin would have been glad to answer, yes. If a north-west gale, a December gale from the Aleutians, from the Siberian coast, caught her to leeward of the Reef, why then—then truly the *Tosca* would need the Twin Brethern at her masthead to live through and make her port.

Sherrin derived still further insight into centers of maximum velocity during the next two days. The weather bureau's prophecy was fulfilled to the letter. The nor-wester blew high and low, drove everything in the Gulf to cover. There were casualties. There were vessels caught unaware, coasting streamers that *must* make their schedule, skippers that *would* take a chance. Wireless told the tale. And the wind's screech in the wires, about corners, its wild way with insecure roofing and plate-glass windows, kept dinning that tale into Sherrin's ears. He lay in his comfortable bed at night and felt the house shudder. He walked between house and office, head down, leaning forward, resist-ing the strong pressure of unseen hands. Out there, he thought, out there beyond the landward barriers that wind would heel a small vessel down till she was lee-rail under. Without rest or mercy, hour upon hour, one sea after another would march up and board her and sweep her decks with its watery broom.

Connors the broker came to his office when the gale had worn to a chill whisper, and the sleet-thickened air had cleared so that Sherrin could see the North Shore again.

"I guess we lose," He said glumly. "You know the *Crusader?*"

Sherrin nodded. He knew her. He knew her business and where she berthed. A sidelong glance out the window showed him her heavy spars and low deckhouse. His glance flicked back to Connors. The man's face was an advertisement of calamity.

"She just got in," Connors went on heavily. "Her captain tells me the blow struck him forty miles off Flattery. He seen the *Tosca* go down—least he thinks he did. Don't see how she could live it out, he says. Took him twenty hours to make the Straits, and didn't think he'd make it at all, for awhile."

The *Crusader* had sighted the *Tosca* at a distance, laboring heavily. Then suddenly she seemed to vanish. The *Crusader's* captain had been so impressed by that disappearance that he had come about and started for her, and only desisted upon conviction that the *Tosca* had foundered and that he was imperilling his own vessel with no chance of picking up any survivor of the other. No ship's boat, and no swimmer born of woman could live ten minutes in such waters. The sea were smoking, the wind a screaming fury, the bottom had fallen out of the glass.

"So I guess she's gone to Davy Jones," Connors mourned. "We're out our money."

"Damn the money," Sherrin cried. "Think of the men."

"Thinkin' don't help 'em none," the broker frowned. "Damn the luck! After they'd turned the trick and pretty near brought home the coin, to get caught in the worst weather of the season. *I'm* out two thousand cold. We'd more than doubled our money if they'd got in."

"Oh, money, money," Sherrin exclaimed hotly.

"Well, maybe I ain't a good loser," Connors defended. "But two thousand bucks dropped cold kind of hurts *me*. Well, I just thought I'd stop in and tell you. So-long."

Sherrin sat staring at the chart, at the point where the last pin-prick showed, that checking of a course which would never be finished. He felt sick. He felt as if he himself had failed in some supreme test. He was a partner in the enterprise. In spirit he had made that chancy voy-age. Upon him spiritually rested the weight of disaster. He had for-gotten, or perhaps he had never known, that always behind the trip-ping feet of adventure tragedy glides in her somber garments, unseen   29 but ever-present, well-schooled to play her part.

He went home to his warmed slippers, to his comfortable chair, to the buoyant chatter of his children, and the click of his wife's knitting-needles. He buried himself behind the evening paper, wondering, while the print ran into a blur before his eyes, if men drowned at sea sink to the bottom or if they float white-faced and sodden till the flesh falls apart and their bones slide down to fathomless depths.

Sherrin came down to his office in the morning. He hung his overcoat and hat on a hook in the corner. He walked to the window, looked out, looked again, muttered two short words aloud. Then he flung on his coat again, hurried down the stairs, gained the landward end of the wharf, crossed to another and so out a floating slip to the *Tosca's* berth.

He climbed to the deck, stood looking about him a second. She bore many a mark. Yes. Even a landsman could see that she had suffered. The gray stretch of her deck sparkled with stuff like frost. Her wheel-house stood askew. One smashed window gaped under a nailed board. Over the other small panes a piece of sailcloth had been lashed. Her false funnel leaned awry. She had gone out of the harbor with two fourteen-foot lifeboats in chocks on deck. The boats were gone, the chocks splintered, the ringbolts that held the boat lashings had come away from the timber like plants torn up by the roots. One set of davits was twisted out of its fair, shipshape curves, the stout iron bent and buckled. Everywhere on her two thick, stumpy masts hung frayed rope-ends, ruined tackle. The roped and eyed luff of a trysail still stood up and down her mizzen-mast with ragged streamers of canvas left dangling here and there.

Yes, the *Tosca* had crept in, unkempt, weary, forlorn. But she had come in. She was still, very still, under Sherrin's feet, as if she were dead or deserted. He leaned over the after companion hatch.

"Tosca ahoy," he called.

"Come on down," a toneless, languid voice answered.

Sherrin went down the companion steps backward because of their steepness, turned at the bottom and faced the dusky interior.

Two bunks filled the port side of the cabin. In each bunk a man lay stretched full length on tumbled bedding. To starboard, on a spring-cushion settee another sprawled on his back, one hand over his face. And at his feet sat Pete May, looking up at Sherrin out of sleepy, red-lidded eyes.

It was stuffy and damp down there, full of a soggy clamminess. The morbid fancy struck Sherrin that the *Tosca* was like a vessel sunk and newly raised, with all the deep sea smell clinging to her. He understood in a cursory glance about and a tentative sniff or two that some of those boarding seas, the green water that had swept her fore and aft, had got below, through strained seams, through leaky ports. He put his hand against a bulkhead. It was damp. He touched a bit of up-holstering. It was sodden. And the odor of burned oil, engine fumes, bilge-smells – it had all been stirred up and bottled in and diluted with sea-water. Yes, the Tosca had suffered, alow and aloft. And her captain set staring at him after the first greeting, grave as an owl, silent as the ship, in which arose no sound but the creak of a loose-swinging block above and the heavy breathing of one man in his bunk.

"Well, Pete, it was a tough trip, eh?"

Pete May's old familiar grin flickered briefly across his tired face. "Yeah, kinda."

He began to fumble in his pockets. He brought out a pipe – and went on fumbling. Sherrin handed him a cigar. He looked it over, tore off the band, bit the end – went on fumbling in his pockets.

"Here's a light," Sherrin supplied a match.

May puffed for a second or two, till the cigar end glowed red. He looked critically at it down his thin, curved nose.

Suddenly he took the cigar in his fingers and began to talk in short, jerky sentences.

"Got rid of our load all right. Got the money. Figured we better make Ensenada to have the ship's papers in order – best to do that in this game when you've cleared foreign. Struck heavy weather off San Diego. Big sea. Didn't bother us much though. After that there was nothin' to it till we had Flattery about half a day's run ahead. Then she breezed up from the nor-west. Blow in here?"

He put the question lifelessly, as if it were a matter of scant interest.

"Blew hard for two days," Sherrin told him.

"Blew harder out there. Blew hell out of us. Blew us backward of the tops of seas. Yes, she blew. I'll say she blew. Head wind – and sail didn't help. So we plowed into it. Plowed's right. Plowed into it. Plowed under. Like a damned submarine. I guess it blew seventy miles an hour in spots. Breakin' seas comin' across decks. Squirtin' in through seams. You could feel her crack and shiver. Bam! And away went one boat. Whoosh! Away goes the other. Everything that wasn't bolted down carried away. Smashed the pilothouse windows. Loosened the house itself. Regular hell to pay. You bet."

He looked fixedly at the cigar in his hand.

"Then a main bearing burned out, an' we had no power. Just at dusk with dirty wet sleet slashin' at us. Tried to make sail. Couldn't do it. Couldn't stay on deck without bein' lashed there. Rigged a sea-drag. Run it out on a forty-fathom line. Got out an oil-bag too, an' made a slick. An' there we lay. Roll? Pitch? An' every once in a while a big one would bust on deck in spite of the oil.

"How long did we ride to that drag? How long did it take to run in that bearin'?"

He spoke to the man on the settee beside him. Without lifting his head, without taking his hand from his face, the man replied tonelessly, after May shook his foot:

"I don't know. All night. We fixed it."

"Funny," May grunted, turning to Sherrin again. "Seems like it was two nights. I ain't dead sure myself, now. Anyway, next day we got sail up. Not much. Enough for steerageway. Trysail on the mizzen blew up. Second one went to ribbons, too. So we sailed under a stay-sail and a leg o' mutton on the fore. And we sailed her out to sea, 'cause the hungriest place I know is the coast south of Umatilla Reef in a gale. And them guys down in the engine-room tryin' to run hot bab-bit with us standin' first on one ear an' then on the other. One of 'em got sick an' puked all over the floor. You'd a laughed to seen us. Clawin' around here like wet rats.

"Finally they got her together and she hit on all four cylinders an' run cool. 'N' we headed up into it again under a slow bell. Come a clear spot in the dark and we picked up the Umatilla light, the Swiftsure light too, got true bearin's and ran up the Strait of San Juan, seas like young mountains chasin' at our tail. 'N' here we are."

He reached into a locker beside him, hauled out a black tin box, turned back the cover. Flat sheafs of currency lay within. Pete May looked at it a second, closed the lid, put the box in Sherrin's hand.

"That's all that kept me from turnin' in. Glad you came down. I was going' to take it up to you, but didn't seem to have enough ambition to make a move. Put it in the safe for me till to-morrow. There's close on twenty thousand there. Everybody doubles his money. Take it away," he said wearily. "I got to sleep. I'm dead for sleep. Lissen to 'em snore."

He looked at his mates across the cabin, mouths open, asprawl in overalls and jerseys, one with a hand hanging limp over the berth's side. And as he looked his own eyelids drooped, his head began to nod, the half-burned cigar fell from his fingers to the damp, dirty floor. May straightened up with a start, and Sherrin stamped out the smoldering tobacco with his foot.

"Oh, I've got to sleep," he sighed. "Take care of that money, Sherrin. I've *got* to turn in. I'm dead on my feet."

Sherrin halted on the first step. He looked back over his shoulder. May was pulling off his boots.

"You won't make another trip like that – not in the winter season?"

"Eh?" Pete looked up at him. A flash of spirit showed in his tired eyes. "Sure. Once we get rested up, and the *Tosca* gets an overhaul. Sure. Why not?"

And the man stretched on the settee took his hand off his face and lifted his head.

32 "Hell, yes," he said impatiently. "Of course. Winter's the time.

Heavy weather—thick weather—that's our best chance. Think we go to sea for pastime?" he demanded testily. "Pleasure cruising? We ain't in the export trade for our health."

Sherrin climbed slowly up the narrow wharf stairs. He stood before his window, one hand thrust in his overcoat pocket. He looked down on the *Tosca*, at her twisted davits and torn sailcloth and broken gear. His fixed gaze pierced through her hull to the damp, musty cabin and the men deep in the slumber of exhaustion.

He flung the tin box of money on the table with a gesture of repug-nance.

"It isn't worth the price," he whispered. "Not the price they pay."

Yet deep in his heart there stirred a little envy of them, the same wistful admiration as might have troubled a Thessalian shepherd when Jason and his companions sailed the *Argo* home with the coat of the golden ram.

BERTRAND W. SINCLAIR (1881–1972) was born in Edinburgh, Scotland, and was brought to live in the Northwest Territories at the age of eight. He later spent time in Texas, California, and Montana before moving to Vancouver in 1912 and finally settling in Pender Harbour in 1922. His travels and various occupations as a cowboy, logger, miner, and fisherman provided a broad range of settings and experiences upon which to draw for his fiction. Sinclair produced scores of popular novels and stories of Western adventure, beginning in 1908 with Raw Gold *and continuing into the fifties. Among his most popular books were* Burned Bridges *(1919) and* Poor Man's Rock *(1920), the latter a best-seller which sold more than 80,000 copies. In 1919 he acquired a thirty-seven foot salmon trawler, and commercial fishing became his main occupation during the three decades preceding his retirement in 1965. His first-hand knowledge of the waters and conditions of the Pacific Coast contributes to the realism of stories like* "The Golden Fleece."

PHYLLUS

JEAN BURTON

There was nothing particularly pastoral about Phyllus, though her fragility might perhaps have appeared Dresden-like with proper care and proper clothes. This was a new experience for her, and her shyness choked her. She was excited and unhappy and fearful, and she could not quiet the hard beating of her heart or still its pain, but all these things were as nothing compared with the cruel shyness that held her in its grip and would not let her go.

And should she call him Jake, or Mr. Milton, as usual? What *should* she call him?

She tried to say his name, but it came only as a whisper.

Phyllus felt all earthly woe paled into insignificance beside the appalling fact that she did not know how to address this man.

Phyllus had worked in Jacques' Beauty Parlours—Beauty Salons, really, but Phyllus was uncertain of the pronunciation—on Granville street for five months before Jake had given any sign of noticing her, but Phyllus was accustomed to being unnoticed, and was not hurt or surprised. She was only very tired.

She was tired of heads full of oil and dandruff, and hot sticky marcels, and the smell of shampoo water. She was tired of the irritable old women, and the rich Jewesses, and the giggling girls. The girls were worst. They expected her to keep up a running line of chatter all the time. They expected to be amused. They asked her if she had seen the new show at the Capitol, or the Pantages. God knows she had no money to go to the Capitol, no time to go, no one to go with. But they kept saying oh gee, did you see Colleen Moore at the Capitol, oh gee, did you *see* the new show at the Pan?

Many of them asked for the other girls when they came in to make appointments, for the other girls had seen all the new shows and could imitate the coiffures of the movie stars, and could also, out of the vastness of their personal experience, offer advice and counsel on the subjects nearest the hearts of their clients.

But in spite of the fact that Phyllus was rarely asked for, she worked

This story was published in The Canadian Forum *in October, 1927.*

very hard at Jacques' Salon, harder, it seemed, than the other girls, for when they were through with a manicure or a shadow wave they picked up their True Romances or their Dreamland Tales and promptly buried themselves in its contents, oblivious, apparently, to the outside world; and so remained until the press of customers became so great that they were forced to emerge, swearing beneath their breath, emerge languidly and disdainfully, patting their elaborate curls, carefully gracious and aloof.

But if Phyllus so much as sat down, with a long sigh of weariness, she knew it would not be many minutes before Estella the red-haired would appear, clacking, "C'm on, Phyllus, put away that book! Cust'mer."

Phyllus was very tired. Phyllus had always been tired, but of late, when she had been standing all day, her heart smothered her and she found it difficult to breathe. If it had not been for this, Phyllus would not have commented upon her weariness, but would have taken it for granted, as she had always done.

She said to herself, quoting her mother, "You're tired. Well, what of it? People've been tired before, and they'll be tired again."

She quoted also her mother's fragment of the ultimate philosophy, "We'll all have a long enough rest, some day."

But of late it did not sound convincing to say "What of it?"

It was because Phyllus was so tired that she did not observe conditions in Jacques' Salon very closely for some months after she came to work there. She did not have much to say to the other girls, in any case. But one day she was moved to sigh to the languid blonde beside her, gum slowly revolving in time to the andante passage in the fictional adventures of the heroine: "Gee, I'm tired. Why don't she call you, for a change?"

The languid blond, showing no resentment, opened violet eyes cased in mascara of astonishing blackness and stiffness.

"Dearie," said the languid blond, "we earn our money, same as you. I mean to say, not the same as you."

And the blond put her wise, which showed that she had, at least, a kind heart.

This was the original reason why Phyllus now found herself in a boarding house on Richards street, wondering whether she should address her employer as Jake, or as Mr. Milton, and wishing in either case that he would turn out the lights.

It had really not been difficult, up to this point. Phyllus hardly knew yet just how it had happened. It seemed that as soon as she had known about Jake and the girls, Jake knew that she knew, and that was all there was to it.

She had dashed up the steps with the others from the downstairs parlours to see the procession go by. The band thrilled her, and the 35

marching men, and the flags. But not the crowd, for the crowd was indifferent and apathetic, like all Vancouver crowds. Phyllus pressed her
way to the front, leaving the other girls behind.

She stood, rigid with patriotism, for a long time, for the procession
had been badly arranged, like all Vancouver processions; until the car
with the new governor-general and his wife passed, dutifully cheered
by a number of young men and boys thoughtfully retained in advance
for that purpose, Vancouver crowds being, as those in charge of such
events know, untrustworthy and not to be depended upon in the matter of enthusiasm and noise.

The new governor-general looked about with polite interest, and his
wife, a dark-haired woman with kindly lines about her eyes and mouth,
smiled and bowed.

"Ah, gee," said Phyllus reverently.

She silenced with a glare the small boy beside her who took it upon
himself to make facetious comment on the governor-general's moustache, for Phyllus believed in the British Empire.

But it had been very hot, and she felt tireder than usual when she
turned down the steps again. At the door Jake was standing, medita-
tively surveying his gleaming finger nails.

"Well," said Jake affably, "fine show."

Phyllus agreed gaspingly.

Jake added an even higher lustre to the nails of his right hand, by
rubbing them against the palm of his left.

"They tell me," said Jake in the tone of one who relates well-nigh incredible tidings, "that all them decorations was sent from Seattle up
here! Home firms didn't get a look in! How the hell do they expect to
see Vancouver grow, when all the time they patronize American industry like that, never even giving the home firms a look in?"

Phyllus found herself in fervent unison with these patriotic senti-
ments.

Jake, satisfied with the state of his nails at last, transferred his attention to Phyllus' ankles. She did not move away, for Jake had the air
of one who has not completed his remarks; and she remained standing,
for there was no place to sit. Standing in itself made Phyllus' heart beat
hard and fast, and now, coupled with her excitement, the old smother-
ing sensation began to come upon her again. But Phyllus waited, standing, and in due time Jake said:

"We'll have supper somewhere together to-night. How's that?"

As simple as that.

He took her, finally, after driving her around Stanley Park—ah, how
often had Phyllus envied the flappers in Jacques' Salon who had talked
casually of driving around Stanley Park—to the boarding house on
36   Richards street, and Phyllus, for the first time in the evening, was

afraid. Not that Phyllus herself lived in a much more exclusive neighbourhood, her home being on Jackson Avenue, inhabited mostly by
negroes, and not so very far from the outer fringes of Chinatown. But
it was familiar, and this place was not, and Phyllus had never been
clever at concealing her emotions.

Jake said, "This place is all right. Sure. Under new management now.
And it's clean. Good gosh, did you expect the Vancouver Hotel?"

Phyllus followed him up the stairs, and past the man at the desk,
whom Jake greeted as an old friend. She trembled, but that, she
thought, was due more to her unreasonable heart than to her fear.

The place was clean, as Jake had observed.

Phyllus was totally innocent of sex, although she had a foul-mouthed
father and a mother who, when she was not drunk, was frank enough.
When she was drunk, she was sentimental, with the unpleasant and
insincere sentimentality of her race.

Phyllus clung at this point to the hope that after all, nothing would
happen, maybe. For this hope Jake was responsible. It should be explained that Jake had the soul of an artist. That was why his Salon de
Beauté was such a success that even women and girls from Shaugh-
nessy Heights now came to him and trusted him implicitly in the choice
of hairdressing styles and shades of rouge. Jake was an ardent admirer
of romance and beauty. He read poetry. He had said to Phyllus that
maybe they wouldn't try anything the first night. Just lie together and
talk and get acquainted. This had seemed to Phyllus an admirable idea.

And to do Jake justice he was quite prepared to follow out this pro-
gramme, having a flair for the unusual. Partly because he was an artist,
and partly because he was very sleepy, the weather being hot. But
with his arms about Phyllus his sleepiness departed, and he said, "Kid,
this is simply torture to me. You don't understand."

Phyllus thought this touching, and she had always been the victim of
a nervous desire to please.

Jake regaled her, later, with stories of his previous exploits which
Phyllus did not mind, it being tacitly understood that from now on
Jake was to be true to her alone, although he did happen to have a
wife, to say nothing of the other girls in the Beauty Salon.

Jake said, in addition, "You're as safe as a church, see? I never knew
this to fail, see? Anyways, I know a doctor. Just as good as a doctor,
anyways."

Phyllus had never expected very much of life, which was just as
well; but during the months which followed, she had her taste of the
joy of living. The work, she discovered, was easier. Jake was kind.
Once or twice he gave her money above her wages. He took her out to
eat. Once he took her to a show, so that Phyllus for the next two
weeks was able to exult to every girl she marcelled, delighting in being

able to say the expected, the proper thing, "Gee, did you see Gloria Swanson at the Capitol?" until a *blasé* flapper said, one day, inevitably, "That's old," after which Phyllus did not refer to it again.

Jake even took her to English Bay and gave her money to rent a bathing suit, and they lay on the sand, grimy and happy, and ate hot dogs, and Jake feasted his eyes upon her, having the soul of an artist, as he frequently reminded her.

But the highlight of the summer was the Sunday he took Phyllus to Capilano Canyon.

They started early, as they were going to walk and see the scenery. Jake might have taken his car, which Phyllus would have preferred; but Jake explained that it would be much more original, and also much pleasanter, really, to walk and see the scenery as one could never hope to do from a car. So Phyllus met him at the corner of Main and Hastings, outside the library, and they proceeded to the dock, through odorous streets lined with second-hand stores and Chinese lodging-houses and Greek restaurants, tall bleak warehouses and employment agencies, down under the subway, already, at nine o'clock in the morning, filled with jostling crowds of men and women and children on their way to Capilano Canyon for the day, laden with picnic baskets and raincoats and kodaks and babies, and most of them, like Phyllus and Jake, prepared to walk—to see the scenery.

They bought chocolate bars and bananas and gum at the news-stand, and passed through the revolving gate to the wharf.

The North Vancouver ferry was half way across the inlet, looking, at that distance, clean and glistening.

She boomed a greeting to the West Vancouver ferry, homeward bound. Phyllus, to whom the sound of drums, of whistles, of thunder, always caused a palpitating flutter of the heart, clutched Jake's arm. Jake was indulgently amused and protective. He gallantly held her elbow while he made way for her through the scrambling crowd when the ferry docked, and found seats on what would be the shady side of the boat when she turned, as he explained to Phyllus, very nautical and technical. Later arrivals observed the strategic position enviously, as they wandered vainly about in search of any seat at all, or failing that, a place to deposit their parcels. Jake was always efficient in a crowd. He looked well, too, with his dark eyes and black hair, glistening with brilliantine, and the carefully trained foppish sideburns, and the crisp black moustache. He would have looked well even if he had not been, as Phyllus proudly told him, such a swell dresser. Other girls cast interested glances at him, but Jake, though acutely conscious of their attention, was blandly indifferent, as he explained the principles of the boat's mechanics to Phyllus. Phyllus adored him.

Phyllus felt that it was almost too much. The clear blue water, the sparkling sunshine, and she, Phyllus, going to Capilano Canyon for the day with Jake! She wondered what the people who glanced at her so casually would think if they knew that she, Phyllus, were one of those whom romance and adventure had claimed for their own, lifting her out of the rut of ordinary days and ordinary ways, and setting her apart forever, for had not she, Phyllus, known Life?

Phyllus looked at Jake, unhearing, and glowed.

Jake ceased his exposition of naval mechanics, and transferred his attention to the crowd surging restlessly about them.

"Lotta tourists already," commented Jake. "Great people, the Americans. The tourists are all right. Sure. Bring business."

At North Vancouver they took the tram as far as it went, and then started on their walk, Jake waving aside the taxi-drivers who kept up a continuous and cacophonous chorus until they were out of sight.

Phyllus enjoyed the walk, in spite of the fact that she tired so easily and that the sun was hot. Jake discarded his coat, and strode forward, magnificent in a pink silk striped shirt, over the roads damp and spongy from the summer rains, and Phyllus pantingly followed him. The rich dense green of the trees on either side of the road soothed her and promised coolness and quiet, and Phyllus would have liked to stop and explore their depths, and just for this one day to lie on piled heaps of leaves and rest, rest, and listen to the sound of the wind in the branches, and look at the sky, and forget all that had happened to her before she knew Jake. Phyllus' whole being called out for rest. Just for this one day. The trees yearned toward her as she passed, whispering of the coolness and the peace waiting for her, only a few steps from the hot and crowded road. But had they not planned to spend the day at Capilano Canyon, she and Jake, had they not come to North Vancouver for no other purpose, would it not be foolish and ridiculous to change their plans for so idle a fancy as this, to rest for a day beneath the trees at a spot which had no particular name, and was never visited by tourists? Certainly Phyllus knew how absurd it would be. She did not mention it to Jake, but followed him breathlessly, under the hot sun, stumbling over the rough places in the road.

They came, finally, to the long hill that is climbed by two steep flights of steps, with a log railing worn smooth by thousands of clutching hands.

"Race you to the top," suggested Jake, jocularly.

For a long and horrible moment Phyllus, looking at the steps, thought her heart had stopped beating. She put her hand to her breast, and leaned weakly against the rail.

"It would *kill* me to run up them steps, I do believe," said Phyllus at length, and Jake, alarmed, looked at her.

"Gosh, kid," he said, "you *are* tired. We'll sit down here for a couple 39 of minutes, and take it easy. How's that?"

But even after the rest, Phyllus apologetically explaining how she had always tired easy, and with Jake's hand beneath her elbow as they climbed, Phyllus wondered how she ever got to the top. When she finally accomplished it, they sat again on a fallen log until she had re-covered her breath, and Jake bought ice-cream cones from the old woman at the side of the road, and the remainder of the walk to the Canyon was not so hard.

At the Canyon itself, Phyllus won Jake's admiration by walking steadily across the long swinging bridge, glancing all along the way with mild contempt at the stout American matrons who clutched the rail, shrieking that they couldn't take another step, and Jim, take me back! No, Phyllus told Jake with scorn, it wasn't height as made her dizzy. Not while you could walk along on the level, like this. It was climbing as took her breath away and gave her that stitch in her side.

When they had eaten their lunch and given the scenery its due meed of praise, it was time to start for home, if they wanted to catch the second-to-last ferry.

The walk back to the ferry did not appear so long or so tiring, for it was down hill, and the evening was cooler. But it was with a dusty, exhausted company that they silently filed onto the boat and sank upon the nearest benches.

Phyllus would never forget, she knew, the beauty of that night, not as long as she lived, with the loveliness of the clear stars against the dark sky, the gentleness of the water, the cool fragrant air, and the comfort of Jake's arm about her tired body. All about them in the soft shadowy gloom shopgirls and their men unashamedly petted. Some one strummed a ukulele. They sang snatches of jazz:

"I'll be loving you—always—always."

Jake's hand moved about her breasts, and the pain which lay always in wait beneath them was for the moment quieted and robbed of its power.

Still to do Jake justice, he did know someone who was just as good as a doctor, a specialist, in fact; and if he had not lost so much at poker the week previous he would have seen Phyllus through her trouble, and this, too, without being unpleasant.

But as it was, he had lost the money, and that was all there was to it.

So he said, "Good God, kid. I told you to be more careful. Listen, do you know what this will cost? One hundred in cold cash! One hundred marcels! Two hundred hair trims. Girl, I wish I could do it for you. I sure do. But the truth is, I simply haven't got—why, I can't pay my own bills. Let alone anything like this. And that new drying lamp to pay for! Now listen, Phyllus, you'll be all right. Lots of girls go through with it, and none the worse and no one the wiser, either. And your job is right here waiting for you, when you come back, any time, Phyllus," said Jake, thus concluding their relationship as he had begun it, in a burst of generosity.

Phyllus was very uncomplaining and quiet about it. She really did not say anything at all. At least, Jake could remember nothing afterwards, although he tried.

In fact, Jake said later, "If the kid had only stayed around, I'da helped her out. Sure. I was just thinking how I could manage." Which was probably true.

But Phyllus was tired. Looking back over her life, she could not remember a time when she had not been tired, the result, most likely, of consistent malnutrition.

Phyllus was not excitable or resentful, and she made her plans very carefully and matter-of-factly, insofar as the plans did not seem in some mysterious manner, to be already formed, for she did not have to ponder the question at all. There was only one thing to do, and Phyllus knew how to do it.

Phyllus went for a brief walk by the beach. The water was flat and still and the colour of gun-metal. Phyllus found it soothing.

She felt, on the whole, quite happy, leaving the world with no regrets, which is more than is given to most. But her chief comfort lay in the fact that it seemed inevitable and the only thing to do. There is always a certain joy in doing the right thing at the right time, which is the basis of all convention and civilization; and Phyllus, at this moment, savoured the zest of undeniable correctness.

She drew a long breath and fixed her eyes on the top of the stairs, but as a matter of fact she never reached the top.

She left a note for Jake, feeling that this, too, was the correct thing to do. He received it the next morning, before he had seen the papers, although even so he might have remained unenlightened, for Phyllus did not reach the headlines.

Phyllus merely said, in conclusion, "I was never strong like you," and there was by that time no way of telling whether she had written the words in a spirit of irony or apology, although Jake has sufficient intelligence to wonder.

JEAN BURTON (1905–52) *was born in Abernethy, Saskatchewan. She lived in Vancouver from 1922 to 1926 while studying at the University of British Columbia (B.A. 1924), and again in 1929, after receiving her M.A. from the University of Alberta. During the late 1920s she published several pieces about Vancouver in* The Canadian Forum, *including "Phyllus," whose sexual frankness stirred considerable controversy among* The Forum's *readers. She also contributed to the* Canadian Mercury *and* Willison's Monthly *in 1928 and 1929, and later to* New Frontier. *In 1930 she moved to California, where she tried to launch a literary career as a novelist and playwright. Remaining in the United States, she finally found her niche as a biographer, publishing six books, many of them about unconventional women. Their titles include* Sir Richard Burton's Wife *(1941),* Elisabeth Ney *(1943), and* Lydia Pinkham is Her Name *(1949).*

A CUP OF COFFEE

DOROTHY LIVESAY

He was standing on the corner of Robson and Granville, his hand jingling in the near-empty pocket. What the hell was he going to do now, he wondered, with all his gratuities gone? Sunk into Vet's Fuels, Inc. Might as well have been thrown into a ditch as thrown to that stinker, Eddie. But he might have known it would turn out like this. Everything had turned out black since way back, since before he knew Hilda, even. . . .

Hilda. The name came easily to his mind. His lips opened slightly, as if the name were like taking a breath. What was it the welfare lady had said? Cold, chilly words as he stood there in the hall, hot with sweat.

"I think you would find her changed, Mr. Metka." Maybe she would be. Maybe—He took his hand from his pocket, slowly mopped his brow with it, as if to clear his thinking.

B-r-r-r. A siren blared. A car screeched to a stop as the light changed. A girl, about to cross the street, caught herself back quickly. Then she half turned on her heel, swinging towards him.

"Hilda!"

The girl turned sharply, violently. Seeing him there she made as if to dart across the street. But the traffic was against her. He took a stride towards her and drew back towards the drugstore window.

"So, it's you." That was all she said.

He took her in at a glance. She looked the same, only thinner. Her hair hung long, in yellow ringlets. He did not like it that way.

"Gosh. How locky I been." In the shock of seeing her he lost control over his accent.

"And I suppose you were lucky the first time you saw me. Well, I wasn't. And I'm not now." Yes, she was hard as nails, like the welfare lady had told him. Still, seeing her was a thousand times better than sending messages through the government hook-up. It meant. . . .

This story originally appeared in The Canadian Bookman *in 1939 and was substantially revised for Livesay's* Right Hand Left Hand (1977).

"Now looka here, Hilda. We gotta talk see?" He took her arm and be-gan walking fast up Granville St. "Come and have a cup of coffee."

"Aw, Nick, I haven't got the time. I'm busy."

"Busy? How long you been in town?"

"A coupla days. I lost that job in Kamloops. So I'm looking for one here."

"Well, come and have a cup of coffee on me." He steered her into the cafe, headed for a quiet cubby-hole at the rear.

"Two coffees—and doughnuts, hey Hilda?"

"O.K." Huh. He though likely she'd be hungry. Probably hadn't had any breakfast. He beamed across at her, intoxicated at his good luck. But before he said anything, he'd wait till after she'd eaten.

"What went wrong on your job?"

"Nothin. Business was bad. They didn't need me."

"Well, you're a good waitress. Shouldn't have no trouble here."

"I had trouble enough before."

"Sure. I know that. I mean, gettin' a job. Seen George yet?"

"Uh huh. He's keepin' me in mind. But it's not any of your damn business, Nick."

He flushed hotly. She was still mad, eh? "Well, maybe you don't think it's my business. But I do. Looka here, Hilda. Chust because I kin hardly keep goin' myself don't mean I don't worry about you...."

"Oh yeah? You been workin'. I know."

"Sure I been workin'. Truckin' sawdust. It looked good, too. I put all my gratuities into the outfit. We was workin' it up, me an Eddie. Get-tin' orders for the winter. He had a hookup with a new mill, out East Hastings. It looked O.K."

"Then what?" She didn't sound interested. Just sarcastic.

"I tell you it looked good. Looked like I'd be able to get onto my feet, and make you a real offer. Then the mill folded up—the son of a b---, Eddie he run off with the truck. Just quit cold and left me holdin' the bag. I got nothin'."

"That's an old story—from you. You had enough dough in Nelson last week-end to take a dame to a beer parlor."

"It's a lie." He pounded the table with his fist.

"Well," she countered, "I'd take somebody else's word rather than yours."

"Who told you such a thing?"

"Your own cousin."

"Frank? Oh, so that's it. Is that all? Why, that was *his* girl, Hilda! He had to go out o' town and he ast me to keep an eye on her."

She lit a cigarette, puffing it into his face. She was beginning to get excited. "Huh. Do you expect me to believe that?"

44

He stared at her, mouth gaping. It had been true. It mightn't uv been but it was, for chris' sake!

"Awright, Hilda. Believe what you want. That don't stop the facts from bein' so. And it don't make my bank account any bigger, either. I tell you. I'm flat. I gotta get a job, fast."

"Why don't you go back to the woods?"

"It's my lame back. Ever since Italy, I can't do the work I use to do, and it ain't easy to find jobs no more—in town, that is. Not like it used to be."

Her mouth tightened again. "And d'ya think it's easy for me? If I'm workin', what do I get. Twenty bucks a week. And rent to come out of that, and clothes, and car fare. And seven dollars for Tommy's keep. . . ."

She broke off quickly, biting her lips, but it was there. She had said it. He leaned forward across the table, breathing fast.

"Heelda! Heelda, why won't you let me see him?"

"I've told you why—too damn often."

"But Heelda! *If* I could pay. Look at me, Heelda. Can't you see it's the trut'? Even if I was making twenty a week, I would give you give—for him. If I had it. Last Christmas, didn't I. . . ."

"Ten bucks. Ten little measly bucks. To pay a year's board, I sup-pose?"

It wasn't much. Not much. But he had thought maybe—"You're awful hard, Hilda."

"And why shouldn't I be? Who made me that way? I got fooled once and now I'm not taking any chances. I've got to look out for myself—and for Tommy. Nobody else will."

"But what harm would it be chust for me to see him? Chust once't? Can't a man see what his own kid looks like?"

"Oh. So you *still* want to be sure he's yours? And then, maybe, you'll pay up? Well, for your information, he's the image of you—brown hair, brown eyes—dark skin—poor kid."

"I know that. The welfare lady told me. That's why. . . ."

"Oh! She did? And what else did she tell you?"

"Nothin'. She wouldn't give me the address. Not till you'd o.k.'d my goin' to see him. Aw, Hilda. . . ."

"Well, I give them that much credit. You can trust their word."

"Listen, Hilda. Ever since I left the old country, kissing goodbye to my little mother, ever since, I wanted to have a home of my own, and a little kid, Hilda. What's gone wrong? Why can't we have it?"

She was putting on her gloves. "Do we have to go over all that again? I'd be keeping you too, as well as Tommy. I got more sense."

He sighed, leaned back in the hard seat. She had changed so he 45 hardly knew her. It would be like cat and dog between them now. He had enough sense to see that. But she mustn't go yet. He had one more card to play. His heavy hand reached for the small gloved one.

"Well, I won't ast you that. I won't even ast to see him. But I got a plan, Hilda. It ain't easy for you to keep Tommy, I can see that. And it ain't easy—it ain't possible for me to keep him. But I want to help, and you gotta believe that...." He paused a minute, wondering how to say it.... She fidgeted, pulled out her make-up box. He put his hand over that too.

"Chust a minute, Hilda. O.K. Please listen to me, this once't. You know Jan—my brother, Jan?"

She nodded, her eyes narrowing.

"Jan and Emma they been married six years. They got a good farm, good fruit country. They got a nice, snug house, and a dog, and chickens. But there's somethin' they ain't got, Hilda. Somethin' that you and me's got, see? They ain't got a kid, Hilda!"

"You mean...?"

"Sure I mean. Jan could keep Tommy. He wants Tommy. He'd even adopt him if we liked. You wouldn't have to pay no board. You could see him whenever you wanted. He'd have all the fresh air, and the milk and the strawberries he needed. And he wouldn't be with strangers no more."

He paused, waited. Her face looked empty. She wasn't saying anything.

"Hilda!" He leaned over, his two hands seizing her wrists.

"Don't. Don't touch me!" She yanked herself away. Her coffee cup rolled over and spilled its dregs on the oilcloth. She turned sidewise, pulled herself out of the seat.

"Hilda. You ain't going like that?" He sprang up to face her in the aisle.

"Leave me alone. Let me out of here!"

"No," he said. "No. You gotta answer me, Hilda."

"Answer what?"

"About Tommy—goin' to Jan."

She stood still opposite him. "Give him to Jan? After two years that I've kept him myself? Give him away to *your* folks and probably never see him again? Say, you must be crazy."

"Hilda." He shook her roughly. "It's sense. It's the only sense there is. It'll give the kid a chance't."

"A lot you've cared about his chance—or mine either." A gulp came into her voice. Amazed, he saw that she was crying.

"Hilda. Hilda." Roughly he patted her arm. "Sit down. Sit down a minute."

46

She crumpled into the seat again, burying her head on her arm. He just sat there beside her, at a loss what to do. Gradually the shaking body quieted. She found a handkerchief and blew her nose. He just sat there.

"I didn't mean to cry" she said, in a stifled voice.

"Sure you didn't. You're strong, Hilda. Strong."

"But I couldn't have you take my baby away from me. I couldn't."

"Sure you couldn't."

"He's mine. He's all I have. I don't see him often, but he's mine."

"Sure, he's yours."

"I'm sorry to make a scene on you like this."

"It's awright." He was folding a paper napkin and squeezing it into a small ball.

Gathering together her bag and gloves, she stood up quickly.

"Well, goodbye, Nick. I'll have to fix my face. Get cleaned up. Make the rounds."

"Sure. Goodbye, Hilda."

They shook hands, then she ran out of the cafe.

The waiter brought him his bill. Two bits. That left him thirty-seven cents for the rest of the day.

DOROTHY LIVESAY was born in Winnipeg in 1909, the daughter of writers and journalists J.F.B. Livesay and Florence Randal Livesay. She attended university in Toronto and in France, and by the age of twenty-four had published her first two books of poetry: Green Pitcher *(1928) and* Signpost *(1932). Deeply moved by the misery of the Depression, she worked as a social worker and political activist in several Canadian and American cities before settling in Vancouver in the late 1930s. She remained here for two decades, raising her two sons and writing poetry, winning the Governor General's Award in 1944 and again in 1947. After a three-year stint of teaching English in Zambia and numerous writer-in-residence and teaching positions at universities across Canada, Livesay has returned to B.C. and now lives on Galiano Island. Her major works of poetry include* Day and Night *(1944),* Poems for People *(1947),* The Unquiet Bed *(1967), and her* Collected Poems *(1972). Her prose appears in* Beginnings: A Winnipeg Childhood *(1973) and* Right Hand Left Hand *(1977), her memoir of the thirties, for which she revised "A Cup of Coffee."*

SOPHIE

EMILY CARR

Sophie knocked gently on my Vancouver studio door.

"Baskets. I got baskets."

They were beautiful, made by her own people, West Coast Indian baskets. She had big ones in a cloth tied at the four corners and little ones in a flour-sack.

She had a baby slung on her back in a shawl, a girl child clinging to her skirts, and a heavy-faced boy plodding behind her.

"I have no money for baskets."

"Money no matter," said Sophie. "Old clo', waum skirt—good fo' basket."

I wanted the big round one. Its price was eight dollars.

"Next month I am going to Victoria. I will bring back some clothes and get your basket."

I asked her in to rest a while and gave the youngsters bread and jam. When she tied up her baskets she left the one I coveted on the floor.

"Take it away," I said. "It will be a month before I can go to Victoria. Then I will bring clothes back with me and come to get the basket."

"You keep now. Bymby pay," said Sophie.

"Where do you live?"

"North Vancouver Mission."

"What is your name?"

"Me Sophie Frank. Everybody know me."

Sophie's house was bare but clean. It had three rooms. Later when it got cold Sophie's Frank would cut out all the partition walls. Sophie said, "Thlee loom, thlee stobe. One loom, one stobe." The floor of the house was clean scrubbed. It was chair, table and bed for the family. There was one chair; the coal-oil lamp sat on that. Sophie pushed the babies into corners, spread my old clothes on the floor to appraise them, and was satisfied. So, having tested each other's trade-straightness, we began a long, long friendship—forty years. I have seen Sophie

This story is from Emily Carr's Klee Wyck (1941).

glad, sad, sick and drunk. I have asked her why she did this or that thing – Indian ways that I did not understand – her answer was invariably "Nice ladies always do." That was Sophie's ideal – being nice.

Every year Sophie had a new baby. Almost every year she buried one. Her little graves were dotted all over the cemetery. I never knew more than three of her twenty-one children to be alive at one time. By the time she was in her early fifties every child was dead and Sophie had cried her eyes dry. Then she took to drink.

"I got a new baby. I got a new baby."

Sophie, seated on the floor of her house, saw me coming through the open door and waved the papoose cradle. Two little girls rolled round on the floor; the new baby was near her in a basket-cradle. Sophie took off the cloth tented over the basket and exhibited the baby, a lean poor thing.

Sophie herself was small and spare. Her black hair sprang thick and strong on each side of the clean, straight parting and hung in twin braids across her shoulders. Her eyes were sad and heavy-lidded. Between prominent, rounded cheekbones her nose lay rather flat, broadening and snubby at the tip. Her wide upper lip pouted. It was sharp-edged, puckering over a row of poor teeth – the soothing pucker of lips trying to ease an aching tooth or to hush a crying child. She had a soft little body, a back straight as honesty itself, and the small hands and feet of an Indian.

Sophie's English was good enough, but when Frank, her husband, was there she became dumb as a plate.

"Why won't you talk before Frank, Sophie?"

"Frank he learn school English. Me, no. Frank laugh my English words."

When we were alone she chattered to me like a sparrow.

In May, when the village was white with cherry blossom and the blue water of Burrard Inlet crept almost to Sophie's door – just a streak of grey sand and a plank walk between – and when Vancouver city was more beautiful to look at across the water than to be in, – it was then I loved to take the ferry to the North Shore and go to Sophie's.

Behind the village stood mountains topped by the grand old "Lions", twin peaks, very white and blue. The nearer mountains were every shade of young foliage, tender grey-green, getting greener and greener till, when they were close, you saw that the village grass outgreened them all. Hens strutted their broods, papooses and pups and kittens rolled everywhere – it was good indeed to spend a day on the Reserve in spring.

Sophie and I went to see her babies' graves first. Sophie took her best   49 plaid skirt, the one that had three rows of velvet ribbon round the hem, from a nail on the wall, and bound a yellow silk handkerchief round her head. No matter what the weather, she always wore her great shawl, clamping it down with her arms, the fringe trickling over her fingers. Sophie wore her shoes when she walked with me, if she re-membered.

Across the water we could see the city. The Indian Reserve was a different world—no hurry, no business.

We walked over the twisty, up-and-down road to the cemetery. Casamin, Tommy, George, Rosie, Maria, Mary, Emily, and all the rest were there under a tangle of vines. We rambled, seeking out Sophie's graves. Some had little wooden crosses, some had stones. Two babies lay outside the cemetery fence: they had not faced life long enough for baptism.

"See! Me got stone for Rosie now."

"It looks very nice. It must have cost lots of money, Sophie."

"Grave man make cheap for me. He say, "You got lots, lots stone from me, Sophie. Maybe bymby you get some more died baby, then you want more stone. So I make cheap for you.'"

Sophie's kitchen was crammed with excited women. They had come to see Sophie's brand-new twins. Sophie was on a mattress beside the cook stove. The twin girls were in small basket papoose cradles, woven by Sophie herself. The babies were wrapped in cotton wool which made their dark little faces look darker; they were laced into their baskets and stuck up at the edge of Sophie's mattress beside the kitchen stove. Their brown, wrinkled faces were like potatoes baked in their jackets, their hands no bigger than brown spiders.

They were thrilling, those very, very tiny babies. Everybody was excited over them. I sat down on the floor close to Sophie.

"Sophie, if the baby was a girl it was to have my name. There are two babies and I have only one name. What are we going to do about it?"

"The biggest and the best is yours," said Sophie.

My Em'ly lived three months. Sophie's Maria lived three weeks. I bought Em'ly's tombstone. Sophie bought Maria's.

Sophie's "mad" rampaged inside her like a lion roaring in the breast of a dove.

"Look see," she said, holding a red and yellow handkerchief, caught together at the corners and chinking with broken glass and bits of plaster of Paris. "Bad boy bloke my grave flower! Cost five dollar one, and now boy all bloke fo' me. Bad, bad boy! You come talk me fo' p'liceman?"

At the City Hall she spread the handkerchief on the table and held half a plaster of Paris lily and a dove's tail up to the eyes of the law, while I talked.

"My mad fo' boy bloke my plitty glave flower," she said, forgetting, in her fury, to be shy of the "English words".

The big man of the law was kind. He said, "It's too bad, Sophie. What do you want me to do about it?"

"You make boy buy more this plitty kind for my glave."

"The boy has no money but I can make his old grandmother pay a little every week."

Sophie looked long at the broken pieces and shook her head.

"That ole, ole woman got no money." Sophie's anger was dying, soothed by sympathy like a child, the woman in her tender towards old Granny. "My bloke no matter for ole woman," said Sophie, gathering up the pieces. "You scold boy big, Policeman? No make glanny pay."

"I sure will, Sophie."

There was a black skirt spread over the top of the packing case in the centre of Sophie's room. On it stood the small white coffin. A lighted candle was at the head, another at the foot. The little dead girl in the coffin held a doll in her arms. It had hardly been out of them since I had taken it to her a week before. The glassy eyes of the doll stared out of the coffin, up past the closed eyelids of the child.

Though Sophie had been through this nineteen times before, the twentieth time was no easier. Her two friends, Susan and Sara, were there by the coffin, crying for her.

The outer door opened and a half dozen women came in, their shawls drawn low across their foreheads, their faces grim. They step-ped over to the coffin and looked in. Then they sat around it on the floor and began to cry, first with baby whimpers, softly, then louder, louder still – with violence and strong howling: torrents of tears burst from their eyes and rolled down their cheeks. Sophie and Sara and Susan did it too. It sounded horrible – like tortured dogs.

Suddenly they stopped. Sophie went to the bucket and got water in a tin basin. She took a towel in her hand and went to each of the guests in turn holding the basin while they washed their faces and dried them on the towel. Then the women all went out except Sophie, Sara and Susan. This crying had gone on at intervals for three days – ever since the child had died. Sophie was worn out. There had been, too, all the long weeks of Rosie's tubercular dying to go through.

"Sophie, couldn't you lie down and rest?"

She shook her head. "Nobody sleep in Injun house till dead people go to cemet'ry."

The beds had all been taken away.

51

"When is the funeral?"

"I dunno. Pliest go Vancouver. He not come two more day."

She laid her hands on the corner of the little coffin.

"See! Coffin-man think box fo' Injun baby no matter."

The seams of the cheap little coffin had burst.

As Sophie and I were coming down the village street we met an Indian woman whom I did not know. She nodded to Sophie, looked at me and half paused. Sophie's mouth was set, her bare feet pattered quick, hurrying me past the woman.

"Go church house now?" she asked me.

The Catholic church had twin towers. Wide steps led up to the front door which was always open. Inside it was bright, in a misty way, and still except for the wind and sea-echoes. The windows were gay coloured glass; when you knelt the wooden footstools and pews creaked. Hush lurked in every corner. Always a few candles burned. Everything but those flickers of flame was stonestill.

When we came out of the church we sat on the steps for a little. I said, "Who was that woman we met, Sophie?"

"Mrs. Chief Joe Capilano."

"Oh! I would like to know Mrs. Chief Joe Capilano. Why did you hurry by so quick? She wanted to stop."

"I don't want you know Mrs. Chief Joe."

"Why?"

"You fliend for me, not fliend for her."

"My heart has room for more than one friend, Sophie."

"You fliend for me, I not want Mrs. Chief Joe get you."

"You are always my first and best friend, Sophie." She hung her head, her mouth obstinate. We went to Sara's house.

Sara was Sophie's aunt, a wizened bit of a woman whose eyes, nose, mouth and wrinkles were all twisted to the perpetual expressing of pain. Once she had had a merry heart, but pain had trampled out the merriness. She lay on a bed draped with hangings of clean, white rags dangling from poles. The wall behind her bed, too, was padded heavily with newspaper to keep draughts off her "Lumatiz".

"Hello, Sara. How are you?"

"Em'ly! Sophie's Em'ly!"

The pain wrinkles scuttled off to make way for Sara's smile, but hurried back to twist for her pain.

"I dunno what for I got Lumatiz, Em'ly. I dunno. I dunno."

Everything perplexed poor Sara. Her merry heart and tortured body was always at odds. She drew a humped wrist across her nose and said, "I dunno, I dunno", after each remark.

"Goodbye, Sophie's Em'ly; come some more soon. I like that you come. I dunno why I got pain, lots pain. I dunno—I dunno."

I said to Sophie, "You see! the others know I am your big friend. They call me 'Sophie's Em'ly'."

She was happy.

Susan lived on one side of Sophie's house and Mrs. Johnson, the Indian widow of a white man, on the other. The widow's house was beyond words clean. The cookstove was a mirror, the floor white as a sheet from scrubbing. Mrs. Johnson's hands were clever and busy. The row of hard kitchen chairs had each its own antimacassar and cushion. The crocheted bedspread and embroidered pillowslips, all the work of Mrs. Johnson's hands, were smoothed taut. Mrs. Johnson's husband had been a sea captain. She had loved him deeply and remained a widow though she had had many offers of marriage after he died. Once the Indian agent came, and said:

"Mrs. Johnson, there is a good man who has a farm and money in the bank. He is shy, so he sent me to ask if you will marry him."

"Tell that good man, 'Thank you', Mr. Agent, but tell him, too, that Mrs. Johnson only got love for her dead Johnson."

Sophie's other neighbour, Susan, produced and buried babies almost as fast as Sophie herself. The two women laughed for each other and cried for each other. With babies on their backs and baskets on their arms they crossed over on the ferry to Vancouver and sold their baskets from door to door. When they came to my studio they rested and drank tea with me. My parrot, sheep dog, the white rats and the totem pole pictures all interested them. "An' you got Injun flower, too," said Susan.

"Indian flowers?"

She pointed to ferns and wild things I had brought in from the woods.

Sophie's house was shut up. There was a chain and padlock on the gate. I went to Susan.

"Where is Sophie?"

"Sophie in sick house. Got sick eye."

I went to the hospital. The little Indian ward had four beds. I took ice cream and the nurse divided it into four portions.

A homesick little Indian girl cried in the bed in one corner, an old woman grumbled in another. In a third there was a young mother with a baby, and in the fourth bed was Sophie.

There were flowers. The room was bright. It seemed to me that the four brown faces on the four white pillows should be happier and far more comfortable here than lying on mattresses on the hard floors in the village, with all the family muddle going on about them.

"How nice it is here, Sophie."

"Not much good of hospital, Em'ly."

53

"Oh! What is the matter with it?"

"Bad bed."

"What is wrong with the beds?"

"Move, move, all time shake. 'Spose me move, bed move too."

She rolled herself to show how the springs worked. "Me ole-fashion, Em'ly. Me like kitchen floor fo' sick."

Susan and Sophie were in my kitchen, rocking their sorrows back and forth and alternately wagging their heads and giggling with shut eyes at some small joke.

"You go live Victoria now, Em'ly," wailed Sophie, "and we never see those babies, never!"

Neither woman had a baby on her back these days. But each had a little new grave in the cemetery. I had told them about a friend's twin babies. I went to the telephone.

"Mrs. Dingle, you said I might bring Sophie to see the twins?"

"Surely, any time," came the ready reply.

"Come, Sophie and Susan, we can go and see the babies now."

The mothers of all those little cemetery mounds stood looking and looking at the thriving white babies, kicking and sprawling on their bed. The women said, "Oh my!– Oh my!" over and over.

Susan's hand crept from beneath her shawl to touch a baby's leg. Sophie's hand shot out and slapped Susan's.

The mother of the babies said, "It's all right, Susan; you may touch my baby."

Sophie's eyes burned Susan for daring to do what she so longed to do herself. She folded her hands resolutely under her shawl and whispered to me.

"Nice ladies don't touch, Em'ly."

EMILY CARR (1871–1945) was born and raised in Victoria, British Columbia. Better known for her distinctive paintings of Indian artefacts and the lush coastal forests than for her writing, she studied art in San Francisco and England, returning to Canada in 1904. In January 1906, she moved from Victoria to Vancouver and established a studio in the Fee Block at 570 Granville Street, where she taught painting to children. However, her four and half years in Vancouver were lonely; one of her few friends was Sophie Frank, who became the subject of her story "Sophie." In 1910 Carr went to Paris for a year. Upon her return she briefly maintained a new Vancouver studio at 1465 West Broadway, but in 1913 she returned permanently to Victoria. In the late 1920s her creativity found a new outlet in writing, a medium which proved increasingly hospitable as her painting activities were curtailed by her declining health. Her first book, the collection of sketches and stories (including "Sophie") gathered under the title Klee Wyck, *was published in 1941 and received a Governor General's Award. Subsequent books include* The Book of Small *(1942),* The House of All Sorts *(1944), and her posthumously published autobiography,* Growing Pains *(1946).*

GIN AND GOLDENROD

MALCOLM LOWRY

It was a warm, still, sunless day in mid-August. The sky did not appear so much cloudy as merely a uniform pearly gray, like the inside of a seashell, Primrose said. The sea, where they saw it through the motionless drooping trees, was gray too, the bay looked like a polished metal mirror in which the reflections of the lead-gray mountains were clear and motionless. In the forest it was very quiet, as though all the birds and small creatures had abandoned it, and the two figures of the man and his wife walking along the narrow footpath, and their little cat bounding along beside them, seemed the only things alive, so that when a vermilion and black and white garter snake wriggled off into the dry leaves and twigs it sounded loud as a deer crashing through the bracken.

Primrose was looking everywhere for the pair of goldfinches, whose nest, with its exquisite pale blue-white eggs, they had found in a trammon tree only six feet from the ground in May, and which they had watched all summer with delight, but their birds were nowhere to be seen.

"The dear goldfinches have gone to Alcapancingo," she said.

"Not so early... They're just gone because they don't like it here any more, with all these new houses going up and their old haunts destroyed."

"Don't be gloomy, Sig darling. It'll be all right."

Primrose and Sigbjørn Wilderness were now approaching the few houses on the fringe of the forest. The cat, black and white, with platinum whiskers, sat sniffing at a clump of spring beauty. He would go no further. Then he vanished. Sigbjørn and Primrose came out of the woods into a place where the ground was being cleared, then as by common consent turned off before they reached the store that had come in sight – which was being partly dismantled in order to create a

Lowry's letters indicate that he was working on this story in 1950, although it was not published until four years after his death, in Hear Us O Lord From Heaven Thy Dwelling Place (1961).

larger one – taking another side path to the left. This transverse path had also once led through the woods, but the ground on one side had been cleared for building. The bushes had been allowed to remain, and it was still a pleasant leafy way of thimbleberries and salmonberries, that in winter, in frost, in moonlight, made a trillion moons.

It brought them out abruptly on a dusty main highway, upon either side of which, as far as the eye could reach, lay sections of brown drainpipe and where a signpost said: *To Dark Rosslyn.*

Sigbjørn's emotions now were entirely those of the cat's – or what the cat's would have been had he had the poor sense to accompany them this far: terror, fear, distrust, anger, anguish, and a hatred so pure in its intensity it was almost beautiful to experience. It was mid-afternoon, and Sunday, and now the cars honked and whizzed by in an all but continuous uproar, each sending up its private cyclone of dust from the road, against which the two had constantly to pause and turn their backs. The bus for Dark Rosslyn came past, snarling like a wild beast crashed by, leaving a backwash of air in which the trees thrashed for some moments. For there were trees again now, on either side of the road, for a short distance, then where there had been the woodland, through which they would have continued their path, there was a huge area of rubble, from which stumps of trees, blackened, hollow, some in cactus shapes, protruded as if blasted by lightning. Near at hand, on the highway, with no thought of privacy, some new houses had already been built, but owing to the law, no trees were left near them. Nevertheless, the destruction of the forest had opened up a magnificent view of the mountains and the inlet, that had been invisible from the road before, and you would have thought that all this evidence of growth and rebuilding would have been productive of anything but despair. On either side of the road a shallow ditch fell away to what, in other seasons, was a small brook, now dry and choked with weeds. Primrose, searching for wildflowers wherever a trace of moisture remained in these ditches, was wandering back and forth across the road, or even pausing vaguely in the middle to search the banks on either side. At these times Sigbjørn would shout at her or even seize her by the waist or shoulder and push her into the side. "Look out!" "My God, there's a car –" "Primrose! There's a –" "I know it. Look, darling –" and she was off again, swift and graceful in her scarlet corduroy slacks.

Sigbjørn's anxiety shifted now, as for the moment she walked in single file ahead of him – though every time a car went by he almost jumped into the ditch himself – to their goal in Dark Rosslyn. He doubted his ability to find it in the maze of roads that wandered around the hillside at the edge of the town, wondered if he would recognize the house again, through the heavy dolorous recollections of the previous Sunday, and feeling in his right side still the pain of the fall in the black woods, he began to sweat. Now he wished to take off his shirt, knowing that if he said so Primrose would say brightly, "Well, why don't you?" and somehow unable to do so on this main highway.

They passed the office of the Rosslyn Park Real Estate and Development Company: *Rosslyn Park, Enquire Here, Scenic View-Lots. Approved for National Housing Loans. Cash or Terms:* past the hideous slash of felled trees, bare, broken, ugly land crossed by dusty roads and dotted with new ugly houses where only a few years ago rested the beautiful forest they had loved.

Look Out for Men! said a sign: *Soft Shoulders: Keep away: Private:* and now the road was half torn up and the ditches where the brook had been and the wildflowers of spring once grew were being filled in with a pipe line, bringing water and all the commercial comforts and plumbing of civilization to their once wild and lonely haven. Here, in particularly vicious slash, where some rank thistles and huge dandelions grew, they saw their goldfinches feeding along the thistles, and paused. Among them was a new bird, like a tiny yellow and black striped sparrow, and Primrose ran across the road again, followed by Sigbjørn, looking both ways at once.

"Look! It's a pine martin."

"A martin's a kind of rat."

"Yes, that's right; but there's a bird called a purple martin."

"You mean a pine siskin."

"Of course. But what's it doing here on the coast? They only live in the high altitudes. Oh, isn't it sweet."

The pine siskin darted away and they walked on past, now, thank God, the end of ugsome Rosslyn Park and the little new "coffee bar"–Sigbjorn glanced at it with pure hatred, it was Sunday, but anyhow you could only buy Coca-Cola and Seven-Up–the big new schoolhouse, a great concrete block of mnemonic anguish, and reached a short stretch still comparatively unspoiled. What did he mean by this–"comparatively unspoiled"? Were one's emotions of horror even quite the truth? Canada was indeed a pretty large country to despoil. But her legends, nearly all her most valuable and heroic history was the history of spoliation, in one form or another. But man was not a bird, or a wild animal, however much he might live in the wilderness. The conquering of wilderness, whether in fact or in his mind, was part of his own process of self-determination. The plight was an old-fashioned one, that had become true again: progress was the enemy, it was not making man more happy or secure. Ruination and vulgarization had become a habit. Nor–though they had found a sort of peace, a sort of heaven, and were now losing it again, had they, very consciously, been looking for peace. Nevertheless he could not help think-

58

ing of the green loveliness of their lost woodland, etc. etc., and all
these conflicting clichés buzzed in his head as he followed Primrose,
who had found a deep spot where a pool of water from the brook still
lingered and here, shaded from the dust and heat of summer, a mass of
wild blue forget-me-nots shone fresh and bright among damp emerald
moss and near it some American brooklime.

But Sigbjørn could not climb down and pick them for her, he could
not, even, remember the name, though he himself had first found and
identified this latter flower in June. She didn't want them now, Primrose said, they would be all wilted before they even reached Dark
Rosslyn; perhaps he could pick her some on the way back. And now
she had seen some goldenrod, growing among a great bank of pearly
everlasting; the first goldenrod of the year. They would pick that on
their way back too.

"I'm even more doubtful now," he said.

"Of what?"

"That I can find the house."

"But I phoned the taxi driver this morning. You told me to. I said
we'd be along this afternoon. He knows where it is, doesn't he?"

"I don't think I can face him ... *With his knowing grin,*" he added.

"There's the taxi driver's house just ahead, honey. Come on, it'll
soon be over now."

"Besides, I wanted to save money," Sigbjørn said.

"*Save!*"

"Don't be angry. I'm sure I can find it," Sigbjørn said, standing at the
crossroads. "It's just up there and off to the left, I think."

"Well ... how far is it?" Primrose said dubiously.

"Not too far. Well—perhaps it's a fair distance but if we don't find it
we can always come back and get the taxi."

Primrose hesitated, then took his arm and they went off up the side
road. The road was unpaved and dusty but at least they were rid of
the momentous traffic and the taxi driver, and Sigbjørn felt rather less
sick and almost hopeful. But the intrusion of the taxi driver at all disturbed and confused him. Why had he told Primrose to phone the taxi
driver? He thought he remembered him in relation to last Sunday but
the connection between him and the object of their visit was vague.
Nonetheless he had been sufficiently conscious of such a connection to
think it worth getting Primrose to phone. And then, there was always
the question that he'd thought he would never have been able to make
it walking at all.

The road went downhill briefly toward the sea, turned sharply right,
then left again and now ahead of them was a long steep hill. He gazed
at it in dismay, for it didn't look familiar at all. Had he really come this
way? Or should he have made that other turn off to the left, as Prim-

59

rose suggested was more likely. He hesitated, listening to the distant
sound of traffic: the klaxons sounded like blended mouthorgans.

"No, I'm sure it's this way. Come on," Sigbjørn said, and they started
up the hill doggedly. Now, the traffic behind, a suburban dementia
launched itself at them: flat ugly houses, the cleared land, stricken and
bare, left without a tree to give shade or privacy or beauty; or strewn
with half burned stumps and rubbish. Wy Wurk, Wy Wurry, Amble
Inn (again), Dew Drop Inn, Dunwoiken, Kozy Kot, crowned by the
masterpiece: Aunty So-Shall. But behind each one of these bourgeois
horrors was still the dark forest, waiting, one hoped, for revenge.

They trudged slowly up the hill and now Sigbjørn really began to
sweat, for it was hot here, with a sultry damp heat that made the air
feel thick and hard to breath, and his side was hurting again. He looked
anxiously back at Primrose who had removed her scarlet corduroy
jacket and was panting and scowling behind him, for though she loved
to walk she hated climbing hills, and at this moment she meant him to
know it. Sigbjørn went ahead, but he could already see that it was as
she said: the road wound directly away from Dark Rosslyn and back
toward home. But there, too, just at the turn, was a rustic wood arch
at the left which said *Whytecliffe Resort, Riding Academy, Horses by the
Day or Hour. Refreshments.*

Sigbjørn waited unhappily until Primrose caught up with him.

"Well," she said. "Did you go to Whytecliffe?"

"I don't think so. No."

"Surely you'd remember that thing." She pointed to the arch.

"I don't know ... but we might as well go and see."

"You go then. I'll sit here and catch my breath."

Tall cedars, Douglas firs, grew beyond the arch as he went up the
bridle path, and it was a little cooler, a breath from the sea below
freshened the air, and now he could see the bay beneath him, and for
some reason this made him feel better. There, below him and to the
right were the stables; people were getting on and off horses, calling to
each other, and a young couple mounted and paced up the hill toward
him: "What do I do?" "You just pull on the right rein and it'll do it for
you." And that was true too, once on it, the horse would do everything for you, even to throwing you off. It was hard to be angry with a
place where you could hire horses, or see a riding academy as a symptom of modernity. He and Primrose always talked of riding together,
though they never had. And how much better the money might have
been spent here, with her—well, it was no use looking, he knew it
wasn't here he'd been the previous Sunday, and he turned back.

"Isn't this where Greenslade lives now—at Whytecliffe somewhere,"
she said when he returned to the arch.

"I think so ... Yes."

"We might go and find him then. He'll know where it is."

"No!" Sigbjørn said. "No, I'll find it, for Christ's sake . . . or we'll get the taxi driver. Come on."

"But Greenslade was with you. He'll know—"

"No." Sigbjørn started distractedly down the hill. "You said no your-self. You said you'd rather be in hell than meet Greenslade again."

"He's a horrible man."

"Yapping about the benefits of civilization. How easy it is for people to talk about the benefits of civilization, who've never known the far greater benefits of not having anything to do with it all!"

Halfway down the hill Primrose suddenly took his arm.

"Look, Sigbjørn, there—those birds with the white stripes on their tails."

"Vesper sparrows?"

"No. They don't have so much white. Oh, what are they?"

"Pipits. Some kind of pipits. American pipits," Sigbjørn said, as the birds lighted on a nearby alder tree. "Yeah. See how they're bobbing their tails?"

"How clever you are—" Primrose held his arm tightly to her side. "And brave too. I think you're swell. I know this is perfectly bloody for you."

"Thank you. I think you're very fine too. But all this isn't easy to do. And I don't see why I'm doing it."

"But you said you wanted to make a new start, you said it was to be—"

"Yes it was. *It is.*"

Watz-it-2-U. Opposite this house, a little further on, a narrow rutted road turned off to the right and Sigbjørn halted again; it didn't look familiar yet he had the feeling the place was off in that direction. At the juncture of the road a stone house was in process of being built. The foundations were in, the walls were part way up, the window frames had taken their square or oblong gaping shapes and inside this half-built house three people were standing: a man, his wife, and a little boy about seven or eight. They were walking around it, they leaned on the windowsills, they pointed, now, toward where the roof would be, their every expression and gesture one of such hope and ex-citement and joy that Sigbjørn turned away: even were the fate of this house to be called Amble Inn, it was not right to look at them thus, he felt, gruesome though their odious nest might be.

He walked on quickly, but as the road made a sharp turn he halted suddenly before three houses in front of which there seemed to be a policeman, or a man in shirt sleeves and a navy blue cap like a police-man's. He turned and almost ran back to where Primrose was linger-ing, around the bend, gazing at some more goldenrod.

"I think it's over this way, but there's a policeman there—"

"A policeman? Where?"

Primrose walked on around the bend then turned, beckoning. The policeman was a taxi driver. But he was not "their" taxi driver. He was a strange one, probably from the city, but if not a policeman, why a taxi driver *here* at this place, and why these other people standing nakedly and unguiltily about, but as it were too consciously *unlooking* —but no, the taxi driver was merely shepherding two elderly women who were looking rather too curiously at Sigbjørn, or so it seemed, and he hurried on again past the three houses and began to climb yet another hill that ran out of sight. But at the top of this hill the road stretched out, turning toward the highway with, oh God, yet another long, long, steep hill ahead.

"I won't do it. I won't," Primrose said. She stamped her foot. "If we'd got the taxi driver we'd have been there and had it all over by now. I won't—"

"Please. Oh please, Primrose. Don't be angry. As a matter of fact I'm sure it's just down there," Sigbjørn yelled in a soft whisper. "Look, maybe it's that—"

"I won't—"

"Christ you said you didn't want to see Greenslade. And Christ I'm doing my best. And Christ I think this is the house."

It might be. He hurried on and stopped at a corner where three more houses made a blind T. Here it was—or was it? There was this house on the near corner, a high-roofed, wooden house, in need of paint, with a bare, littered yard in which a little black kitten and a puppy were playing together and a small girl playing with a saw stared at them.

"Well, is this it?" Primrose caught up with him, tight-lipped and pale.

"Oh hush! You insisted on coming with me, now you might be—"

"What?"

"Oh for God's sake, Primrose."

"I never did any such thing. You know you begged me to come, Sigbjørn—"

Sigbjørn, exasperated beyond endurance and smarting under his own unfair and untruthful charge at Primrose, gave one despairing glance around and rushed to the door where he knocked loudly.

"Why not try the back door?" Primrose suggested after a while.

The back door was open and they could see through into a dirty, dark kitchen with dirty dishes and bits of stale bread and food on the floor and sink. A radio played loudly. Sigbjørn knocked again. There was a deceptive air of slatternly innocence in a teapot sitting on the cookstove and though the place had something familiar about it he still couldn't be sure. And if Al—Al? didn't answer the door who on earth was he to ask for? He took the letter out of his pocket and tried again to make out the signature: "Dear Sigbjørn—you asked how you could send that $26.00 Your wife exerted so much pressure for me to be on my way the other morning that I forgot to leave you my address. Which is Yours truly F. Landry (Landing? Fanbug?) P.O. Box 32 Dark Rosslyn." This same pressure he must have felt exerted upon himself, for it seemed he moved from the door, and was contemplating going around to the front again.

Primrose suddenly took his arm, then she kissed his cheek. "There now, Sig darling, it'll soon be over now my brave one."

He took a deep breath and knocked again, loudly; the radio was turned off somewhere in the front of the house and footsteps sounded. Sigbjørn turned around.

"You promised," he whispered, "you promised to be nice—and to have a drink with him, if he offers us one."

And now someone, a man, the man Al, appeared, a short muscular fellow with untidy hair, dressed in unpressed trousers, suspenders over a soiled shirt, while his shoes were curled up at the toes and broken at one sole. Sigbjørn felt Primrose stiffen behind him, taking in every detail of his loose fat mouth, bad teeth and squinting eyes.

"Hello," Sigbjørn said.

"Hello. Come in." He opened the door and they filed into the squalid kitchen where Primrose sat down quietly on a chair and Sigbjørn stood beside the sink. "Haven't got a thing in the place," the man was saying, "but Al can get you a bottle."

Sigbjørn, who had thought this man was Al, was confused, and now the beacon, the pharos, of the possible drink at the bootleggers' that had shone before him all the way was gone. He remembered the rather hopeless, nearly empty bottle at home and glanced at Primrose, but she was gazing out the door, her clear, cold profile and glassy polite smile gave him no hope on this plane.

"I came to pay you the debt I owe you from last Sunday," Sigbjørn said. "I got your letter."

"Yeah? I've quit. Well, I've quit for a while anyways. After last Sunday. But there was no hurry about that. You could have sent me a check or something."

"Do I really owe you twenty-six dollars?"

"That's right. There was eight bottles of gin drunk up here last Sunday. First time I ever served drinks in my house. I tried to get you to go, you know, but then the Indians came."

"Indians?"

"Yeah."

"But I paid for the first two bottles. I had the money, remember?" Sigbjørn said. "And Greenslade paid for his didn't he? Or didn't he?"

"He paid. But he went, after the first bottle was gone. He didn't   63 drink so much. He took his bottle and left. But you wouldn't go. You wanted to take them two bottles home to drink with your wife, re-member? But then them Indians came and you started buying them drinks and that's bad stuff. You know. Indians. It ain't safe. I was on hot bricks."

"I'm sorry if I caused you any trouble," Sigbjørn said.

"Oh, that's all right, bud. But I never saw a man drink so much and stay on his feet. Them Indians passed out—one was laying on the floor over there, remember? And he was getting tough—you know how they do when they're drinking. They feel insulted."

"They do," Sigbjørn said. "And by God—"

"Giving drinks to Indians, that's bad. I tried to get you out, then to get you to lay down a little and you says: I'm going to lay down and sleep for exactly twenty minutes and then I'm going to get up and have another drink. And by God you done just that. Never saw anything like it, Missus." He turned to Primrose. "That's just what he done. Exactly twenty minutes."

"Yes," she said.

"Well now, I hate to see a man get taken advantage of. Them Indians ought to of paid for some of it. You know when you get it from me on a Sunday, like, when the liquor stores is closed, I gotta charge a bit more and all. Tell you what, though, suppose we settle for twenty, how's that?"

"Thank you . . . How did I spend thirty-nine dollars?"

"Well, brother, you drank it. Never saw a man drink so damn much and stand on his feet. I got a taxi and took you home, remember? That is, I let you off there by the store and you said you'd make it the rest of the way all right. And I put a bottle in your pocket, you wanted to take to your wife, did you get home with that?"

"I got lost in the forest."

"It's the first time you've every done it," Primrose said.

"Well I'm damned." The man grinned. "You sure had a time for your-self, bud. But you got home O.K.?"

"Yes, I got home O.K. You saw me the next morning. I mean the morning after the next morning." Sigbjørn stared at the floor: but not that night. Where, actually, had he spent that night? Had he slept on the ground? drunk the bottle? where had he fallen? And the new sports jacket, precious because Primrose had given it to him for his birthday, worn only the second time that night—

"I've quit," the man was saying to Primrose now. "The person next door is very religious . . . one of them Indians fell down outside and he was quite obscene in his language . . ."

And why not, Sigbjørn thought, Christ why not! and he remem-
64 bered the time when the deer used to come down through the woods

and swim across the bay and there hadn't been any bootlegger in Dark Rosslyn to sell you firewater on Sunday, or, come to that, any reason for drinking it. How easy to make a judgment here. The deduction made, another lie would speed to its total doom, were it wholly un-true: the evil is in its half-life, where it coalesces with all the other half-truths and quarter-truths to confuse us, the esemplastic medium of oversimplifications in which we live. The bootlegger, in times of pro-hibition, in great cities, has one function. The bootlegger, in times of partial prohibition, has another. The bootlegger, on Sundays, where there is Sunday prohibition, is a secular savior. The bootlegger, in rural places is as fundamental as the prostitute in the city—

"I've been batching it for three weeks—the wife's in Saskatoon. That's why the place is in such a mess," the man was saying apolo-getically to Primrose, and then to Sigbjørn: "Well, we'll settle for twenty dollars, is that O.K.? And I'll tell you what, there's one of them Indians I know pretty well and maybe I can get a bottle out of him to pay his share. If I can I'll bring it along, how's that?"

"O.K." Sigbjørn said, handing over the twenty dollars.

Primrose went to the door. "It looks like rain," she said, "perhaps we'd better get started."

"Well, good-by."

"So long, bud. See you in jail."

"Ha ha."

"Ha ha."

Sigbjørn and Primrose Wilderness walked silently side by side down the road toward the long hill until they felt themselves out of sight of the houses. Then Primrose suddenly threw her arms around Sigbjørn.

"Darling Sig. Please forgive me for being so foul. I really was perfectly foul and God I'm sorry! Say you forgive me."

"Of course. I was disgusting too."

"You weren't. You were brave. I know how awful that was for you and I—I thought you were gallant!"

"There are the pipits again—there."

"So they are."

Watz-it-2-U... Walking hand in hand they came to the bottom of the long hill and there was a new footpath branching off through the woods toward the highway, a short-cut which would eliminate the hill. "But Primrose, honey, maybe it's private property. What if it ends up in somebody's garden?"

"It doesn't say so. Oh come on, Sigbjørn, let's try it anyhow."

Primrose started down the path which, at first fairly wide, became more and more narrow and overgrown though now, just ahead, they could hear the snorting obscene traffic of the highway. Then suddenly the path debouched into a garden and there in front of them was a woman, hoeing. Sigbjørn and Primrose started to apologize together but the woman straightened up and smiled.

"Oh, that's all right. Somebody comes in here every once in a while from that path. You can get through to the road. Just go round the garage there and down our drive."

They thanked her and Sigbjørn led the way, Primrose following behind.

Once more they were on the highway, pushed into the side of the ditch by the passing cars. Primrose was gathering pearly everlasting and tall dusty purple asters, she gathered them, for Sigbjørn could scarcely bend for the pain in his side, so he carried them for her and walked behind. Kozy Kot. Amble Inn.

The rain began to fall, soft and gentle and cool, a benison. They came to the little boarded shelter of the bus stop and halted for a moment as they saw the bus approaching.

"Shall we take the bus?"

"Oh no. Let's walk."

"But you'll get wet. Won't it spoil your clothes?" Sigbjørn said, for he loved her scarlet corduroy slacks and jacket.

"Not these. I don't think it's going to rain very hard anyhow. And I do want some goldenrod!"

The bus whizzed past and they turned their heads from that disgusting smell and blast which progress has schooled us to believe—as Proust observed—was nostalgic too. A silent ambulance looking, Sigbjørn thought, like a hearse, came up the road from the city and stopped before a house on the corner.

"Look—" Primrose said. "Do you remember that chap who used to sit on that porch typing every time we came by?"

"Oh yes—on the big heavy office typewriter. I hope he's not—"

They lingered, watching the ambulance driver in conversation with a gray-haired woman on the porch, but it appeared he was only inquiring his way, and they started on, obscurely relieved that it wasn't the man of the typewriter, to whom they'd never spoken a word.

Primrose walked ahead, carrying a single stem of scarlet bunchberries, that species of tiny dogwood they had discovered one spring, and Sigbjørn behind, carrying the goldenrod. He was watching Primrose in her scarlet slacks and the scarf she was wearing now over her head against the rain, which was of scarlet and cobalt and emerald and black and white and gold in the design of a curious bird with a cobalt beak and emerald feet.

"I have a confession to make, Sigbjørn," she said.

"May I know what?"

"You didn't lose that bottle of gin. You gave it to me when you came back the next morning. But I put it away and then you thought you'd lost it."

"Then we have it now."

"Sure. And we can have a cocktail when we get back."

"Good girl."

They stepped into their own woods and the cat came leaping to meet them. In the cool silver rainy twilight of the forest a kind of hope began to bloom again.

MALCOLM LOWRY (1909–57) was born into comfortable circum-stances in Birkenhead, England. He early proclaimed his unconventional-ity when he shipped out as a deckhand before attending university. After his graduation from Cambridge in 1932, *he followed an itinerant and er-ratic literary career through Europe, Mexico, and the United States, even-tually settling in the Vancouver area. For much of the time between* 1939 *and* 1954 *he and his wife, Marjorie Bonner, lived in a shack in the squat-ters' colony at Dollarton—the site of present-day Cates Park on the north shore of Burrard Inlet and the setting of "Gin and Goldenrod." During his lifetime Lowry published only two books:* Ultramarine (1932) *and* Under the Volcano (1947). *His alcoholism contributed to his early death in Eng-land, after which many of his voluminous manuscripts were edited and published by his widow and his friends, including* Hear Us O Lord From Heaven Thy Dwelling Place (1961), Lunar Caustic (1963), *and* October Ferry to Gabriola (1970).

LOVE IN THE PARK

WILLIAM McCONNELL

He could never conceive of the Park not being there, never having existed, with its sheards of grass, too-long by necessity in the small stream which ran through its centre, and the evergreen hedge trees which looked clipped but really grew that way with time, as if the monstrous gods tired of licking their bases and really slirruped at their peaks. The Park must, at one time, of course, have not been there, for the city was not old, perhaps one hundred years, and even sixty years ago away out here on the edge of the beach and crowding suburbs there had been a real creek where the stream now was, and evergreens so high and thick that many an oxen team had been hullooed and chivvied and goaded before they were skidded away to the first mill on the inlet.

He had often thought of the Park always being there, from the time he was a boy and his wizened nurse, whom everyone but himself called Panky, let him roll on the undulating bank which led to the stream, while she read *The Woman's Companion,* or some sort of companion which was its predecessor, for of course he wasn't able to read even titles in that long ago time. He called Panky a stink when she cut his visit short to walk further to the beach, but to her face, particularly when she let him nestle against the ratty fur neck-piece which garrotted her neck, he called her Grey Anne – why, God alone knew in retrospect, for it sounded even then like one of the makes of English biscuits his mother placed so much credence in as nourishment between meals, or even a heavy butterfat yielding cow, though Panky, of course, had no milk in her or to her or even a suggestion of lactation when she seldom smiled. In fact, she was a woman of so little emotions and those so thoroughly diced and shredded into her imagined duties that one could almost call her a person of curried emotion, except there was no real seasoning, not even anger, for she didn't shout or grow cross but merely snapped. Yet, whatever her nature or lack of it, she

 This story was published in Klanak Islands *in* 1959.

did introduce him to the Park, and its small three acres, seeming huge then, had since been vested with the oblique-rayed charm of childhood discovery. So much so, that in later years on repeated walking through it and over it and around it and by it his senses simply refused to believe that it was encompassed by backs of three story wooden homes of Victoria's reign and a strong batter might easily hit any of its boun- daries if the batting of baseballs in its centre were allowed by the always elderly caretaker.

Now, of course, the houses were old and leaned on their acquired wooden fire escapes with which authorities decreed their senility as rooming houses must be fortified if thirty instead of eight or ten per- sons were to be rent-cozened in each. His home had been of stone for most of its way up three storeys. Yet it, too, had changed, even though not backing on the Park, as there were red paint-covered varicoses of never-used stairs from its height over the beach almost to the ground. He seldom walked by it, even though he often visited the Park, yet when he did his mouth would tighten a little wryly at the wooden strip-tease the city hall by-lawed that stairs, even fire-stairs never used, should almost but never quite touch the ground which afforded safety.

For some never ascertained reason—certainly not aesthetic—none of the houses could be called a home (just as he couldn't call his deserted house by the beach home, or for that matter call the place he now lived in a home, or any place which didn't have his anxious long-dead mother, his sporadically absent father and Panky-the-stink and himself and his brother and perhaps some dog he vaguely remembered as Sport, a half-dozen toys the sight of which would now sprout either tears or a yawn of boredom or even both, and finally the self of him which had long since died far more successfully than mother, father, Panky, brother, Sport and toys).

Perhaps, he thought, as he scuffed the autumn turf, that is why he couldn't conceive the Park as never having been there. Not because it physically remained while the others had mouldered as fast or faster than the beach leaves sticking to his wet soles. Nor even that its sides and size refused to shrink as he grew older and less magical and less real. But (and here he was only pondering, with no real outcome to lure him on, or even fantasy to bewilder and bewitch) because it was here he first loved, loved first, loved often and loved always and where he never failed to return. The Park wasn't approximate, or time-filled, as everything else was, even the pulsing race of physical love itself, but actual and equating. The very placing of each and every house which surrounded it on all but two sides proved this, for they all looked wrong and the Park was exactly right.

This was true when the weeping willows, hedge pines, bush maples, and mountain ash were tiny, probably newly planted, for then they were monstrous to his three, four, then five and six feet. His growth didn't match theirs, but it was so commensurate that when he died he knew for certain if he were laid in their middle boughs as the Indians buried their dead, he would be lifted gently and inexorably to the clouds and beyond, for it would be commensurate then. It was not that he felt communion with the Park – that, in his nature, was impossible – but it was the place of love and rightness and, unlike the surrounding houses, would never need props to make it bear age.

It had had its dangers. Once, when he lingered too long with his romping and Panky (as the others insisted on calling her with callous disregard for associations) had left him without a call, the spring eve-ning had suddenly wavered into near-darkness, and the smoke from dozens of garden fires curled and blued into the quiet air so that, with a little effort, he knew he would be able to roll up-hill, even up-air, much more smoothly than down. When he leaped across the brook and toiled up the green slope to where Panky was sitting a huge man step-ped from behind a monkey tree and said,

"Wait!"

The voice was neither cold nor warm, loud nor soft, commanding nor entreating, but an empty sound inviting him to step into it and rattle around and make its sides echo for the first time of his experience.

He would have obeyed but Panky suddenly appeared and shrieked at him to hurry and the man disappeared around the monkey tree with-out another word. Panky had chewed the man's presence to pieces all the way home, filling him so full of terror that even now he himself couldn't approach children, even one he knew (except of course his own, and even with him it was always a cautious process) unless there was first a litany of court formalities which killed all interest in himself and the approached and turned their freckles grey.

Again, when he was almost in his teens, he was walking after park-ing his bicycle at the entrance, when he saw Belknapp, the wheezing dandruffian neighbourhood cop, creeping about the far hedging, uni-formed knees almost touching the grass in his obvious anxiety to sti-fle his own presence, then suddenly pounce like a scrofulous cat and pull a shamed struggling couple from a niche and shake them with glee so that their loosened clothing fell from their white terrified shanks. This time he was old enough, however, to respond. With Belknapp's cycle held by his right hand, he careened past the night-stalker and on, right to the footpath of the beach with the unmajestical law heaving in pursuit, where he sent the bicycle sideways into deep tide-water and cursed because he was too thin and little to hurl its owner, too.

Over the stream which ran through the Park, not too far from the covey of vine maples which hid the sun, no matter how hot the sum-mer day, there was a log bridge so hugely hewn that it might have served for a niagara underneath, yet instead the stream merely widened and quietened and formed a large pool where he and the others when he was growing swore there were trout. There might have been, for then, even as now, it was clear, with a sand bottom and enough gnats and bluebottles stitching the air just above its surface to feed a thousand fish. If you trotted over the bridge there was a slight rumble, as the planks were always giving non-uniformly with age, and replacements only muted the sound for a while till they, themselves, gained character and sedate looseness. It was perpetually cool under the bridge and it was pleasant, no matter what your age, to sit there, chew the tender stalks of stray grass and see the Rubens-like hams of the summer-dressed housewives out for a stroll before their husbands came home.

The Park never prompted chance matings, for it was too formal and chastely dressed with underbrush. Yet it was a place for lovers, and even he had loved there, under the sympathetic scorn of a cheese moon and with the white beginning of hoar frost on the close-clipped grass. He had loved by walking slowly over the brittle stubble of grass, touching her arm, her fingers, suddenly clutching her when passing a benign bare tree trunk, only to have the magic swilled down the drain when she whispered,

"No, no. Let's go home."

And her voice, till then compared to the stream, was neither loud nor soft, cold nor warm, commanding nor entreating, but an empty sound inviting him to step into it and rattle around and make its sides echo, with the difference that the long-forgotten man belonged to the Park and she didn't for she wished them somewhere else.

It had been many months before he knew that hand-gropings, like word-gropings, were not love, any more than acres and trees with interspersed shrubs could ever duplicate the Park. For fortunately, they returned many times and it was he who was at fault in trying to mesmerise the shadings of feeling which must grow and never become detached. They wandered each evening for many months through and along the chance walks. It was autumn and the huge seas only a block away in their casting in of spindrift and roar, though muted, still caused the air about them to smell strongly of salt, and each tree trunk, seemingly secure, tremored from the blows in its upper branches, trying to warn the two below of the violence elsewhere.

When he left for war they met for the last time in five years. He remembered his own false puckishness as he kicked snow, crystal by crystal it seemed, for it was so cold, about her protected ankles, and talked vaguely and wildly of how she must retrace every step each evening and recount in her daily letters how many steps she paced for him, a promise she did not make but which he imposed. This night it was his voice which was the empty sound, his invitation to treat him like an empty gourd and shake him hard, while she was dreamy and tactile and seemingly too engrossed by their trysting place to let him matter whatever he intended to do.

Each day she wrote and for many months there was always a reply. The seasons in their minutest changes were transmuted for him although he was five thousand miles away where climate dropped its seasons like badly-handled stage curtains—so sudden they shocked changelessness from its seat and galled one into age. And unlike him, she always walked alone.

Away, some alchemy worked a change in him. Blood, strange bruising images, hills instead of mountains and sand dunes where there should have been a sea, all gnarled and twisted so that he never walked alone, or talked alone, or bedded alone, or talked or walked or bedded at all but crowded in with a thousand others a frenetic activity that was neither life nor death and frosted every root of existence till one became a sad-gay corpse giving out and receiving death and life with drugged abandon.

And although his letters stopped, and long after hers did, too, almost stopping with an audible sigh, she still walked daily to the Park, rescued shoaled boats in the stream, talked gravely and low with neighbours, hoped and sustained by what it had meant to him, till it grew the same for her, and gave the strength which caused her certainly not to forget, but to grow and supplant till there was another walking the self-same paths, learning slowly the identical mysteries (which wonderously never changed) till he, too, was accepted.

This, the first one learned when he returned. Learned, not from her, for they never spoke, though they nodded solemnly each day when they met. He learned from the shrubs, the changing sky, the moist descent of rain when everyone who walked but he carried an umbrella or at least a hat. Yet he was happy as he limped along, his shattered left leg adding a new sound to the packed clay walk—happy to know his earliest knowledge of the Park always being there and always holding his love inviolate was now confirmed, and to see there her two grave children, shy at his uneven walk, glancing up and into him.

WILLIAM MCCONNELL was born in 1917 in Vancouver, his home for much of his life. After riding the rods during the Depression and rising from private to sergeant in the Canadian Army during the Second World War, he studied at the University of British Columbia and practiced law in Vancouver until his recent retirement. His short stories, mostly written during the forties and fifties for the CBC and a wide range of periodicals, including Queen's Quarterly, the Canadian Forum, and First Statement, remain uncollected. McConnell is also editor of Klanak Press, which published Klanak Islands (1959). This collection of stories by Vancouver writers includes "Love in the Park," which is set in Tatlow Park in Kitsilano.

A DRINK WITH ADOLPHUS

ETHEL WILSON

"Well I can't do both," said Anne Gormley. "If I go with you I can't go
to the Moxons'" ("What you mean is you can't go with that Thibeau-
deau boy to the Moxons'," said her mother) "and if I don't go with you
I *can* go with Tibby and I like going to the Moxons' and it *is* a party
and it'll go on and on the way I like it. I'm sorry of course," said the
beautiful girl shaking back her hair, "that you'll have to take a taxi but I
do hate that kind of party that goes home at seven, sheer waste, and
you know that's when you'll want to come home because you're scared
of being late for dinner—you darling darling," she said, almost surrounding her mother with sudden cajoling love, "we like different parties. Okay by you?"

"I suppose so but this isn't a party. It's just us." And, as so often, she
stopped herself saying out loud to her youngest child, "I'd like you to
have been brought up in my generation, my young lass, just for about
two years."

"I'll order your taxi for you."

"Not yet," said Mrs. Gormley who was lame and had to do her hair
and make the best of herself and go downstairs rather slowly.

"Oh why do you go!" said Anne, her affection smiting her a little.
"You don't *hafto!*"

"Yes," said her mother at the mirror, "that's three Saturdays now. I
do have to. It's just us. To see the view. The house is old but he's mad
about the view on Capitol hill. That's why Adolphus bought it. I can't
not go and your father'll be delighted not to have to."

Before walking downstairs, crabwise, Mrs. Gormley looked in on her
husband but there was nothing to see except a great lump in the bed.
"I'm going to have a drink with old Adolphus. Goodbye Hamish," she
said, but only a muffled sound came from the bed. In the hall she met
Ah Sing the cook.

This story was published in The Tamarack Review *in 1960 and in Wilson's* Mrs. Golightly and Other Stories *in 1961.*

"I takem hot lum Mister Doctor," said Ah Sing. "I fixem he cold."

"Yes do, Ah Sing," said Mrs. Gormley in the rather effusive way that she had the habit of employing to the Chinese cook whom she and the children had loved, feared, and placated for twenty years.

The taxi, proceeding eastwards, sped through mean streets and then began to climb. Mrs. Gormley looked towards the north at the salt waters of the inlet, gently snoring against the foot of the hill. The thought of going all this way to have a drink with Adolphus bored her and the fact of paying for a taxi both ways bored her still more; but she would enjoy the view. Adolphus was not a friend by selection, rather by happening. He was the kind of person that she had known, for-tuitously, for so many years that he was designated "friend". They had lived near each other in childhood and Dolly had played with her big brothers and had survived to be called Adolphus. That was all. There-fore Mrs. Gormley was bored in anticipation and it was expecting too much of Hamish who had not been brought up with Dolly Bond to want to spend one of his precious Saturday afternoons admiring Dolly's new house. Now that the years spun faster and faster, Saturdays came hurtling towards Mrs. Gormley like apples thrown. She was still a fool for optimism and thought each week (after all these years with the chil-dren), But next Saturday Hamish and I will really "do" something, even if it's only staying at home. But come Saturday, and Hamish would say "I may be late home from the hospital and then I have some calls to make." He would arrive home late for dinner (he – the only one permitted by Ah Sing) and Saturday spun past them again without even being seen.

"Please stop," said Mrs. Gormley to the taxi-man, "and I'll have ten cents' worth of view."

The view was certainly superb and worth more than ten cents. She looked down the slope at the configuration of the inlet and on the wooded shores which now were broken by dwellings, by sawmills, by small wharves, by squatters' houseboats that were not supposed to be there, by many little tugs and fishboats moored and moving with vees of water in their wakes. But her eyes left the shores and looked down across the inlet, shimmering like silk with crawling waves where the tidal currents through the Second Narrows disturbed the waters. She looked farther on to where the dark park lay, dark green and black with pines and cedars against the bright skies of coming evening, at the ocean and islands beyond (so high she was above the scene), and across at the great escarpment of mountains still white with winter's snow. In ten cents' worth of time, she thought – and she was very happy islanded, lost, alone in this sight – there's nearly all the glory of the world and no despair, and then she told the taxi-man to drive on.

Adolphus Bond's new house was nice and rather shabby but, Mrs.

Gormley told herself, it was a credit to Adolphus and it had something that these flat caricatures of houses hadn't got, although their insides were charming. The taxi arrived, and she was greeted by Adolphus and other sounds.

"It's so good of you to come," said Adolphus kindly as he helped her out of the car.

"So sorry about Hamish," said Mrs. Gormley at the same moment, stepping down not gracefully but with care.

"Too bad you had to get a taxi, someone would have fetched you," said Adolphus, kindest of men.

"You see it came on so suddenly," said Mrs. Gormley simultaneously. "One moment no cold, the next moment the worst cold you ever saw in your life but as usual he refuses inhalations. Ah Sing is giving him a hot rum and lemon and butter and honey, good enough to make anyone have a cold on purpose," but Adolphus did not hear. Neither of them listened to the other.

"This is the cupboard," he said. "Let me."

"I see you have a party," said Mrs. Gormley, "I thought it was just us. If I'd known I'd have worn a smarter dress. In honour of the new house. Who have you?"

"Oh, some people," said Adolphus vaguely. "So I see," she said for how could it be otherwise; but Adolphus was steering her towards wide and wide-open doors and then across a room towards a fine long and deep window which intimated a sloping lawn, a fir tree perhaps, and some lovely scene beyond. "This is the library," he said although nothing corroborated the statement.

Sounds of voices came from all around. Guests had scattered, and some had gone out of the french windows on to the lawn, adding to and subtracting from the view. Mrs. Gormley felt herself seized round the waist from behind. Two hands clasped themselves in front of her and a man's voice said (breath fanning the back of her neck), "At last, little one, at last! At last I have you!"

"Well really! How unfamiliar!" said Mrs. Gormley, wishing she were still slender, "this is very pleasant but who do you suppose it is? Is there some mistake?"

"Pay no attention. He's been to a wedding," murmured Adolphus rather crossly in her ear. Mrs. Gormley stood still and tried to avoid falling over backwards upon the person to whose body she was firmly clamped in an unusual manner.

"Perhaps if you'd tell me . . ." she began, unable to do anything about it.

"This is the view, you see," said Adolphus frowning at the view.

"Yes but . . ." said Mrs. Gormley perceiving that she was now 76 unclasped. A tall slight fair man in a gray suit stood in front of her.

"Jonathan Pascoe..." remarked Adolphus,... "you see how the garden slopes away, affording..."

"How do you do Mr. Pascoe... Yes I do see, Dolly, and what trees!"

"At last we have met!" said the man in the gray suit, indicating
something somewhere with his long hands and smiling gently.

"But I have never seen you before!" said Mrs. Gormley.

"Neither have I," said the wedding guest and was no longer there.
Adolphus explained the view.

"It is beautiful, beautiful, but I should like to sit down somewhere,"
said Mrs. Gormley and Adolphus led her back into the centre of the
room and to a large high chair from which she could see out of the window. A black poodle dog, walking on his hind legs, pushed past them,
strode down the library, out of the french windows, and disappeared.

"What a peculiar thing for a dog to do! I didn't know you had a dog,
or whose dog is it?" she asked.

"What dog," said Adolphus, "this is Mr. Leaper."

"How do you do," said Mrs. Gormley and was surprised when Mr.
Leaper said he was well. He's very literal, she thought. She sat down
upon the high comfortable chair and looked around her. The wedding
guest was not among the vivacious strangers in the room which though
solid enough had a dream-like irrelevance. The large black rims of Mr.
Leaper's glasses intimidated her.

"I have just been in Spain and my wife has been in Portugal," he said.

"Have you a dog?" asked Mrs. Gormley and Mr. Leaper said, "We
used to have a monkey but it stole and we became involved in legal
difficulties." Someone put a glass in her hand. Adolphus was fulfilling
his duties elsewhere.

A young man who had the appearance of a hired waiter stood in
front of her. On the tray were familiar-looking pieces of coloured food
that she had seen somewhere before and some small spheres unfamiliar
in appearance but, it seemed, edible.

"What are these do you suppose?" asked Mrs. Gormley tentatively.
The young man became suffused by a dark spreading blush.

"I think," he said, speaking very low, "I heard some person call them
hot ovaries."

"Did you really say hot ovaries?" said Mrs. Gormley very much interested and looking at him affectionately because he was so young, so
awkward, blushing there. "Uh-huh," said the young waiter who was
some mother's son.

"I wouldn't if I were you," said Mr. Leaper as if to a child. "When we
were in Spain..."

"Parmee parmee," said a maid with a tray, pushing between them.

"What does she mean—'parmee'?" asked Mr. Leaper.

"I think she means 'pardon me'," said Mrs. Gormley. "You were saying when you were in Spain?"

"We had too many eggs."

"I thought so too," she said, "but" (warmly) "there are compensa-tions – what about the El Grecos?"

"We never had any of those," said Mr. Leaper gloomily. "Of that I am sure, as I noted down our meals very carefully in my diary."

"In your diary?" enquired Mrs. Gormley. "What else do you write in your diary?"

"I write my personal reflections and impressions," said Mr. Leaper looking very queer.

"Do you mean after a party like this? How alarming."

Mr. Leaper looked at her intently through his black-rimmed glasses and Mrs. Gormley felt uneasy. From the next room came shrieks of laughter.

"Parmee parmee," said the maid, pushing back again. There was Adolphus, looking engagingly kind. He brought up a nut-brown girl, a sad man, and a young friend of Mrs. Gormley's with a dark beard. Beards are usually dark, she thought, why. They do not even know they have legs,these people, she thought with a pang, smiling at them. They do not know how pleasant it is at a party to move, move on, move on, negotiate yourself elsewhere, get away from Mr. Leaper who does not like eggs in Spain and will write about us in his diary, give him a chance poor thing. "I am going to show them the house," said Adolphus.

"Oh, do" said Mrs. Gormley in her gushing way, and Adolphus, the nut-brown girl, the sad young man, and the young man with the beard went to look at the house. Mrs. Gormley and Mr. Leaper began to talk in earnest about Spain and the prices there. God, thought Mrs. Gormley, what would I give to have Hamish's cold, ". . . but cheaper still in Portugal!" she said, smiling, mustering pleasure and charm if any.

Evening had really fallen now. People had drifted away, to look at the house, to fill their glasses again in the dining-room, and wasn't the drawing-room full of music or something? The maid stood at the library door and threw a quick glance into the nearly empty room. Then she turned away. Mrs. Gormley, talking to Mr. Leaper, looked beyond him through the long windows unobscured now by people, on to the garden which was only faintly green in the twilight. A pale moon hung high, and upon the inlet the moonlight fell, and fell upon the garden, casting still faint shadows from a great cedar tree. The garden and the moonlight and the cedar shadows were made to walk in, but Mrs. Gormley, continuing to sit, continued also to fabricate things like "the Savoy . . . Dorchester . . . a quite humble little place on Ebury Street

78   . . . Claridge's" (how snob can we get, talking like this, impressing each

other but probably not. I sound as if Hamish and I stayed in these places, and she mimicked herself "a quite humble little place"). In the garden something moved. It could not be a large moth, but like a large moth the wedding guest danced all alone under the moon. His gray flannel arms rose and fell again. Perhaps he was flying. He advanced, flapping his arms in the haunted mystical evening, he retreated, stepping high and slowly below the cedar tree. How beautiful he was and he must have been happy. Mrs. Gormley longed to be out there dancing with the free slowly dancing wedding guest. She longed it until (sitting there smiling, with immobile hips and legs) she nearly burst, but she did not say to Mr. Leaper, "Look, there is Jonathan Pascoe whoever he is dancing in the scented moonlight like a large gray flannel moth." She could not share the wedding guest (whom she loved to see dancing under the moon) with Mr. Leaper. As she turned to agree that one could not do better than a good small hotel she saw that the young man with a beard had come to sit as if exhausted in a large chair opposite.

"Where's Anne, I suppose she wouldn't come. Your dog bit me," he said morosely.

"It's not my dog whose dog is it?" said Mrs. Gormley, "you know I haven't got a dog, Ozzie!"

"I think the government will be out in six weeks," he said, "and serve them right."

"Oh why do you think that? Whatever makes you think that?" she asked eagerly but he looked suspicious and did not answer.

"Let me fill your glass," said Mr. Leaper and did not return. Mrs. Gormley and the young man with a beard sat at peace and looked for some time at the very good carpet. She raised her head and saw that Jonathan Pascoe was leaning against the doorway.

"Little one," he said, "you are so beautiful, may I kiss you?"

"Yes, please do," said Mrs. Gormley laughing, "I need a kiss badly. I think it would do me good. How did the moonlight feel? And then will you get me a taxi. I want to go home."

Upon his return home from Mr. Bond's party, Mr. Leaper did not write in his diary as usual. He was agitated. Perhaps some part of his thin protective covering had been abrased, split, broken. However, a few nights later, he wrote:

"As you know, I make it a rule to write up my diary just before retiring at night. Mabel knows this and respects my privacy for a time which varies from a few minutes (I make registers of the seasons, bursting of buds, etc.) to quite a protracted period, even an hour. She then knocks and says in that clear voice of hers Beddy-byes and I bring my writing to a conclusion, that is, I stop writing. I hesitate to commit

to paper the effect of that word Beddy-byes (which I even find it difficult to write) upon me. There may have been a time when it did not
cause me to wince, but I do not remember. I cannot bring myself to tell
Mabel (for whom I have such a regard) to say something else, nor can I
be unmoved by it. I have no doubt that in the larger things of life Religion is a great comfort, but I do not think that Religion provides an
answer in a relatively small matter like this. However.

Some years ago Mabel gave me a nicely bound book with the spe-
cially embossed words *Diary—S. B. Leaper* upon the cover. Although I
appreciated the gift, it has not been useful, as I find a pad of typing
paper easier on the whole. The book had a feeling of permanence
which did not put me at my ease, and I found that I could not cross out
what I had written without a sensation of waste.

Last night I was in a disturbed frame of mind owing to an unpleasant
experience on the previous evening and I did not write my diary.
However, tonight I have adjusted my feelings somewhat and will re-
cord the evening party which Mabel and I attended, given by my
friend Mr. Adolphus Bond, one of the kindest of men. When I say "my
friend", perhaps I overstep and should rather say acquaintance. A
cousin of mine married a cousin of his who has since passed away.

Mr. Bond lives in a charming house complete with garden. He is a
bachelor of many interests and has a wide and scattered social and
business acquaintance and so Mabel and I did not see many familiar
faces. In fact none. Mr. Bond, a genial host, introduced me to a young
man with a dark beard whose name seemed to be Ozzie who was talking to a handsome lively girl. I did not hear Ozzie's other name but I
thought I heard Mr. Bond say before he left us that he was a nephew
of the Leader of the House. I was going to say by way of joke What
House? because I had noticed in the telephone book that very day the
House of Liqueurs, the House of Charm, the House of Drapes and the
House of Sport but decided not to. Although I make it a rule never to
bring up the subjects of politics and religion in strange company, it
seemed safe to refer to my satisfaction at the recent elections, with a
passing reference to the young man's uncle Mr. Robertshaw. The
young man Ozzie became almost violent and referred to his uncle's
party as a lot of bloody fools. I was silent, but the girl was amused and
laughed heartily. It seems that Ozzie is an artist which one might have
suspected from his beard, but as Mabel says, that is no proof.

There was a slight lull in the conversation and turning to the window I remarked on the lengthening of the days. I said that I made the
practice of recording the position of the sun in my diary. The young
man Ozzie said, very rudely I thought, "Your *what?* Do you mean you
write a diary?"

I said, "Certainly I write a diary," whereupon he said, "If I can believe that I can believe anything." Silence fell and then the girl said, "Ozzie you great oaf some day somebody's going to hit you. You'd better apologize," and Ozzie said to me, "I beg your pardon. I had no business to say that but I never met anyone who wrote a diary before."

I received his apology as best I could and as I heard Mabel's clear voice ringing out from the neighbouring room I thought I would join her. I smiled and withdrew but I must confess that I was shaken as I had always regarded the writing of a diary as a natural affair and apparently there are some people who find it strange. The uncomfortable feeling of not resembling other people persisted with me and that is one reason why I did not feel in the mood for writing yesterday.

Before I reached the door I was stopped by my host who had on his arm an elderly woman who appeared to be lame, by the name I think of Gormley or Gormer. He introduced us and found her a chair and we were left together. Thinking the matter over later, I came to the conclusion that Mr. Bond, unintentionally no doubt, had left me—as Mabel sometimes says—holding the bag, for owing to Mrs. Gormley's lameness a certain sense of "noblesse oblige" made me spend most of the rest of the time at the party conversing with her. I did not find her an interesting woman and Mabel remarked afterwards that I seemed embittered at the close of the evening.

In an endeavour to avoid inflammable subjects I told this Mrs. Gormley that we had recently been in Spain. That conversational opening usually promotes lively response. People either wish to go to Spain or they have been in Spain, and a certain enthusiasm follows. Mrs. Gormley's only response was to make some enquiry about a dog. I saw at once that she must be a very unintelligent woman. I mentioned the monkey Chiko which we had some years ago but did not go further as Chiko led us into very unfortunate legal proceedings. I well remember that we had to give Chiko to the Monkey House in Stanley Park. Mabel and I have often remarked that when we went to visit Chiko there, it was impossible to distinguish him from the other monkeys. They all seemed to have the same anxious expression and a similarity of feature. I did not tell Mrs. Gormer anything further.

An embarrassing moment occurred at once. Owing to the strike among waiters, all available experienced waiters are employed in the various hotels and restaurants and very few can be found for private parties. This accounts, I think, for the young hobbledehoy who served us at Mr. Adolphus Bond's party. When this Mrs. Gormer asked him (very rudely, I thought) what certain of the hors d'oeuvres contained, he said he did not know but thought they were hot ovaries. Mrs. Gormer seemed very much amused at this, but that shows the kind of woman she is.

We then had a long conversation on foreign travel. I said that in   81

Spain we had too many eggs and she said Yes, but what about the el grecos. I had to admit that we did not have any. We then spoke about hotel accommodation. While I was telling her my impressions of the hotels in London she looked past me and at the windows behind my head, looking into the garden. I would, at any other time, have thought she was in a trance, but she responded with moderate intelligence to my remarks. I think it must be a bad habit of hers and I must say it is very disagreeable.

We were just discussing the Royal York Hotel in Toronto when the young man Ozzie entered the room. He flung himself down in a large chair opposite us and appeared quite exhausted. He too said something about a dog. I did not stay to enquire but gladly made this an opportunity to leave on the pretext of bringing Mrs. Gormer another drink. When I arrived at the bar which had been set up in the dining-room I saw Mabel leaning against the bar surrounded by other people, and talking very loudly. I was instantly alarmed, remembering that occasion in Winnipeg. She saw me and shouted "Hi!" (a greeting I particularly dislike) and went on laughing and talking. I did not join them but filled Mrs. Gormer's glass and my own. I drank my own and then decided to have a re-fill. I then carried Mrs. Gormer's glass and my own back to the library. I stopped at the door because it was partially blocked by a tall thin man in a gray suit who spoke the following words to someone in the room: "Little one, little one, you are so beautiful, may I kiss you?"

I looked under the extended arm of the man in gray, taking care not to spill the drinks, in order to see whom he might be addressing, but only Mrs. Gormer looking different and the man called Ozzie were in the room. The remark of the man in the gray suit then seemed unintelligible as Mrs. Gormer is far from beautiful but he may not have been quite sober.

What was my surprise to hear this Mrs. Gormer thereupon urge the man in gray to kiss her which he did with, I must say, considerable respect, but without passion which was understandable. She made the plea that she needed a kiss. I found the whole episode quite incomprehensible. I decided to drink Mrs. Gormer's whiskey as well as my own —did not re-enter the room but returned to the bar.

On the way home I have never known Mabel so outrageous except on that occasion in Winnipeg. She called me a sour-puss and used other terms which I shall never be able to forget. I went so far as to say that a little attention always goes to her head which seemed to annoy her excessively. She was driving the car and I must confess that some very strange thoughts came into my mind. You can imagine that on our arrival at home I was in no condition to write my diary. I sometimes think that whereas some people are born to joy, I was born to sorrow.

This morning I purchased a small safe and brought it home. I told Mabel that I had been asked to keep some of the Firm's papers in a safe in our house. I shall also keep my diary there which permits me the freedom of expression that I sometimes require but which in daily life I seem unable to enjoy. A man must have a friend even if it is only himself.

Before I stop, I will mention an item in the paper that has touched and moved me very much tonight. A man in Illinois or is it Iowa is undergoing trial for the murder of his wife. The thing that impressed me was that he and his wife had seemed to live a devoted and harmonious life together.

"I must have another party," said Adolphus, busy with his lists.

ETHEL BRYANT WILSON (1888–1980) was born in South Africa and spent her early childhood in England. Orphaned at the age of ten, she was brought to her relatives in Vancouver where she was raised by her maternal grandmother, Ann Malkin. Her youthful experiences in this city later prompted the delightful stories of The Innocent Traveller *(1949). In 1921, after thirteen years of teaching school, she married Dr. Wallace Wilson. Although she wrote a children's serial for several months in 1919 to promote her uncles' tea and coffee importing firm (Malkins Best), she did not begin writing seriously until the late 1930s. Eventually collected in 1961 in* Mrs. Golightly and Other Stories, *her stories, like her novels, reveal her great attachment to the landscape and ethos of British Columbia. Her other books are* Hetty Dorval *(1947),* The Equations of Love *(1952),* Swamp Angel *(1954), and* Love and Salt Water *(1956).*

AQUARIUS

AUDREY THOMAS

They had been warned what to expect; yet the explosion – what else could you call it? – and the quantities of water which leapt at them – for as the whale descended the water did, indeed, seem to leap, as though it had almost taken on the shape, or at least the strength, of the great beast which had violated its calm – there was a collective "aaahh" from the little group of spectators, and a band of elementary-school children drew in closer to their teacher and shrieked in fearful delight.

"Brian, Daniel," called out the honeyed, public voice of the teacher, "Settle down now; come away from the side."

The man started, as if he had heard a voice calling to him from a dream. He felt disoriented, his glasses spattered with water – as though he were looking out from the lower port-holes of the whale pool, not in and down from outside – and his head still echoed to the sound of the whale's re-entry into the pool. And disoriented in another way as well, for something had happened to him as the whale leapt up toward the sound of the keeper's whistle: like the water, he, too, had felt the shape and thrust of all that energy and had been strangely thrilled by it and strangely envious. Standing there now, still only vaguely aware of the schoolteacher, the children, the other spectators, blinking as he rubbed his glasses clean, terribly conscious of his thin body and his pale, scholar's hands, he felt abandoned, cast down from some unimaginable height of strength and brute beauty and thrust. Wished, for a moment, to be one of the children who could close up, like delicate petals, around the tight bud of their teacher's serenity. He felt his separation from the whale. "O Ile leape up to my God," he remembered, "who pulles me downe?"

As if in answer he heard his wife give a low laugh and murmur something to her neighbour, an American who was worriedly examining the water-splashed lens of his camera and paying no attention to

This story was first published in The Fiddlehead *in 1971 and was reprinted in Thomas's* Ladies & Escorts *in 1977.*

the whale who was now circling the pool, faster and faster, just below the surface of the water. Occasionally a brief island of dark, rubbery back would rise up above the surface and then disappear again, as the whale plunged deeper and deeper into the heaving water. The attendant, perched on his little platform like a circus artist, explained through a hand mike that the whale could reach speeds of up to 30 miles an hour. Mentally he went round and round with the rushing whale, faster and faster, five, ten, fifteen, twenty–he riding the slippery back as though it was the easiest thing in the world, waving his hand to Erica as he passed, casually, as one might wave to an old, almost forgotten friend seen suddenly from a taxi window; then up and up with the whale, out away from the blue water of the pool, which burned upward after them like transparent, ice-blue fire. A truimph against gravity, captivity, everything. "O Ile leape up to my God."

Erica laughed again. Before the performance began she had moved around to the other side of the pool, almost directly under the platform so that she could be in front of the whale as it leapt. He took off his glasses once more, nervously, for he did not need his eyes to see her: long hair tied back artful carelessly with a bright silk scarf, the top button of her cardigan undone, a mannerism he had observed in her for almost twenty years. He knew the shape of her neck as it rose from the cardigan, and the texture of that neck, with its tiny orange mole, like a rust spot, and the texture of her pale, coarse hair. She would be smiling up at the attendant, of whom she had already asked one or two extremely intelligent questions, amused no doubt by the boy's look of amazement and respect. How could *he* know the way her mind worked, or the extraordinary talent she had for seeming to know more than she really did. He had watched her leaf quickly through the paperback on whales which had been on display in the souvenir shop as they came in. But the boy was not to know this, or to know that years before she had typed for him an article on the reality factor in *Moby Dick*. She would look up at him, leaning back a little, and ask her questions with an air of polite apology, as though only too aware that *everyone* knew the answer except her; and the attendant (or museum guide or gallery official) would regard her with a kind of wonder–as if he had heard a flower speak. Yet sex was not really her game–not in these casual encounters at any rate; she simply wanted, had to be, always, on the side of the professionals.

And that, he thought, (his mind reflecting, ruminating, while his body still unconsciously swayed slightly in a circle, in time to the rhythm of the whale), was precisely where he had failed her. A serious poet–a new Eliot if not a wild, new, apocalyptic bard–was one thing; a scholar who wrote poetry for a hobby was quite another. What was this fellow's name? Perry or Percy–something like that. The little mini-skirted girl had announced him at the beginning of the show. Something Frenchified and out of keeping with his T-shirt and sneakers and buckets of raw herring. What had his mother been thinking of when she gave her son that name? Perhaps she hoped he'd grow up to be a poet. His name should have been Harry or Dan or even just Red.

"Now I'll get Skana to give me a kiss," the boy said, descending from his perch and standing next to Erica, but in front of the low glass breakwater. He blew his whistle twice.

The whale stopped circling immediately and sped over toward her master, lifting her great blunt head up toward his inclining cheek. They touched and the spectators "aaahhed" again. Then the young man held up a fish directly over the whale's head, so that her mouth gaped open and her 44 teeth, blunt and sawdust-coloured ("George Washington must have looked like that when he smiled," he thought irreverently) were exposed. The boy patted her on the head and gave her the herring. She thrust her head up again and the audience duly chuckled. He gave her another fish and another friendly pat.

Again the watching man felt a strange thrill of identification and envy. There was nothing patronizing in the boy's attitude: he and the whale were a team—they complemented one another. The boy explained that the teeth were used only for holding and grasping. The man felt his tongue move almost involuntarily in his mouth, trying to imagine the tactile sensation of a mouth full of those quaint, wooden-looking molars, trying to imagine the stress of those molars against something they had chosen to grasp and hold. And suddenly he remembered the feel of Erica's teeth that first time, and how something had willed him, just for a moment, to set his teeth against her determined seeking, a something that had been almost immediately forgotten in the great conflagration of his desire.

Tipping the rest of the bucket into the water, the attendant thanked them all for coming, switched off the mike and prepared to walk away. The older man, on the other side of the pool, watched his wife touch the boy lightly on the arm (just one more intelligent question for the road). The man moved back toward the door where he stood idly, used to waiting, rubbing his index finger against his thumb and still feeling that terrible sense of loss. He decided he would have to come again, without her, and try to define more explicitly what it was he really wanted from the whale. For he wanted something, that much he was sure of: maybe a new poem; maybe only reassurance; maybe something more. As his wife turned he noticed that her sweater and the front of her slacks were wet. He was annoyed—not because she would insist upon going home, but rather because she would stay, moving unconcernedly and triumphantly amongst the curious. And she would have a story to tell the children or her friends.

"My dears, I was nearly *swallowed up,* like a female Jonah or Pinoc-chio or someone!" and still later he would watch her bury her face in the wrinkled clothes, inhaling the faint aroma of her triumphal morn-ing, before she tossed them in the hamper. Suddenly he was thoroughly disgusted and decided to ignore her smile and wave (was he mistaken, or was the redheaded young man beginning to look just a trifle bored?), moved out with the last of the stragglers, back into the aquarium proper. Now just Erica and the boy were out there by the pool. Erica and the boy, and somewhere below them, Skana, the killer whale. The children, pulled along by their teacher's authority, as though by an earnest tug, had long since disappeared to look at other things.

Had Erica experienced a genuine thrill when the whale leapt? She might have, once. And the creature was powerful and female, sleek and strangely beautiful—like the woman herself. He had always as-sociated her, too, with the sea—because of her name and her pale blond hair and cold blue eyes. When he first loved her he even saw himself as something Scandinavian, a Siegfried, and exulted in her restrained, voluptuous power and her ice-blue eyes. ("Except for that one moment," he thought, "when I set my teeth against her thrusting tongue. Strange I had forgotten that.") Later, because the Siegfried role was not his true self-idealization, he allowed himself to be mothered by her. She had been lonely when he met her and he sensed she needed to be needed. She had taught him all he ever knew of sex (he never asked her where she got her knowledge), and cooked for him thick homemade soups in a huge copper kettle she had discovered at the Salvation Army shop. And she it was, too, who willed him to be a poet, encour-aged him, made do with bare floors and tipsy, mismatched chairs. She was afraid of nothing, neither accidents nor poverty nor death. "I am terrified only of the mediocre," she told him once, and he had thrilled to hear her say it, wrapped in his old dressing gown, drying her long, pale hair by firelight. It had all been heaven then: the thick soups, the crazy chairs, the bottles of cheap wine, the crusty bread, the basement flat which—with her incredible luck—had contained a fireplace and a priceless, abandoned, Hudson Bay "button blanket" on the wall.

She had seemed the ultimate in womanhood, the very essence of female with her full, Northern figure and her incredible self-assurance and practicality, so different from the flat-bosomed, delicate foolishness of his own well-bred female relatives. And what excited him most, although he would never have admitted it, and indeed felt actually ashamed, at first, even to himself, was a certain sluttishness about her—the top button of her inevitable cardigan always left undone or missing, her legs crossed thigh over thigh, quite casually—his mother and sisters had always crossed only at the ankles. Her strange desire to

87

make love when she had her period. But even more than this, the things she said. Once, in the very early days, she had run her hands along his thin flanks and kissed him there and laughed with delight at his thinness.

"I will fatten you with kisses," she had cried. And indeed, he could feel his body firmer, fuller, where she had traced her fingers and her lips. Then suddenly she had grabbed his head between her hands, kneading his scalp in her beautiful capable fingers and licking his face with her warm tongue – as though he were her kitten. He had already grown a beard, even then, and she had whispered, rubbing her cheek against him, "Your beard is all soft and springy – like pubic hair." So that his face flamed up at her bold words and for days he found it difficult to go outside, to expose his face to others, so deep was his sensual delight, so wanton his happiness.

He walked slowly along the illuminated displays and admired the care that had been taken with the lighting and accessories of each exhibit. Shells, sand, gravel, anemones and kelp: like with like or nearlike. Everything conspired to give the illusion of a real beach or cove or lake or ocean home. It was spacious, tasteful, and most effective. Yet he felt cold and claustrophobic in the aquarium, as though it were he who was shut in, not the fish and other specimens. An iguana observed him wipe his forehead with a cynical, prehistoric eye; the octopus flattened his disgusting suckers against the harsh reality of glass; the alligators slept with tourists' pennies clinging to their heads and backs. The wolf-eel, however, looked as if a mere quarter-inch of glass would not stop *him*. "Fishermen will sometimes cut the line," he read, "rather than handle this fish." He believed it. The thick, sensuous lips, the small eyes, the conical front teeth convinced one that here was evil incarnate, a creature who would not hesitate to attack. Erica, he thought, would have laughed loudly and squatted down with her nose against the glass, grinning, daring the eel to pit his aggression against hers.

He read that they had been captured up to a length of eight feet. Taller than a man. Imagine finding *that* on the end of your line! Where was Erica?

Had it all been a trick, her violent lovemaking which somehow was in keeping with her Nordic looks – a love like waterfalls and mountain torrents, a love that suggested terrible deeds to be done for love or hate or kinship, quite in contrast to his own, soft, dreamlike attitude. But in those early days she could rouse him up until he forgot that he was thin and lank and weak of vision; and he would take into himself her passion and her fury until the little flat rang with their cries, like the harsh, triumphant cries of eagles or giant sea-birds, and he thought his heart would burst from excitement and exertion. He was trans-

88

formed, transfigured, under her incredible shaping hands. He entered her as Siegfried leaping through a wall of fire. He lived.

But she had never been able to rouse him to the heights of poetry. All his best work was done before he met her. He felt, now, that this was as much a failure in her as it was in him. Vampire-like she had renewed herself with his passion; and then, having won him and worn him out, she had begun to cast him off as worthless – to shed him as a snake might shed its winter skin. On the strength of the acceptance of his first book they had married. When his second group of poems had been repeatedly rejected she initiated her first affair. Her children, tall and blond like her, came to take the place of the poems she had urged him to create, just as her anonymous lovers (sometimes he could even smell them on her skin – what a bitch she was!) had taken his place in her body. It was as if, after the first wild, dream-like years when he made poetry all day and love all night (she blond and buxom, like a seventeenth-century genre painting then in her spotless kitchenette, with the first child, round and rosy-cheeked, hugging the backs of her knees; and at night a rich dim honey-coloured nude), it was as if she had peered down into a well, assessed the amount of liquid remaining there, and then, with a practical shrug of her shoulders, had shut up the cover and gone elsewhere for her water.

And the water in the well became stagnant, scum-covered, un-drinkable. Noises from outside filtered down, as distant as summer thunder – and as deceptive. When he tried to write about his anguish he found that he was no longer interested in the old preoccupations with beauty and order and truth. He could only dryly mock himself, forsaken merman, and mocking, failed again. The money from his mother's estate, the small advance from his first book: these vanished even more quickly than his dreams. He had always taught part-time, to guarantee they wouldn't starve. Now Erica suggested coldly that he apply for a full-time job; and he, with a sinking heart, accepted his defeat. He began to see himself as a man walking slowly toward the exact centre of a low-walled bridge. He had not yet reached the centre but it would draw him on and on and someday – over. He taught rea-sonably well, but he was always tired; and the mountains just beyond the city, mountains which had always thrilled him, began to oppress and even frighten him. They seemed to be growing larger, hemming him in against the sea. A worrisome phrase kept running through his mind: "with one stride came the dark." Often, lately, he had had to leave his class for a few minutes and light a cigarette in order not to weep. Sometimes he wished that Erica were dead.

"Open water fishes," he read, "are darker above than below." To fool the enemy. Not the wolf-eel though. But is an eel a fish? And where was Erica?

89

But the paleness might be a camouflage, not a symptom. Like Erica's pale hair and honeyed skin. "The good heroines of the Western world are always blond and fair," he thought, "like Erica." But the Vikings were blond too, or red-haired and fair. The "Rus." And destructive. Ravenous in appetite if not appearance. "The fish's pallor is a mask," he said to no-one in particular. Where was Erica? Not making love to the young attendant, even if he had turned out to be a novice marine biologist. Oh, no. Her taste ran now to higher things: historians, art critics, young writers (especially poets) on fellowships. A boy in a T-shirt, whose hands smelled of herring, would no longer physically excite her. And he remembered again, "The only thing I'm afraid of is the mediocre."

He hesitated in front of the Mozambique Mouth-Breeder, attracted by its name. Were the young fry snug or struggling—which?—behind the closed gate of their mother's teeth, coming awake in the slimy warmth of their mother's mouth? How did she eat without swallowing them? How catch her food? Or did she not eat at all while she carefully manoeuvred the African waters, aware of her incredible mouthful. He had always felt the aloneness of his own infant children, had carried the first strapped to his back in a harness of his own devising—his unique example of mechanical inventiveness. He had told her it was to save money—for he had been slightly afraid of her, even then—and she had been very proud of him. They had been, he reflected now, naïvely picturesque as they padded along the busy streets on Friday mornings. Friday had always been a day of reorganization for them, of doing the weekly shopping and changing the bed and answering any letters. Later she would wash her long blond hair while he worked on the latest poem, the child asleep on his lap. They were poetic about their poverty too, acting out the romantic role of the artist and his barefoot wife, for she had given up shoes (at least indoors) long before it was fashionable to do so. And had named their first child Darius. It was all so transient: money and fame were not beneath them but just ahead of them; and they accepted their poverty with style and good grace because they knew it was only temporary, accepted it the way the wise accept the bitter winter, knowing of the spring.

But it was not to be. Wherever he sent his work it came back rejected: first (on the strength of his book) accompanied by a kind and sometimes helpful letter, later by the now-familiar oblong of paper or card, clipped to the upper left-hand corner. Thank you for your submission. Thank you for giving us the opportunity to read ... Thank you but no thank you. He couldn't believe it. Eventually he had to. Once he had received his manuscript back with a letter, quite a long one, only to discover it was from a fellow-struggler who had received the two manuscripts clipped together under a single message of dismissal.

The writer of the letter was ironic and amused; but he was furious, and felt publicly exposed in front of this stranger from Brickchurch, New Jersey, USA, who had also offered inadequate libations to the gods. He even thought of writing to the editors. Surely there was an ethical principle involved? But in the end he didn't—it was too humiliating.

And so, finally, she took a lover and he a full-time job. That night he had shaved off his beard in a fury of bitterness—a mask for the wrong dance. Why had he ever let it grow again?.

He looked at his watch. Where the hell was she? Surely she couldn't be *still* talking to that boy. And he was bored with all these strange, slippery creatures that surrounded him, lost in their own dream-like, antiseptic coffins. The vague bubbling noise and shifting light had given him a headache. And it was nearly lunchtime. She would want to go to Chinatown and have a meal, knowing he hated the kind of restaurant she always chose—the dirtiest, tackiest one she had not yet tried, with peeling, musty oilcloth-covered tables and slimed menus, where the lukewarm soup was served in heavy, cracked white bowls and the smells from the kitchen made him gag. "Ahh," she would exclaim, giving him a wicked smile, "Now this isn't one of your bloody tourist traps, my darling; this is the real thing!" She would enjoy watching his discomfort, would eat quickly and with great show of appetite, scooping the liquid up toward her bent, blond head, almost lapping it up like a cat, in her haste to get on to the next course (which was usually a revolting and expensive something that was not on the regular menu), afterward licking the film of grease from her upper lip with one sweep of her tongue. He couldn't bear it, not today. He'd have to find some excuse.

She always laughed when he told her such places disgusted him—"You weren't always so discriminating!" And it was so. He felt a physical revulsion now for anything that smacked of foreignness or dirt or unclean, hidden things. Three nights before she had unexpectedly thrown her heavy, blue-veined thigh over his as she was getting into bed, and had cried out in triumph, "Look how thin you are getting! I could crush you!" And his sudden leap of desire had been quenched by a smudge of lipstick on her teeth. He couldn't bear it if someone forgot to flush the toilet.

He was beginning to feel a little giddy, and turned back toward the fish, as if seeking some answer or relief. Perhaps she had simply gone home without him? She liked to mock him, now, in front of their nearly-grown children, and she had to work out the story of her wet clothes. "Darlings, I was nearly drowned! This morning—at the aquarium—you nearly lost me!" She was afraid of nothing and she despised him. The Pacific prawns, delicate as Venetian glass or transparent 91 drinking straws, moved gently just ahead of him. How beautiful. He wondered at their strange reversal of sex and envied them their beauty and, for a long moment, their eternally ordered environment. He and Erica had had a reversal too—but ugly, unnatural. She had dominated him always, more and more, had emasculated his body and his soul and having done so, cast him aside, an empty shell. Even this trip to the aquarium was her suggestion. He had wanted to cross the bridge and drive out to Horseshoe Bay, have a quiet lunch beside the water. It appeared to him now that even the exhibits he had seemed to choose at random had been chosen first by her, as living illustrations of her strength and his incredible, female, weakness.

He remembered how she had told him, captive, everything about her labour during the birth of their third child. Had described it in such detail he had sickened and begged her to desist—this in the semi-private room at the hospital, while the woman in the other bed remained an implied smile behind the plastic curtains. She had raped him—truly—as the Vikings raped their conquered women. And she has desecrated him and everything he dreamed of. That night, while he sat wretchedly with his head between his knees, she talked of herself and the young doctor who assisted her as if they had been lovers who created the child between them. And he had visualized the gloved hands of the doctor reaching forward between her bloody thighs to draw out the thing that was *his,* and had fallen from the chair and onto the coolness of the hospital floor. That story was one of her best ones.

He decided to go home. Let her walk or take the bus. Let her disappear forever. Let her get knocked down by a taxi cab or knocked up by the chairman of the Symphony Committee: it was a matter of indifference to him. But out in the corridor he saw the door to the pool was standing open and felt irresistably drawn to the dark shadow of the whale, floating down there somewhere below the surface of the water. No-one was about. A bucket of fish and the big pink plastic ball stood ready beneath the empty platform. The red-haired boy was nowhere to be seen. He was vaguely aware, through the glass, of the back of Erica's cardigan and her bright scarf near the counter where they sold the shells.

At the water's edge he hesitated, peering down uncertainly, then stuck his fingers in his mouth and whistled twice, a high, thin sound that came back to him out of his childhood, a sound that would reach down and pierce the heavy blanket of the water and draw the big whale up to him. He inclined his cheek, waiting. "Skana," he whispered, "Skana." But the surface of the pool remained a calm, indifferent blue. The whale did not hear or did not choose to answer.

He got up, slowly, awkwardly, and went to join his wife.

AUDREY CALLAHAN THOMAS was born in 1935 in Binghamton, New York, and graduated from Smith College. In 1959 she emigrated to Canada. With the exception of two years in Ghana (1964–66) and later extensive travels, she has made her home in British Columbia, in Vancouver and on Galiano Island. Thomas did graduate work at U.B.C., receiving her M.A. in 1963. Her third daughter and her first book, Ten Green Bottles, *both appeared in 1967. Thomas's fiction is characterized by a strong sense of place: Africe in* Mrs. Blood (1970) *and* Blown Figures (1974); *upstate New York in* Songs My Mother Taught Me (1973); *Crete in* Latakia (1973); *and British Columbia in* Munchmeyer and Prospero on the Island (1972), Intertidal Life (1984), *and many of the stories in* Ladies & Escorts (1977) *and* Real Mothers (1981).

FORGIVENESS IN FAMILIES

ALICE MUNRO

I've often thought, suppose I had to go to a psychiatrist, and he would want to know about my family background, naturally, so I would have to start telling him about my brother, and he wouldn't even wait till I was finished, would he, the psychiatrist, he'd commit me.

I said that to Mother; she laughed. "You're hard on that boy, Val."

"Boy," I said. "*Man.*"

She laughed, she admitted it. "But remember," she said, "the Lord loves a lunatic."

"How do you know," I said, "seeing you're an atheist?"

Some things he couldn't help. Being born, for instance. He was born the week I started school, and how's that for timing? I was scared, it wasn't like now when the kids have been going to play-school and kindergarten for years. I was going to school for the first time and all the other kids had their mothers with them and where was mine? In the hospital having a baby. The embarrassment to me. There was a lot of shame about those things then.

It wasn't his fault getting born and it wasn't his fault throwing up at my wedding. Think of it. The floor, the table, he even managed to hit the cake. He was not drunk, as some people thought, he really did have some violent kind of flu, which Haro and I came down with, in fact, on our honeymoon. I never heard of anybody else with any kind of flu throwing up over a table with a lace cloth and silver candlesticks and wedding cake on it, but you could say it was bad luck; maybe everybody else when the need came on them was closer to a toilet. And everybody else might try a little harder to hold back, they just might, because nobody else is quite so special, quite so center-of-the-universe, as my brother. Just call him a child of nature. That was what he called himself, later on.

I will skip over what he did between getting born and throwing up at

This story first appeared in McCall's Magazine *in 1974 and was reprinted the same year in Munro's collection of stories,* Something I've Been Meaning to Tell You.

my wedding except to say that he had asthma and got to stay home from school weeks on end, listening to soap operas. Sometimes there was a truce between us, and I would get him to tell me what happened every day on "Big Sister" and "Road of Life" and the one with Gee-Gee and Papa David. He was very good at remembering all the characters and getting all the complications straight, I'll say that, and he did read a lot in *Gateways to Bookland,* that lovely set mother bought for us and that he later sneaked out of the house and sold, for ten dollars, to a secondhand book dealer. Mother said he could have been brilliant at school if he wanted to be. That's a deep one, your brother, she used to say, he's got some surprises in store for us. She was right, he had.

He started staying home permanently in Grade Ten after a little problem of being caught in a cheating-ring that was getting math tests from some teacher's desk. One of the janitors was letting him back in the classroom after school because he said he was working on a special project. So he was, in his own way. Mother said he did it to make himself popular, because he had asthma and couldn't take part in sports.

Now. Jobs. The question comes up, what is such a person as my brother – and I ought to give him a name at least, his name is Cam, for Cameron, Mother thought that would be a suitable name for a university president or honest tycoon (which was the sort of thing she planned for him to be) – what is he going to do, how is he going to make a living? Until recently the country did not pay you to sit on your uppers and announce that you had adopted a creative life-style. He got a job first as a movie usher. Mother got it for him, she knew the manager, it was the old International Theater over on Blake Street. He had to quit, though, because he got this darkness-phobia. All the people sitting in the dark he said gave him a crawly feeling, very peculiar. It only interfered with him working as an usher, it didn't interfere with him going to the movies on his own. He got very fond of movies. In fact, he spent whole days sitting in movie houses, sitting through every show twice then going to another theater and sitting through what was there. He had to do something with his time, because Mother and all of us believed he was working then in the office of the Greyhound Bus Depot. He went off to work at the right time every morning and came home at the right time every night, and he told all about the cranky old man in charge of the office and the woman with curvature of the spine who had been there since 1919 and how mad she got at the young girls chewing gum, oh, a lively story, it would have worked up to something as good as the soap operas if Mother hadn't phoned up to complain about the way they were withholding his pay check – due to a technical error in the spelling of his name, he said – and found out he'd quit in the middle of his second day.

Well. Sitting in movies was better than sitting in beer parlors, Mother said. At least he wasn't on the street getting in with criminal gangs. She asked him what his favorite movie was and he said *Seven Brides for Seven Brothers*. See, she said, he is interested in an outdoor life, he is not suited to office work. So she sent him to work for some cousins of hers who have a farm in the Fraser Valley. I should explain that my father, Cam's and mine, was dead by this time, he died away back when Cam was having asthma and listening to soap operas. It didn't make much difference, his dying, because he worked as a conductor on the P.G.E. when it started at Squamish, and he lived part of the time in Lillooet. Nothing changed, Mother went on working at Eaton's as she always had, going across on the ferry and then on the bus; I got supper, she came trudging up the hill in the winter dark.

Cam took off from the farm, he complained that the cousins were religious and always after his soul. Mother could see his problem, she had after all brought him up to be a freethinker. He hitchhiked east. From time to time a letter came. A request for funds. He had been offered a job in northern Quebec if he could get the money together to get up there. Mother sent it. He sent word the job had folded, but he didn't send back the money. He and two friends were going to start a turkey farm. They sent us plans, estimates. They were supposed to be working on contract for the Purina Company, nothing could go wrong. The turkeys were drowned in a flood, after Mother had sent him money and we had too against our better judgment. Everywhere that boy hits turns into a disaster area, Mother said. If you read it in a book you wouldn't believe it, she said. It's so terrible it's funny.

She knew. I used to go over to see her on Wednesday afternoon – her day off – pushing the stroller with Karen in it, and later Tommy in it and Karen walking beside, up Lonsdale and down King's Road, and what would we always end up talking about? That boy and I, we are getting a divorce, she said. I am definitely going to write him off. What good will he ever be until he stops relying on me, she asked. I kept my mouth shut, more or less. She knew my opinion. But she ended up every time saying, "He was a nice fellow to have around the house, though. Good company. That boy could always make me laugh."

Or, "He had a lot to contend with, his asthma and no dad. He never did intentionally hurt a soul."

"One good thing he did," she said, "you could really call it a good turn. That girl."

Referring to the girl who came and told us she had been engaged to him, in Hamilton, Ontario, until he told her he could never get married because he had just found out there was a hereditary fatal kidney disease in his family. He wrote her a letter. And she came looking for him to tell him it didn't matter. Not at all a bad-looking girl. She worked for the Bell Telephone. Mother said it was a lie told out of kindness, to

spare her feelings when he didn't want to marry her. I said it was a
kindness, anyway, because she would have been supporting him for
the rest of his life.

Though it might have eased things up a bit on the rest of us.

But that was then and now is now and as we all know times have
changed. Cam is finding it easier. He lives at home, off and on, has for a
year and half. His hair is thin in front, not surprising in a man thirty-
four years of age, but shoulder-length behind, straggly, graying. He
wears a sort of rough brown robe that looks as if it might be made out
of a sack (is that what sackcloth is supposed to be, I said to Haro, I
wouldn't mind supplying the ashes), and hanging down on his chest he
has all sorts of chains, medallions, crosses, elk's teeth or whatnot.
Rope sandals on his feet. Some friend of his makes them. He collects
welfare. Nobody asks him to work. Who could be so crude? If he has
to write down his occupation he writes priest.

It's true. There is a whole school of them, calling themselves priests,
and they have a house over in Kitsilano. Cam stays there too sometimes. They're in competition with the Hare Krishna bunch, only these
ones don't chant, they just walk around smiling. He has developed this
voice I can't stand, a very thin, sweet voice, all on one level. It makes
me want to stand in front of him and say, "There's an earthquake in
Chile, two hundred thousand people just died, they've burned up
another village in Vietnam, famine as usual in India." Just to see if he'd
keep saying, "Ve-ery ni-ice, ve-ery ni-ice," that sweet way. He won't
eat meat, of course, he eats whole-grain cereals and leafy vegetables.
He came into the kitchen where I was slicing beets—beets being forbid-
den, a root vegetable—and, "I hope you understand that you're com-
mitting murder," he said.

"No," I said, "but I'll give you sixty seconds to get out of here or I
may be."

So as I say he's home part of the time now and he was there on the
Monday night when Mother got sick. She was vomiting. A couple of
days before this he had started her on a vegetarian diet—she was always promising him she'd try it—and he told her she was vomiting up
all the old poisons stored up in her body from eating meat and sugar
and so on. He said it was a good sign, and when she had it all vomited
out she'd feel better. She kept vomiting, and she didn't feel better, but
he had to go out. Monday nights is when they have the weekly meeting at the priests' house, where they chant and burn incense or cele-
brate the black mass, for all I know. He stayed out most of the night,
and when he got home he found Mother unconscious on the bathroom
floor. He got on the phone and phoned me.

"I think you better come over here and see if you can help Mom,
Val."

"What's the matter with her?"

"She's not feeling very well."

"What's the matter with her? Put her on the phone."

"I can't."

"Why can't you?"

I swear he tittered. "Well I'm afraid she's passed out."

I called the ambulance and sent them for her, that was how she got to the hospital, five o'clock in the morning. I called her family doctor, he got over there, and he got Dr. Ellis Bell, one of the best-known heart men in the city, because that was what they had decided it was, her heart. I got dressed and woke Haro and told him and then I drove myself over to the Lions Gate Hospital. They wouldn't let me in till ten o'clock. They had her in Intensive Care. I sat outside Intensive Care in their slick little awful waiting room. They had red slippery chairs, cheap covering, and a stand full of pebbles with green plastic leaves growing up. I sat there hour after hour and read *The Reader's Digest*. The jokes. Thinking this is how it is, this is it, really, she's dying. Now, this moment, behind those doors, dying. Nothing stops or holds off for it the way you somehow and against all your sense believe it will. I thought about Mother's life, the part of it I knew. Going to work every day, first on the ferry then on the bus. Shopping at the old Red-and-White then at the new Safeway—new, fifteen years old! Going down to the Library one night a week, taking me with her, and we would come home on the bus with our load of books and a bag of grapes we bought at the Chinese place, for a treat. Wednesday afternoons too when my kids were small and I went over there to drink coffee and she rolled us cigarettes on that contraption she had. And I thought, all these things don't seem that much like life, when you're doing them, they're just what you do, how you fill up your days, and you think all the time something is going to crack open, and you'll find yourself, *then* you'll find yourself, in life. It's not even that you particularly want this to happen, this cracking open, you're comfortable enough the way things are, but you do expect it. Then you're dying, Mother is dying, and it's just the same plastic chairs and plastic plants and ordinary day outside with people getting groceries and what you've had is all there is, and going to the Library, just a thing like that, coming back up the hill on the bus with books and a bag of grapes seems now worth wanting, O God doesn't it, you'd break your heart wanting back there.

When they let me in to see her she was bluish-gray in the face and her eyes were not all-the-way closed, but they had rolled up, the slit that was open showed the whites. She always looked terrible with her teeth out, anyway, wouldn't let us see her. Cam teased her vanity. They were out now. So all the time, I thought, all the time even when she was young it was in her that she was going to look like this.

They didn't hold out hope. Haro came and took a look at her and put his arm around my shoulders and said, "Val, you'll have to be pre-pared." He meant well but I couldn't talk to him. It wasn't his mother and he couldn't remember anything. That wasn't his fault but I didn't want to talk to him, I didn't want to listen to him telling me I better be prepared. We went and ate something in the hospital cafeteria.

"You better phone Cam," Haro said.

"Why?"

"He'll want to know."

"Why do you think he'll want to know? He left her alone last night and he didn't know enough to get an ambulance when he came in and found her this morning."

"Just the same. He has a right. Maybe you ought to tell him to get over here."

"He is probably busy this moment preparing to give her a hippie funeral."

But Haro persuaded me as he always can and I went and phoned. No answer. I felt better because I had phoned, and justified in what I had said because of Cam not being in. I went back and waited, by myself.

About seven o'clock that night Cam turned up. He was not alone. He had brought along a tribe of co-priests, I suppose they were, from that house. They all wore the same kind of outfit he did, the brown sacking nightgown and the chains and crosses and holy hardware, they all had long hair, they were all a good many years younger than Cam, except for one old man, really old, with a curly gray beard and bare feet—in March, bare feet—and no teeth. I swear this old man didn't have a clue what was going on. I think they picked him up down by the Salvation Army and put that outfit on him because they needed an old man for a kind of mascot, or extra holiness, or something.

Cam said, "This is my sister Valerie. This is Brother Michael. This is Brother John, this is Brother Louis." Etc., etc.

"They haven't said anything to give me hope, Cam. She is dying."

"We hope not," said Cam with his secret smile. "We spent the day working for her."

"Do you mean praying?" I said.

"Work is a better word to describe it than praying, if you don't understand what it is."

Well of course, I never understand.

"Real praying is work, believe me," says Cam and they all smile at me, his way. They can't keep still, like children who have to go to the bathroom they're weaving and jiggling and doing little steps.

"Now where's her room?" says Cam in a practical tone of voice.

I thought of Mother dying and through that slit between her lids—who knows, maybe she can see from time to time—seeing this 99 crowd of dervishes celebrating around her bed. Mother who lost her religion when she was thirteen and went to the Unitarian Church and quit when they had the split about crossing God out of the hymns (she was for it), Mother having to spend her last conscious minutes won-dering what had happened, if she was transported back in history to where loonies cavorted around in their crazy ceremonies, trying to sort her last reasonable thoughts out in the middle of their business.

Thank God the nurse said no. The intern was brought and he said no. Cam didn't insist, he smiled and nodded at them as if they were granting permission and then he brought the troupe back into the waiting room and there, right before my eyes, they started. They put the old man in the center, sitting down with his head bowed and his eyes shut—they had to tap him and remind him how to do that—and they squatted in a rough sort of circle round him, facing in and out, in and out, alternately. Then, eyes closed, they started swaying back and forth moaning some words very softly, only not the same words, it sounded as if each one of them had got different words, and not in English of course but Swahili or Sanskrit or something. It got louder, gradually it got louder, a pounding singsong, and as it did they rose to their feet, all except the old man who stayed where he was and looked as if he might have gone to sleep, sitting, and they began a shuffling kind of dance where they stood, clapping, not very well in time. They did this for a long while, and the noise they were making, though it was not terribly loud, attracted the nurses from their station and nurses' aides and orderlies and a few people like me who were waiting, and nobody seemed to know what to do, because it was so unbeliev-able, so crazy in that ordinary little waiting room. Everybody just stared as if they were asleep and dreaming and expecting to wake up. Then a nurse came out of Intensive Care and said, "We can't have this disturbance. What do you think you're doing here?"

She took hold of one of the young ones and shook him by the shoulder, else she couldn't have got anybody to stop and pay atten-tion.

"We're working to help a woman who's very sick," he told her.

"I don't know what you call working, but you're not helping any-body. Now I'm asking you to clear out of here. Excuse me. I'm not ask-ing. I'm telling."

"You're very mistaken if you think the tones of our voices are hurting or disturbing any sick person. This whole ceremony is pitched at a level which will reach and comfort the unconscious mind and draw the demonic influences out of the body. It's a ceremony that goes back five thousand years."

"Good Lord," said the nurse, looking stupefied as well she might. "Who are these people?"

I had to go and enlighten her, telling her that it was my brother and what you might call his friends, and I was not in on their ceremony. I asked about Mother, was there any change.

"No change," she said. "What do we have to do to get them out of here?"

"Turn the hose on them," one of the orderlies said, and all this time, the dance, or ceremony, never stopped, and the one who had stopped and done the explaining went back to dancing too, and I said to the nurse, "I'll phone in to see how she is, I'm going home for a little while." I walked out of the hospital and found to my surprise that it was dark. The whole day in there, dark to dark. In the parking lot I started to cry. Cam has turned this into a circus for his own benefit, I said to myself, and said it out loud when I got home.

Haro made me a drink.

"It'll probably get into the papers," I said. "Cam's chance for fame."

Haro phoned the hospital to see if there was any news and they said there wasn't. "Did they have—was there any difficulty with some young people in the waiting room this evening? Did they leave quietly?" Haro is ten years older than I am, a cautious man, too patient with everybody. I used to think he was sometimes giving Cam money I didn't know about.

"They left quietly," he said. "Don't worry about the papers. Get some sleep."

I didn't mean to but I fell asleep on the couch, after the drink and the long day. I woke up with the phone ringing and day lightening the room. I stumbled into the kitchen dragging the blanket Haro had put over me and saw by the clock on the wall it was a quarter to six. She's gone, I thought.

It was her own doctor.

He said he had encouraging news. He said she was much better this morning.

I dragged over a chair and collapsed in it, both arms and my head too down on the kitchen counter. I came back on the phone to hear him saying she was still in a critical phase and the next forty-eight hours would tell the story, but without raising my hopes too high he wanted me to know she was responding to treatment. He said that this was especially surprising in view of the fact that she had been late getting to hospital and the things they did to her at first did not seem to have much effect, though of course the fact that she survived the first few hours at all was a good sign. Nobody had made much of this good sign to me yesterday, I thought.

I sat there for an hour at least after I had hung up the phone. I made a cup of instant coffee and my hands were shaking so I could hardly get the water into the cup, then couldn't get the cup to my mouth. I let it go cold. Haro came out in his pyjamas at last. He gave me one look and said, "Easy, Val. Has she gone?"

"She's some better. She's responding to treatment."

"The look of you I thought the other."

"I'm so amazed."

"I wouldn't've given five cents for her chances yesterday noon."

"I know. I can't believe it."

"It's the tension," Haro said. "I know. You build yourself up ready for something bad to happen and then when it doesn't, it's a queer feeling, you can't feel good right away, it's almost like a disappointment."

Disappointment. That was the word that stayed with me. I was so glad, really, grateful, but underneath I was thinking, so Cam didn't kill her after all, with his carelessness and craziness and going out and neglecting her he didn't kill her, and I was, yes, I was, sorry in some part of me to find out that was true. And I knew Haro knew this but wouldn't speak of it to me, ever. That was the real shock to me, why I kept shaking. Not whether Mother lived or died. It was what was so plain about myself.

Mother got well, she pulled through beautifully. After she rallied she never sank back. She was in the hospital three weeks and then she came home, and rested another three weeks, and after that went back to work, cutting down a bit and working ten to four instead of full days, what they call the housewives' shift. She told everybody about Cam and his friends coming to the hospital. She began to say things like, "Well, that boy of mine may not be much of a success at anything else but you have to admit he has a knack of saving lives." Or, "Maybe Cam should go into the miracle business, he certainly pulled it off with me." By this time Cam was saying, he is saying now, that he's not sure about that religion, he's getting tired of the other priests and all that not eating meat or root vegetables. It's a stage, he says now, he's glad he went through it, self-discovery. One day I went over there and found he was trying on an old suit and tie. He says he might take advantage of some of the adult education courses, he is thinking of becoming an accountant.

I was thinking myself about changing into a different sort of person from the one I am. I do think about that. I read a book called *The Art of Loving*. A lot of things seemed clear while I was reading it but afterwards I went back to being more or less the same. What has Cam ever done that actually hurt me, anyway, as Haro once said. And how am I better than he is after the way I felt the night Mother lived instead of died? I made a promise to myself I would try. I went over there one day taking them a bakery cake—which Cam eats now as happily as anybody else—and I heard their voices out in the yard—now it's summer, they love to sit in the sun—Mother saying to some visitor, "Oh yes I was, I was all set to take off into the wild blue yonder, and Cam here, this *idiot,* came and danced outside my door with a bunch of his hippie friends—"

"My God, woman," roared Cam, but you could tell he didn't care now, "members of an ancient holy discipline."

I had a strange feeling, like I was walking on coals and trying a spell so I wouldn't get burnt.

Forgiveness in families is a mystery to me, how it comes or how it lasts.

ALICE LAIDLAW MUNRO was born in 1931 in Wingham, Ontario, and attended the University of Western Ontario for two years. She sold her first story at the age of eighteen, but did not achieve recognition until her first collection, Dance of the Happy Shades, *won the Governor General's Award for fiction in 1968. In 1951 she moved to Vancouver, where she lived for twelve years, and then to Victoria. Her British Columbia years were taken up with her family of three daughters and the writing of the book for which she is best known,* Lives of Girls and Women (1971). *In the mid-seventies she returned to Ontario, the setting of most of her work. Her other collections of stories are* Something I've Been Meaning to Tell You (1974), The Moons of Jupiter (1982), *and* Who Do You Think You Are? (1978)—*published in the United States as* The Beggar Maid—*which won its author a second Governor General's Award.*

THE FIRST WOMAN

GABRIEL SZOHNER

From his window Franz could see the illuminated clock of the C.N.R. railway station. Already, it was after two a.m. The hands of the clock seemed to chase each other, running a wild race against his nerves, disjointing his thoughts.

Franz came to Canada more than three years ago, rented this two room apartment across from the station. The huge red clock became the focal point of the landscape. He looked at it a dozen times a day and at night, when loneliness engulfed him, he watched the dragging hands and the numbers trapped in their places. And he imagined his paintings exhibited in the world's largest galleries. He would have good clothes, good food and beautiful intelligent people for companions. Damn, when you're famous, it doesn't matter that you have rusty red hair, small yellow eyes, a body like a skeleton, or that the skin on your face is like worn concrete. When you're famous you don't have to prove what a good human being you are. This night Franz could not go into those dreams. There was a girl in his bed. After three long years, this was the first woman to come so close, to share his food, his bed.

Earlier, around ten p.m., Franz had thrown his paint brushes against the kitchen wall in frustration, had run down from his apartment, out to the cold rainy streets. Everything seemed hopeless. The few paintings one small gallery had accepted from him, lay against the back wall of the storage room. They didn't ask him outright to take them all back, but that was a very small consolation. The sum of money he had in reserve was wearing away very fast. What was left? To join the eight to five slaves, labour his muscles, his senses away? Go home tired and thinking of nothing but how long this job would last, what would the next job be, or join the miserable decaying line of the welfare collectors? Pounding out hard decisions over every penny, should he buy a can of beans or a tube of paint, half a dozen eggs or a paint brush? This on his mind, he wanted to get soaked to the bone, catch cold, pneumonia, to get hit by a drunken driver, fall into a workman's hole, or

 This story appeared in The Canadian Fiction Magazine *in* 1976.

something; he yearned for something bad to happen. He walked slowly and with the rebellious mind of a person who's losing the last days of his freedom, he talked out loud. He yelled and cursed at the passing cars, "Go, go, slimy mad insects! Turning, twisting worms! You impulsive predators! Spiritless damn coffins!" Desperately, he tried looking up against the rain without blinking an eyelid. His bearded face, soaked, beaten with heavy drops. His shirt open, the colorful neon lights danced on his long skinny body, and sang a melancholy tune on his wet white skin.

He saw his own reflection in the huge glass doors of the Bank of Montreal. A clown stared back at him. A clown dressed in the hand-out faded colours of the streets. The image had no laughter to offer. It shrugged off Franz's outraged stare. It shouted every insult back at him.

A companion has to be either above or below you, Franz compromised. We can't be friends or enemies. With this thought Franz turned away, thinking he sure would have liked to kick the other right on the bony knees, if that glass door wasn't so expensive to replace.

At this time of night, there wasn't a soul walking on the street, despite the rushing traffic, despite the neon lights, to him the street was dead. This was the end of Main Street, four or five blocks away skid road began. At times he walked over there to find some alcoholic. At least, sometimes, they listened. Tonight, he didn't want to see any of those people, he wanted to be alone, to feel sorry for himself alone. The broken down buildings, junkyards, trashy dirty second-hand stores, sick old warehouses, created a painful awareness. Suddenly a hand reached out to him and a face came so close, that he stopped promptly to avoid collision.

"Can you spare some change?"

A girl stood there, old leather jacket, blue jeans, hair soaked tight to her scalp.

Franz searched in his pockets. He knew he had no money on him at all, but he felt a refusal, a simple no, even if true, would sound cruel. "I'm sorry," he muttered finally. "Uh ... Where are you going? Perhaps I can help ... help some other way."

"Forget it," she said firmly, turning away.

"Where you going?" Franz asked again. "It's uh ... sure is miserable. Could I walk you somewhere?"

"I'm going no place."

"I haven't got a cent, believe me."

"Don't apologise." She stepped back, as if this was all she wanted to accomplish, nothing mattered now, like a child hiding away behind a chair, humming a three-four note tune over and over, just wrapped up in her own thing.

"I live only two or three blocks away. Couldn't stand the smell of paint any longer ... I can make you a cup of coffee. At least you could dry off ... get a little warmer." The girl turned to face him, "And what after?"

"After?"

"Yeah, after your cosy coffee?"

"Oh," smiled Franz, "You can trust me. I'm just not the type, and to be honest, I wasn't thinking of anything like that."

"You got some accent," the girl stated.

"Yes, I'm German."

She looked away. "I don't like immigrants. I don't trust them. You know Tony?"

Franz shook his head. "Tony? Tony who?"

"Everybody knows Tony. He's an immigrant. He thinks he's a smart one. Fancy clothes, penthouse and all that. That Tony. A goddamn sonofabitch. That's why I don't like immigrants."

"I don't know him." Franz went on shaking his head. "Never heard of him. Did he do bad for you?"

"He's a pig."

In spite of her strong words, she looked helpless to Franz. At least he could speak a few warm words to show that he cared. They stood there silent for a while, Franz looking at the girl. The girl looking all over the place, except back at him. Finally Franz spoke, "You sure you don't want me to walk you somewhere? It's getting late. I can walk you down town at least. There are more people on the streets. Easier to find someone to help."

"I'll go for the coffee."

She said it so simply that this change, this surrender cut short the emotions building up in Franz. Nervously, he offered a hand. "Let's run, before we melt."

"I'm too goddamn stiff to run," she answered. "I couldn't get more soaked anyway."

Rejecting Franz's hand, she walked beside him dangling her arms awkwardly, looking straight ahead.

"It's a horrible smell," Franz apologized, opening the door to his apartment. "I do my paintings in the kitchen."

"You some kind of an artist?"

"Oh, just a fake. I fool around, cheat myself. Take your coat off if you like. I'll make the coffee. My name is Franz."

The girl looked around. "Is that radiator working? Is it hot?"

"Yes," Franz answered. "You can put your coat on it." In the kitchen he made coffee, toast, found cheese and some sausage in the fridge. The girl sat on the radiator, on top of her coat staring down at the floor. Franz looked at her, holding the plate in front of him. "Not much, but it's all I could come up with. What're you thinking?"

"I'm not thinking," replied the girl. "I'm just warming my bum."

"You thinking about Tony?"

"Tony who?"

Franz handed her the coffee. "Sometimes I drink it with rum," he explained. "Want some in it? Warms you up faster."

"Wanna get me drunk?" she looked up. "I don't mind, I'm used to booze. I drink like a fish. What's one more alcoholic, huh?"

Franz poured some rum in both cups. "I have to admit," she started. "They have some charisma, don't they? I mean they're different than what you grow up with around here." She took a deep breath and emptied her hot coffee with one drink. "There are no Italian men without that charisma," she went on. "I don't know how to explain it. Tony sure had it. He gave me speed the other day. Sure beats liquor. Oh man, does it ever."

"I've never tried any of that stuff," Franz smiled. "I'm just afraid of those things."

"Wow. Like orgasm, a thousand times over," she stated.

"Are you not afraid of it?" Franz asked.

"Why would I be? Who cares?"

"What if you get hooked on it?"

"Jesus, you're something! You sure you live around here?" Then she carelessly added. "Hope you don't think I'm rotten, or something."

"I think you're a lovely girl."

"Wow. You sure don't know me, man."

"Your parents live around here?"

"Yeah, they're here alright."

"What happened?"

"They gave me the boot. Don't think they liked me. I sure as hell didn't like them, so I went with Tony. Any more of that coffee?" She bent forward while Franz filled her cup. "He was older, sophisticated, big shot, you know, made me proud, the way he cared for me . . . at first, that is."

"Why did you leave him?"

The girl's face became troubled as if the time had come for her to stand up against some injustice. "He was a rotten prick, that's why . . . bringing all these monkeys home, hairy, stinking beasts, guys who couldn't piss straight into a toilet bowl, speaking their own language all the time, playing cards, showing off their muscles to each other, like a bunch of freaks. Then he started to ride on me. 'Come on,' he said. 'Gino is a nice guy.' Then came Luigi . . . Martino . . . you know what? You know what he told me? He said 'Oh, come on, they don't take any away from your little thing, do they? They only just add to it!'" She was angered, yet she laughed. "The sonofabitch was charging them for my services."

Franz wanted to put a stop to her anger. "Hey, how old are you?" The girl was going to answer hurriedly, but she stopped. "Oh shit, I won't lie to you. I'm fifteen. Gonna throw me out now?"

"No, I won't," answered Franz. "But there is only one bed and one blanket."

She looked around. "Where is the bed?"

"The chesterfield. It opens up."

"Gonna make it, then?"

Franz opened up the old chesterfield, took a sheet, a blanket, a pillow out, and by the time he turned toward her, she stood there nude. "I always sleep on the right side," she said. "Do you snore?"

Franz was too shy to look at her body and afraid to show his inexperience with women, but she had a body Franz couldn't turn away from. She didn't look like any girlchild, she had a strong, rich woman's figure, full breasts, with nipples standing upward; stubborn, blonde, curly pubic hair, growing thick outward onto her thighs, strong curving hips. A warm satisfaction vibrated through Franz's body. How lonely he felt. Just a couple of hours ago, how empty everything was; his apartment rigid and hostile, his soul hopeless, his mind frustrated. Now the place looked and felt like home. In the bathroom, he brushed his teeth, combed his hair, turned off the light, and lay down beside the girl. Already she was lost in a deep sleep, motionless, heavy, like a huge stone on the ocean floor...

He should put his arm around her, hug her, or just touch her skin, to transfer the warmth of his palm to her flesh, just to make her feel, at least in her subconscious being, assured of his sincere friendship. In the hours since he'd met her it had developed into a strange feeling for Franz. All at once, he wanted to protect, provide, to take and weave her future into his dreams. At times he reached out to touch her; his skinny long white arm trembled in the dark blue-grey air and stopped inches away from the girl's shoulder. She wouldn't understand.

He held his arm in mid-air until his muscles knotted into one long pain. Then he pulled back and sighed, admitting to himself that he was also yearning to kiss that strange girl. He wanted to hold her head between his hands and kiss her young pale lips, kiss away her sadness, her stubborn rebellion, her feeling of rejection. He had a burning desire to make love to her, cover her with his feverish body. What if he just reached out and did all that? Would she kiss him back? Would she hug him and open up for him? Would she? She would be angry and start to yell at him. She would scream. At his bravest moment, Franz reached out and just touched her fine blonde hair with his finger tips, whispering in his overwhelming outburst of kindness, "God be with you, girl."

The red blaze of the clock proudly implied a victory. It was three forty-five, and with the morning, this night would become just a dream. Everything looks and feels different in the morning. The reality of the girl's presence started to shift and slowly slip away, leaving Franz stranded. He put on his paint-smeared overcoat and went into the kitchen. His canvas stood on the table, leaning against the wall, displaying some colour patches, the beginning of some odd still-life. Taking his biggest brush and turpentine, he painted the whole thing into a mess. He began a new composition, a bed, a woman's figure.

She would have laughed at him, just like other people, like everybody, if she wasn't so tired, he thought, there were a few seconds when she had that fiendish glint in her eyes... when she saw him standing by the bathroom door in only his underwear.

The turpentine, linseed oil and paint bit into his nostrils, his lungs. There were only a few scrubby lines on the canvas, and already, he didn't like it. After three more tries, disgusted with his surroundings, the smell, the pounding rain on the rooftop, he sat and watched the grey mess floating off the canvas, onto the kitchen table, under some dirty dishes, then dripping down to the floor.

She would have laughed. She didn't appear to be much of a considerate, polite person, not an educated one, either. She had a face with a kind of dumb innocence, though, that inflamed the soul of Franz.

It was already morning when Franz went back to the living room, to open the only window and change the air in the old apartment.

The girl felt the cold, but didn't wake, just pulled her knees up tight against her belly, leaving her pale, fleshy back uncovered. In the dim morning, it looked to Franz like marble. Franz tucked in the dirty grey sheet and blanket, carefully covering the girl; again, touching only her hair. He imagined himself with the girl back in his country, the places of his childhood. Holding hands while walking the gentle slopes and valleys, the peaceful meadows, oak forests carpeted with soft moss. Wild poppies on a hillside swaying their bright red heads in the tender mid-summer breeze. She laughs, and runs, pulls him close and whispers, "So beautiful," and he answers "Yes. Everything you see, everything you touch, is like what I feel for you. I give you all this, out of my body."

As she opened her eyes, almost with the same motion, she sat up and threw her legs down over the side of the bed, sitting there a few seconds, motionless. Then with a sudden movement, she reached for her clothes on the radiator, jerking them all into her lap. "At least they're all dry," she muttered.

Franz watched her dress. "I was awake all night," he stated. "Just couldn't go to sleep. I hope I didn't bother you." The girl twitched a corner of her mouth.

"I wanted to tell you a lot of things," Franz went on, "Oh... I don't think I could tell all that now."

"Would you pass my shoes? I sure hope those damn things dried." 109

Franz bent down for the shoes, puzzled and hesitant. After handing them to her, he walked to the window. "I know how stupid I look . . . " stuttered Franz. "That's all anybody notices about me . . . how I look."

She was all dressed. Her coat, shoes, everything on, she walked to the bathroom, combed her hair with her fingers, then took a long disap- proving look at the fuzzy blonde split ends. She stood there for a long time, taking her hair ends, strand by strand. Finally, disgusted, she threw them all onto her back, and walked toward the door. "Thanks, huh?"

Franz stood with his back to the window and listened to the old dried out wooden stairs, screaming under her clunky steps. He turned and closed the window, watching her walk by underneath, rain beat- ing down on her scalp, her arms dangling free. She walked slowly. At the corner, she stopped, facing an empty lot scattered with debris, just stood there, staring at that broken old Chevron station sign as if wait- ing for it to light up.

Franz tried to paint again but he couldn't stand more than ten minutes in the kitchen. He wanted to go after her, bring her back. The apartment was, once again, cold, empty. He rushed to the window. She was still there, facing the oncoming traffic — her thumb high in the air.

GABRIEL J. SZOHNER was born in Hungary in approximately 1936 and suffered a traumatic wartime childhood. After his arrival in Vancou- ver in 1957 he wrote stories and poetry for Hungarian-Canadian news- papers and won several Canada Council grants to support his writing. In addition to "The First Woman," reprinted here, he has published a novel, The Immigrant *(1978), and he is now developing a career as a painter.*

SPANS

GEORGE BOWERING

The impenetrable author of it all smiled down on a bending sea that separated the old world from the new, and mused, we may assume, on the past which for him was simply in another pocket. Some, onlookers, took advantage of this quiet moment to distort and distend themselves, and among them was the schoolboy called Eduardo Williams, wanderer among cork trees and vineyards, and dabbler in the oddly cool southern sea. In the city of Oporto one could hide from the eyes above, because they were so concerned with the people in their black loose clothes, skulking in and out of the cathedral.

"Eduardo Williams? Who the fuck is that?" the Impenetrable Author would have asked had anyone, ethereal or muscular, brought up the name.

"Eddie Williams hasn't sent in an official notice of withdrawal as far as I know," said Mr. Arthur Boggs, Registrar of the university on the hill.

"He's pretty withdrawn, though," said some young person, purportedly a friend.

Upon hearing the news that his son Edward had been caught with his hand inside the elastic band of a native girl, Mr. Clifton E. Williams, M. Sc. (Oxon.), told his wife that it was not the sort of thing to get riled about. For one thing, this is not England, nor even Wales, and for another, he's going to be a man, not some blushing poof, and the wife of the industrialist submitted that her mate might be more right than herself, and resolved not to seem to have heard of the incident. There was some money that went to Portuguese hands.

"It was ever thus," said Eduardo Williams, examining his officially innocent hands.

But now I, someone, that voice speaking to you at last, the intrusion you will probably call it, though I have been here all along, of the first

This story appeared in Descant *in 1977 and in Bowering's* Protective Footwear *in 1978.*

person, that voice is, nevertheless, by my will alive; I can insert all I want of me without fear that either you or Eduardo Williams will be able to respond with either rancour or disgust, or impatience. I. I. I. I. I. I indulge myself, at your expense, though you may attempt to make it mine.

I was going to say:

Now I am attempting to tell the story (the?) of Eduardo Williams and the puzzle of what it is he wants, though the problem could be simplified by taking his word that he wants another cigarette, or a seven-letter word beginning with T and defining a Mediterranean deity. The story of Eduardo Williams is already well known, perhaps, to those people, at least, who would bother to hear it anyway. So what is the point of listening to it again? It could be to hear the voices. A distraction, then. Or a curiosity.

The psychiatrist guy said it would be a good idea to pay a visit to a guy called Williams. A college kid.

"I didn't move away from my own country and work all my life to turn my son into a wastrel," said Mr. Williams, senior.

Where the hell did he pick up a word like that, wondered Mr. Williams, Jr. The vestige of a classical education. Mr. Williams, Jr., himself, had been reading Samuel Butler, out of perversity. That too may have been attendant upon his earlier recollection of the little Portuguese girl and her loose underwear.

She was the daughter of a wealthy Portuguese businessman, and so there was no serious question when he chose to frequent her father's house.

I will have tried and she will refuse me but I will have tried, he thought, not very old at thirteen and fresh from his books that he read on the yellow second-storey verandah overlooking the ocean.

Eduardo, you were to make your mistakes early, and the worst one never to become someone else.

It was not noteworthy that he should go over to the girl's place, nothing the culture said against it, her father only a native but fully as wealthy as Mr. Williams, and his house too overlooked the ocean, and was better furnished, many of the pottery pieces and such in the family since the early nineteenth century at least. So it was quite acceptable to call her by her own name. Maria. Also to tell about her. She was thirteen as well, though she was as the custom had it dressed to appear younger than Eduardo, who was after all English, and not the English of short grey pants, skuff knee, Hampstead at all, but expatriate, deemed to learn young as he could have in Trinidad or Southern Rhodesia. She, to return to Eduardo's eye, had dark skin and black hair that looked always as if it had moisture combed into it, and she wore white clothes, and especially white were her cotton socks next to dark skin of her straight girl legs. Her eyes were of course dark and it was impossible to tell where the pupils met the irises, and they were so big as to give her that one appearance of a slightly greater age, the eyes, though innocent of course in approved expatriate poet terms, but also large and moist, and always there to remind the viewer (Ed.) that there was a woman waiting behind them; and weren't Latin women supposed to get ready for that sort of thing much younger than we do, asked Mr. Williams.

His wife felt constrained to assent that that was what she had heard among the white ladies of the city.

So one day they were there at her house with no one home but ser-vants, who did not pay any more attention to Maria than they had to when her mother as well as her father was out of the house. The yel-low and thick walls of the old house had here and there pikes of wrought iron sunk into them, for balconies and windows, and against some of these Maria was leaning when he first kissed her on the mouth, and as he pressed against her the wrought-iron bars sank slightly into her flesh even through the white blouse she wore. It was a little girl's blouse, though very fine with very fine lace. He was wear-ing a sweatshirt put on after a swim at the beach, and the rougher ma-terial was pressed against the front of the white blouse while the bars pressed into the back, his mouth was awkwardly but fully pressed on her lips, and finally she had to pull her face away in order to take a breath. That gave Eduardo time to think, though he was too nervous to say any words, either English or Portuguese. He didn't know much Portuguese, as it happened.

She spoke English very well, though quite formally, the way she danced during her dancing lessons. The letter that Mr. Williams, Sr. received from her father a little later was of a similar formality. Formal anger, then, of the natives forced to address even negative feelings to the foreigners in the foreign language, complicated as it all was by money of still another foreign country.

Young Eduardo had an intimation that he was rushing things. He thought he should do no more than just kiss her upon this occasion, and on some others, before proceeding. But there was also the chance that he would not be with her for too long, and then the preparation of the kissing would have worn away, and he would have to start over again.

Thus at first he felt her arch away against the wrought iron when he put his hand on the blouse, wondering exactly where they were. Now one was under the palm of his hand. Thirteen years old, a gentle slope, hard still and still growing like a volcano. He managed to kiss her again, and he felt his thing lying long against his thigh under the short beach pants. Then he lifted her skirt without looking, and he found that he 113 could put his fingers inside the loose elastic of her underwear.

The shame was a lot like delight, he remembered after his talk with his father. When the letter had come he had been ready for it or at least for something. Some time had transpired since that moment when he had run blind from the house where the maid was shouting a lot of Portuguese words with which he was not familiar. He wondered whether he had the right image of Maria – slipping to the floor or remaining pressed against the wrought iron? His father had smiled a little, one of the infrequent smiles ever seen on his father's face, and put his heavy thick-fingered hand on his back and told him to

"Just watch it, just be careful."

He decided after a week on the beach that he would go back to the house and apologize. He expected to be barred from the house, but the same maid met him at the door and conducted him inside, and pretty soon Maria gave him a kiss. He never did get to say sorry. He gave her a kiss and touched her breast through the white blouse, but he never again put his hand inside her skirt.

"Work hard. Work up to your ability. Just watch it."

"I'm going to be all on my own at Columbia," said his friend Sammy Blossom.

In Vancouver the warm winter made it easy to walk around and to wait for buses. The sky was cloudy, but low and familiar. The streets were straight, and there was nothing easier than getting around town in winter under the edge of the Pacific sky. The climate makes the outside layer of the skin soft. When it rains it rains for several days. The first day is for going into a selfish depression that can be carried, nurtured and developed for the following days of stepping through puddles, hands in raincoat pockets, face down under the dripping awnings. Either way, rain or no rain, it is gratifying weather. So Edward Williams finds it, entering the university on the hill, not a hill really, on the land above the clay cliffs that hold off the wide bend of the world's biggest ocean.

Not the comfortable though cool ocean in the south of Europe, but comfortable because Vancouver is a long way from anywhere, on the last reach of the new world, and too far from the Orient for the imagination, no matter how white.

Boy, if he would just work up to his abilities.

If he would work up to his abilities he would get the highest marks I ever gave in this course.

A pen in his shirt pocket, he walked around, looking for a place to have coffee. If he just wouldn't cut so many classes.

Mike Rice the pretty-well-known Vancouver painter had coffee with Edward Williams once in a while. Eddie looked at the paint that stuck in the creases at the edges of Mike Rice's thumb nails and decided that dedication knows no time for sticking your thumb into a jar of turpentine. Mike Rice didn't take much time to finish his coffee, and Eddie was left, usually, looking for a table of people he could move to.

Once apart, neither of them thought of the other. Mike Rice went home to listen to Indian wedding music, and Eddie Williams walked across the campus to the cliffs, and down them to the narrow beach cluttered with smooth driftwood logs, old grey things that had presumably been trees a couple hundred kilometres up the Fraser River. The ocean had always smelled particularly salty here and he was surprised. He had never imagined that this sea would be salt, the Atlantic should be thick with salt and this one should be only blue, and with white liners sailing from San Francisco docks with orange and wide sunsets, into the Orient and the islands of nut-brown people.

Maria is brownish, and probably as fat as a Tahitian, a berry on the Iberian bush, quiet and still between forefinger and thumb of another blond, northern chappie.

What is a four-letter word for the spiritual seat of man. Oh sardonic college boy.

The late-winter sun glittered off the small waves as he walked on the beach, taking care not to step on the green-weeded clumps of black shells, and when he lifted his eyes he saw the dazzling young long-hair poet of the campus, George Delsing, and with him was a young woman lying on her back upon the sand. Delsing was sitting on a log with his bare toes poked into the grey sand, and that was all there was to see about him. The young woman was one he had never seen before. She didn't seem to have much to do with Delsing, only there beside him as the slanting sunlight bounced off the poet's glasses. The kind of scene you are likely to encounter during any break in the rain. Well, poetry. Eddie Williams didn't like poetry and he didn't care much for Delsing. This country boy making gestures like Shelley in the city.

She had her shoes off too, but more important, she had tied her maroon shirt into a kind of halter, with a raggy bow made from the tails of it, tied under her breasts. This could be pretentious or carefree on her part. It wasn't *that* warm. The sun was also shining on her skin where it sloped down between her ribcage and the top of her jeans. Her skin was white as the wings of seagulls swooping between him and the sun, and she was thin. He could see the length of her bottom rib, but her belly was not flat. It made a knoll just below the beltless top of her jeans. What colour was her hair. Could be brown, could be black. Short, anyway, thus proper to the beach.

Eddie Williams had never had a girl during his time in Canada. George Delsing, the poet, never seemed to have a girl, not this one, anyway. So she was in all likelihood something to do with poetry, or at least with Delsing's poetry classes. The beach is, after all, also one of those poetry places, especially in the late winter, before it becomes a place for frisbee-throwing swimmers and loungers. Late winter fog-horns and all that, except on days like this. The sun was falling past the ocean.

"What are you doing on my beach," said Eddie Williams.

"Shit," said the poet.

"No one with an English accent can have this beach," said the young woman.

It could be that he was making too much of her. But when she spoke he happened to be looking at her belly. It moved up and down with revulsion at her own words. That at least was a good sign.

"Have a cigarette," said the poet.

"Oh? Defile nature?" said the critic.

"Suit yourself," said Delsing, and put a cigarette into the corner of his mouth.

"Okay, I'll have one."

"Me too," said the young woman.

"You don't smoke," said Delsing.

"Yes, but you don't wade, and you've got your shoes off."

That's the way she was then.

Later he did manage to see her breasts, very white once out of the loose wrappings, and even jiggled them with his hands, and covered them with kisses, and positioned his wet mouth over each nipple, and finally patted them with the soles of his bare feet like a circus goon. As they became more familiar she was less the brash nymph of the cig-arette-strewn beach. She became a serious and quiet woman, and per-haps overly concerned for him. She made him change his socks, or wear both from the same pair at once. She washed his grimy ashtrays. She wrapped her cool fingers around his penis and held him like a baseball bat, laying down a sacrific bunt. Even before coming to the new world he had been a baseball fan. It was a logical game, unlike the racing and pelting and booting of soccer.

"Eddie Williams—"

Ted Williams. There was a great baseball player, old man now standing tall and thin still over the plate, lightly swinging his bat, cool fingers curled around the handle.

"—why don't you wash your face more often? You've got grease all over your nose and forehead.'

"Back home among the Portagee we washed on the vernal equinox and on Whitsun morning."

A fastball they called it, though they all looked pretty fast, high up on the letters, a graceful barely upward swing, a satisfying crack, and the ball lifted over the outfield even with the roar of the crowd.

HR number 36 for Eddie Williams. The Splendid Splinter. Insolent son of a bitch.

But the season is the sea's son, natural progeny of the strength in the tide, the moon its mother, measurer of his life. Just watch it. Eddie Williams had met her in late winter at the edge of the sea, and each spring was the worst time of the year even while it was the best. There were every year more suicides in the spring than any other season, and that is because there is more visible life, the green stems that rise from the ground, the winter-whitened stems under women, suddenly one day visible as winter coats are left open and finally discarded. It is obvious that as the season progresses more and more clothes will be left on the hangers of home, till the summer's hottest day when the young women wear scant bathing suits (once again at the beach, son of the sea) and just when it appears that even the bathing suits will be wriggled off, the mornings grow cool, and the Hudson's Bay catalogues come out with fur coats right at the front, and it will all begin again, the decline of the flesh, the decline also of those earlier green stems to brown mulch frozen under rain, and the probing headlights of Volkswagens, at five in the afternoon.

But to return to spring, as we must, spring was the season Eddie Williams wanted never to arrive, though he loved little better than to rest with the back of his uncombed head on the scented grass. Because it was the end of the year, the end of the college year—while spring should be the beginning, the refreshment. So as for the nearby suicides, the burgeoning as they say of life only brings homeward the rot of death in those who are not a part of nature, but have chosen for themselves, or have had chosen for them, to be going down the wrong street in the wrong direction—conscious always of the minutes that yank one toward the grave, doubly bastard thought because young women are swishing by in organdy dresses.

Spring means in such a place, exams, which are easy, cutting loose from school, the university on the hill no longer a place to visit except for trips to the job office where there are no jobs except for the people who tell you there are no jobs. He had little expectation of getting a summer job. Sorry, nothing today, but we have your phone number. Plus the other fear of suddenly acquiring a job, rising *every morning* at six or seven, amassing money to dispense in the fall for further courses that only bring the spring closer, and the final spring a bachelor of arts, and then what do you do, because he had always thought that by the time he got out of university he would know what he was going to be when he grew up. Now it was that spring, the final spring, or insecticide and graduation, unless.

"Eddie, I wish you could tell me, or tell anyone, what is it you want?"

"I wish."

"I wish you would wash your face more often."

In the spring? Feel spring air on it? Maureen.

Season of death.

The sea is the source of all life. Big deal. In Vancouver of the bridges the sea often took the bodies of those who had moved as far west as they could where opportunity crooked its finger till the beckoning of each wave that slid off the rocks like a hand off a ledge, and they jumped off the bridges into the source of all life. Hello again. Especially in the spring, you could look it up. The bridges.

The Lions Gate Bridge. The Granville Street Bridge. The Burrard Bridge. The Cambie Street Bridge. The Second Narrows Bridge. The Patullo Bridge. The Oak Street Bridge. The Georgia Viaduct. The Mutilation Bridge.

Spring from a bridge.

GEORGE BOWERING was born in 1935 in Penticton and grew up in the Interior of British Columbia, where he worked as an RCAF aerial photographer for several years before attending the University of British Columbia. He completed his M.A. in 1963 under the supervision of poet Robert Creeley, a visiting professor at the time. A busy and prolific writer, editor, teacher, and critic, Bowering was one of the founders of the important little magazine Tish *in 1961, founded and edited* Imago *(1964–74), and was a contributing editor to* Open Letter. *Now a full-time member of the English Department at Simon Fraser University, he has produced some forty books of poetry, fiction, and criticism. Bowering has twice received the Governor General's Award: for poetry in 1969 and for fiction in 1980 for* Burning Water, *an imaginative re-creation of George Vancouver's voyage and arrival at Burrard Inlet.*

THE JADE PEONY

WAYSON CHOY

When Grandmama died at 83 our whole household held its breath. She had promised us a sign of her leaving, final proof that her present life had ended well. My parents knew that without any clear sign, our own family fortunes could be altered, threatened. My stepmother looked endlessly into the small cluttered room the ancient lady had oc- cupied. Nothing was touched; nothing changed. My father, thinking that a sign should appear in Grandmama's garden, looked at the frost- killed shoots and cringed: *no, that could not be it.*

My two older teenage brothers and my sister, Liang, age 14, were embarrassed by my parents' behavior. What would all the white people in Vancouver think of us? We were Canadians now, *Chinese- Canadians,* a hyphenated reality that my parents could never accept. So it seemed, for different reasons, we all held our breath waiting for *something.*

I was eight when she died. For days she had resisted going into the hospital . . . *a cold, just a cold* . . . and instead gave constant instruction to my stepmother and sister on the boiling of ginseng roots mixed with bitter extract. At night, between wracking coughs and deadly silences, Grandmama had her back and chest rubbed with heated camphor oil and sipped a bluish decoction of an herb called Peacock's Tail. When all these failed to abate her fever, she began to arrange the details of her will. This she did with my father, confessing finally: "I am too stub- born. The only cure for old age is to die."

My father wept to hear this. I stood beside her bed; she turned to me. Her round face looked darker, and the gentleness of her eyes, the thin, arching eyebrows, seemed weary. I brushed the few strands of gray, brittle hair from her face; she managed to smile at me. Being the youngest, I had spent nearly all my time with her and could not imag- ine that we would ever be parted. Yet when she spoke, and her voice hesitated, cracked, the sombre shadows of her room chilled me.

This story was published in the UBC Alumni Chronicle in 1979.

Her wrinkled brow grew wet with fever, and her small body seemed even more diminutive.

"I–I am going to the hospital, Grandson." Her hand reached out for mine. "You know, Little Son, whatever happens I will never leave you." Her palm felt plush and warm, the slender, old fingers boney and firm, so magically strong was her grip that I could not imagine how she could ever part from me. Ever.

Her hands *were* magical. My most vivid memories are of her hands: long, elegant fingers, with impeccable nails, a skein of fine, barely-seen veins, and wrinkled skin like light pine. Those hands were quick when she taught me, at six, simple tricks of juggling, learnt when she was a village girl in Southern Canton; a troupe of actors had stayed on her father's farm. One of them, "tall and pale as the whiteness of petals," fell in love with her, promising to return. In her last years his image came back like a third being in our two lives. He had been magician, acrobat, juggler, and some of the things he taught her she had absorbed and passed on to me through her stories and games. But above all, without realizing it then, her hands conveyed to me the quality of their love.

Most marvellous for me was the quick-witted skill her hands revealed in making windchimes for our birthdays: windchimes in the likeness of her lost friend's only present to her, made of bits of string and scraps, in the centre of which once hung a precious jade peony. This wondrous gift to her broke apart years ago, in China, but Grandmama kept the jade pendant in a tiny red silk envelope, and kept it always in her pocket, until her death.

These were not ordinary, carelessly made chimes, such as those you now find in our Chinatown stores, whose rattling noises drive you mad. But making her special ones caused dissension in our family, and some shame. Each one that she made was created from a treasure trove of glass fragments and castaway costume jewellery, in the same way that her first windchime had been made. The problem for the rest of the family was in the fact that Grandmama looked for these treasures wandering the back alleys of Keefer and Pender Streets, peering into our neighbors' garbage cans, chasing away hungry, nervous cats and shouting curses at them.

"All our friends are laughing at us!" Older Brother Jung said at last to my father, when Grandmama was away having tea at Mrs. Lim's.

"We are not poor," Oldest Brother Kiam declared, "yet she and Sek-Lung poke through those awful things as if–" he shoved me in frustration and I stumbled against my sister,"–they were beggars!"

"She will make Little Brother crazy!" Sister Liang said. Without warning, she punched me sharply in the back; I jumped. "You see, look how *nervous* he is!"

I lifted my foot slightly, enough to swing it back and kick Liang in the shin. She yelled and pulled back her fist to punch me again. Jung made a menacing move towards me.

"Stop this, all of you!" My father shook his head in exasperation. How could he dare tell the Grand Old One, his aging mother, that what was somehow appropriate in a poor village in China, was an abomination here. How could he prevent me, his youngest, from accompanying her? If she went walking into those alley-ways alone she could well be attacked by hoodlums. "She is not a beggar looking for food. She is searching for – for...."

My stepmother attempted to speak, then fell silent. She, too, seemed perplexed and somewhat ashamed. They all loved Grandmama, but she was *inconvenient*, unsettling.

As for our neighbors, most understood Grandmama to be harmlessly crazy, others that she did indeed make lovely toys but for what purpose? *Why?* they asked, and the stories she told me, of the juggler who smiled at her, flashed in my head.

Finally, by their cutting remarks, the family did exert enough pressure so that Grandmama and I no longer openly announced our expeditions. Instead, she took me with her on "shopping trips," ostensibly for clothes or groceries, while in fact we spent most of our time exploring stranger and more distant neighborhoods, searching for splendid junk: jangling pieces of a vase, cranberry glass fragments embossed with leaves, discarded glass beads from Woolworth necklaces.... We would sneak them all home in brown rice sacks, folded into small parcels, and put them under her bed. During the day when the family was away at school or work, we brought them out and washed every item in a large black pot of boiling lye and water, dried them quickly, carefully, and returned them, sparkling, under her bed.

Our greatest excitement occurred when a fire gutted the large Chinese Presbyterian Church, three blocks from our house. Over the still-smoking ruins the next day, Grandmama and I rushed precariously over the blackened beams to pick out the stained glass that glittered in the sunlight. Small figure bent over, wrapped against the autumn cold in a dark blue quilted coat, happily gathering each piece like gold, she became my spiritual playmate: "There's a good one! *There!*"

Hours later, soot-covered and smelling of smoke, we came home with a Safeway carton full of delicate fragments, still early enough to steal them all into the house and put the small box under her bed. "These are special pieces," she said, giving the box a last push, "because they come from a sacred place." She slowly got up and I saw, for the first time, her hand begin to shake. But then, in her joy, she embraced me. Both of our hearts were racing, as if we were two dreamers. I buried my face in her blue quilt, and for a moment, the whole world seemed silent.

"My juggler," she said, "he never came back to me from Honan...

perhaps the famine. . . ." Her voice began to quake. "But I shall have my sacred windchime. . . I shall have it again."

One evening, when the family was gathered in their usual places in the parlor, Grandmama gave me her secret nod: a slight wink of her eye and a flaring of her nostrils. There was *trouble* in the air. Supper had gone badly, school examinations were due, father had failed to meet an editorial deadline at the *Vancouver Chinese Times*. A huge sigh came from Sister Liang.

"But it is useless this Chinese they teach you!" she lamented, turning to Stepmother for support. Silence. Liang frowned, dejected, and went back to her Chinese book, bending the covers back.

"Father," Oldest Brother Kiam began, waving his bamboo brush in the air, "you must realize that this Mandarin only confuses us. We are Cantonese speakers. . . ."

"And you do not complain about Latin, French or German in your English school?" Father rattled his newspaper, signal that his patience was ending.

"But, Father, those languages are *scientific*," Kiam jabbed his brush in the air. "We are now in a scientific, logical world."

Father was silent. We could all hear Grandmama's rocker.

"What about Sek-Lung?" Older Brother Jung pointed angrily at me. "He was sick last year, but this year he should have at least started Chinese school, instead of picking over garbage cans!"

"He starts next year," Father said, in a hard tone that immediately warned everyone to be silent. Liang slammed her book.

Grandmama went on rocking quietly in her chair. She complimented my mother on her knitting, made a remark about the "strong beauty" of Kiam's brushstrokes which, in spite of himself, immensely pleased him. All this babbling noise was her family torn and confused in a strange land: everything here was so very foreign and scientific.

The truth was, I was sorry not to have started school the year before. In my innocence I had imagined going to school meant certain privileges worthy of all my brothers' and sister's complaints. The fact that my lung infection in my fifth and sixth years, mistakenly diagnosed as TB, earned me some reprieve, only made me long for school the more. Each member of the family took turns on Sunday, teaching me or annoying me. But it was the countless hours I spent with Grandmama that were my real education. Tapping me on my head she would say, "Come, Sek-Lung, we have *our* work," and we would walk up the stairs to her small crowded room. There, in the midst of her antique shawls, the old ancestral calligraphy and multi-colored embroidered hangings, beneath the mysterious shelves of sweet herbs and bitter potions, we would continue doing what we had started that morning: the elaborate windchime for her death.

122   "I can't last forever," she declared, when she let me in on the secret

of this one. "It will sing and dance and glitter," her long fingers stretched into the air, pantomiming the waving motion of her ghost chimes; "My spirit will hear its sounds and see its light and return to this house and say goodbye to you."

Deftly she reached into the Safeway carton she had placed on the chair beside me. She picked out a fish-shape amber piece, and with a long needle-like tool and a steel ruler, she scored it. Pressing the blade of a cleaver against the line, with the fingers of her other hand, she lifted up the glass until it cleanly *snapped* into the exact shape she required. Her hand began to tremble, the tips of her fingers to shiver, like rippling water.

"You see that, Little One?" She held her hand up. "That is my body fighting with Death. He is in this room now."

My eyes darted in panic, but Grandmama remained calm, undisturbed, and went on with her work. Then I remembered the glue and uncorked the jar for her. Soon the graceful ritual movements of her hand returned to her, and I became lost in the magic of her task: she dabbed a cabalistic mixture of glue on one end and skillfully dropped the braided end of a silk thread into it. This part always amazed me: the braiding would slowly, *very* slowly, *unknot,* fanning out like a prized fishtail. In a few seconds the clear, homemade glue began to harden as I blew lightly over it, welding to itself each separate silk strand.

Each jam-sized pot of glue was precious; each large cork had been wrapped with a fragment of pink silk. I remember this part vividly, because each cork was treated to a special rite. First we went shopping in the best silk stores in Chinatown for the perfect square of silk she required. It had to be a deep pink, a shade of color blushing toward red. And the tone had to match—as closely as possible—her precious jade carving, the small peony of white and light-red jade, her most lucky possession. In the centre of this semi-translucent carving, no more than an inch wide, was a pool of pink light, its veins swirling out into the petals of the flower.

"This color is the color of my spirit," she said, holding it up to the window so I could see the delicate pastel against the broad strokes of sunlight. She dropped her voice, and I held my breath at the wonder of the color. "This was given to me by the young actor who taught me how to juggle. He had four of them, and each one had a centre of this rare color, the color of Good Fortune." The pendant seemed to pulse as she turned it: "Oh, Sek-Lung! He had white hair and white skin *to his toes! It's true,* I saw him bathing." She laughed and blushed, her eyes softened at the memory. The silk had to match the pink heart of her pendant: the color was magical for her, to hold the unravelling strands of her memory....

It was just six months before she died that we really began to work   123 on her last windchime. Three thin bamboo sticks were steamed and bent into circlets; 30 exact lengths of silk thread, the strongest kind, were cut and braided at both ends and glued to stained glass. Her hands worked on their own command, each hand racing with a life of its own: cutting, snapping, braiding, knotting.... Sometimes she breathed heavily and her small body, growing thinner, sagged against me. *Death,* I thought, *He is in this room,* and I would work harder alongside her. For months Grandmama and I did this every other evening, a half dozen pieces each time. The shaking in her hand grew worse, but we said nothing. Finally, after discarding hundreds, she told me she had the necessary 30 pieces. But this time, because it was a sacred chime, I would not be permitted to help her tie it up or have the joy of raising it. "Once tied," she said, holding me against my disappointment, "not even I can raise it. Not a sound must it make until I have died."

"What will happen?"

"Your father will then take the centre braided strand and raise it. He will hang it against my bedroom window so that my ghost may see it, and hear it, and return. I must say goodbye to this world properly or wander in this foreign devil's land forever."

"You can take the streetcar!" I blurted, suddenly shocked that she actually meant to leave me. I thought I could hear the clear-chromatic chimes, see the shimmering colors on the wall: I fell against her and cried, and there in my crying I knew that she would die. I can still remember the touch of her hand on my head, and the smell of her thick woolen sweater pressed against my face. "I will always be with you, Little Sek-Lung, but in a different way... you'll see."

Months went by, and nothing happened. Then one late September evening, when I had just come home from Chinese School, Grandmama was preparing supper when she looked out our kitchen window and saw a cat—a long, lean white cat—jump into our garbage pail and knock it over. She ran out to chase it away, shouting curses at it. She did not have her thick sweater on and when she came back into the house, a chill gripped her. She leaned against the door: "That was not a cat," she said, and the odd tone of her voice caused my father to look with alarm at her. "I can not take back my curses. It is too late." She took hold of my father's arm: "It was all white and had pink eyes like sacred fire."

My father started at this, and they both looked pale. My brothers and sister, clearing the table, froze in their gestures.

"The fog has confused you," Stepmother said. "It was just a cat."

But Grandmama shook her head, for she knew it was a sign. "I will not live forever," she said. "I am prepared."

The next morning she was confined to her bed with a severe cold.

Sitting by her, playing with some of my toys, I asked her about the cat: "Why did father jump at the cat with the pink eyes? He didn't see it, you did."

"But he and your mother know what it means."

"What?"

"My friend, the juggler, the magician, was as pale as white jade, and he had pink eyes." I thought she would begin to tell me one of her stories, a tale of enchantment or of a wondrous adventure, but she only paused to swallow; her eyes glittered, lost in memory. She took my hand, gently opening and closing her fingers over it. "Sek-Lung," she sighed, "*he* has come back to me."

Then Grandmama sank back into her pillow and the embroidered flowers lifted to frame her wrinkled face. I saw her hand over my own, and my own began to tremble. I fell fitfully asleep by her side. When I woke up it was dark and her bed was empty. She had been taken to the hospital and I was not permitted to visit.

A few days after that she died of the complications of pneumonia. Immediately after her death my father came home and said nothing to us, but walked up the stairs to her room, pulled aside the drawn lace curtains of her window and lifted the windchimes to the sky.

I began to cry and quickly put my hand in my pocket for a handker-chief. Instead, caught between my fingers, was the small, round firm-ness of the jade peony. In my mind's eye I saw Grandmama smile and heard, softly, the pink centre beat like a beautiful, cramped heart.

WAYSON CHOY was born in Vancouver in 1939, where he lived for his first twenty-two years, attending Gladstone High School and the University of British Columbia. Now a Teaching Master at Humber College of Applied Arts and Technology in Toronto, he returns to Vancouver every summer, which to him remains "that mythical place where dragons and lions dance, in a fire-cracker mist, that celebrated the end of World War II." His work has been published in Prism, River's Bend Review, *and* Best American Short Story.

1941–1942

JOY KOGAWA

The darkness is everywhere, in the day as well as the night. It threatens us as it always has, in the streetcars, in the stores, on the streets, in all public places. It covers the entire city and causes all the lights to be turned out. It drones overhead in the sounds of airplanes. It rushes unbidden from the mouths of strangers and in the taunts of children. It happens to my eight-year-old brother Stephen even more terrifyingly than it does to me.

One day he comes home from school, his glasses broken, black tear stains on his face. My aunt, Obasan, is hanging up clothes on the line from the back porch. When she sees him, she does not cry out but continues hanging up the laundry, removing the pegs from her mouth one at a time.

"What happened?" I whisper as Stephen comes up the stairs.

He doesn't answer me. Is he ashamed? Should I go away?

"What happened?" It is Obasan asking this time and her voice is soft.

He still does not reply and Obasan takes him by the hand into the kitchen and wipes his face. I stand hesitantly in the doorway, watching.

"I told you," Stephen says at last.

I am encouraged that he is speaking to me. "Oh," I say wishing to show that I understand, but I do not.

"You know, Nomi."

Stephen is in grade three at David Lloyd George School. There are "air raid drills" at school, he tells me, which means that when a loud alarm sounds, all the children line up and file out of the classrooms as quickly as possible. They lie flat on the ground, crouch by hedges or in ditches, to hide from the bombs which may drop on us all—not just on the school, but anywhere at any time out of enemy aircraft overhead. We may be killed or maimed, blinded for life or burnt. We may lose an arm, or a finger even. To be safe, we must hide and be still so they will not see us.

 This piece is taken from Joy Kogawa's novel, Obasan (1981).

The girl with the long ringlets who sits in front of Stephen said to him, "All the Jap kids at school are going to be sent away and they're bad and you're a Jap." And so, Stephen tells me, am I.

"Are we?" I ask Father.

"No," Father says. "We're Canadian."

It is a riddle, Stephen tells me. We are both the enemy and not the enemy.

Riddles are hard to understand. Only Stephen knows what they mean. Neither Aya Obasan nor Grandma and Grandpa Nakane under- stand the jokes in Stephen's riddle book. But Grandpa Nakane pats Stephen on the head and laughs when Stephen does.

When Grandpa Nakane walks, he bends forward from his waist and his right arm dangles loose from his shoulder close to his knees like some of the monkeys at Stanley Park. The monkeys are swift and hop and swing acrobatically from wall to ceiling and around in great arcs. But Grandpa Nakane is no leaping dancer and lopes along at his own pace.

During the Christmas concert, I look up and see Grandpa Nakane coming down the aisle of the church to sit in front, his hoary white eyebrows lifted high so he can see better.

Under his left arm he is carrying a present wrapped in rustly white tissue paper. He is watching intently as Stephen and I stand around the manger singing carols with the other white-robed cherubs, our hands folded like church steeples and our eyes gazing down at the little Lord flashlight Jesus asleep in the hay. Nakayama-sensei, the round-faced minister, is standing beside the organ smiling widely and nodding in time to the music. When I peek up at the audience, I can see short Grandpa Kato sitting in the aisle near the back, his round belly like a ball with his gold watch-chain draped in front. I know Aunt Emily and Uncle Dan are somewhere in the crowded church watching and I am filled with a need to hide but there is nowhere to go. If the wooden manger in front were bigger I could dive into the hay and be buried from view.

All the lights except for the flashlight in the hay go out and the room is suddenly so still and dark that it seems almost to have disappeared. In a moment a candle appears high up in the air in the middle of the aisle at the back and I can hear Father's high clear notes on his wooden flute, playing the *Gloria in Excelsis Deo*. After this, Father's voice, rich and tender, sings the beginning of the hymn and candle after candle comes through the archway from the hall, around to the back and, in a steady advancing stream of light and song, up to the front, engulfing us.

All of Christmas is like this. A mixture of white lights and coloured twinkling lights in the dark, surprises, songs, and streams and streams of people, up and down the escalators, in the crowded stores and on the green and red decorated sidewalks.

Even on New Year's, Stephen and I are so showered with gifts that our rooms bulge with new toys. I have a wonderful set of entirely red things — an apple-fat shiny red purse that clicks open and shut like Aunt Emily's with a shiny red change purse inside, a red bead necklace, bracelet, comb, brush, and a gold and red kitten brooch with green jewel eyes. Stephen has a Meccano set and a wine-coloured encyclopedia — *The Book of Knowledge* — which Aunt Emily exclaims over and reads aloud with excitement.

"Look, Nomi," she says, pointing to the picture of a little girl carrying a candle and walking in the dark to get a secret message to her father in a dungeon. It's a story in a part of the encyclopedia called "The Book of Golden Deeds", which is filled with tales of martyrs and brave children and people going through torment and terror. Could I, I wonder, ever do the things that they do? Could I hide in a wagon of hay and not cry out if I were stabbed by a bayonet?

Mother, it seems to me, could. So could Grandma Kato or Obasan. But not, I think, Aunt Emily, though perhaps that is not so. She is too often impatient and flustered, her fingers jerking her round wire-rimmed glasses up her short nose. And Stephen? Who among us would last the longest in a torture chamber without betraying the rest? Sometimes, in the dark, I send my finger digging deep into my arm or chest, imagining the bayonet's bloody stab.

At night I lie awake thinking of dangerous people wielding hooks and prongs, but during the day there is another danger, another darkness, soft and mysterious. I know it as whispers and frowns and too much gentleness. Then, one spring evening, the two shadows of day and night come together in a white heavy mist of fear.

I am in the basement playroom making folding paper cranes, each one tinier than the one before. I can hear Father coughing lightly in his study, over and over. He coughs almost all the time and he sits in his study writing at night. When I talk to him he smiles but he stares away as if I am not there. He is never cross. He is alone these days. Where has everyone gone? There used to be friends visiting us and staying for meals. They brought me little toys or toffee. Uncle Dan was almost always here in the evenings, his horsey face flung back in laughter and his shoulders pumping up and down. Where is he now? No one ever visits us in the evenings any more.

But tonight Aunt Emily is here. I hear a groan and a thump as someone pounds — what? The wall? The desk?

I tiptoe out of the playroom and past the furnace to the door of the study. The room has a cot in it. Aunt Emily is pacing back and forth, her arms folded tightly and her black skirt swishing. No one sees me standing by the door and I take my smallest paper crane and crawl under the bed. From there, lying on my belly, I can see one of Father's legs crossed at the knees, moving back and forth like a pendulum. His black boot with the hooks lined up along either side of the tongue kicks the leg of his roll-top desk – tick, tick, tick, like a clock.

Then suddenly the crash again of a fist against the wall and I hear their voices speaking as I have never heard before – tight, low, dark. I half thought I would shout "boo" and jump up at them, but now I am afraid to move. I wish I had not thought to hide.

"What next, Mark?" Aunt Emily is whispering in a hoarse voice.

Father's fit of coughing begins again. When he speaks, his voice is thin as the wind. "It can't be helped. It can't be helped."

"But we can get them out. I'm sure we can," Aunt Emily says. I have never heard such urgency. "Your father won't last in the Sick Bay. And he'll be left behind after the rest of us are gone. He'll be alone. The orders are to leave everyone in the Sick Bay behind. It's a death sentence for the old ones."

Grandpa Nakane at Sick Bay? Where, I wonder, is that? And why is it a cause of distress? Is Sick Bay near English Bay or Horseshoe Bay? When we go to Stanley Park we sometimes drive by English Bay. Past English Bay are the other beaches, Second and Third Beach where I once went to buy potato chips and got lost. Grandpa Nakane came ambling out of all the crowd that day and took my hand in his one strong hand without saying a word and I fed him my potato chips one by one as if he were one of the animals at the zoo. If Grandpa Nakane is at the beach now, could he be lost the way I was? Should we not go to find him?

"They must have rounded up everyone on Saltspring Island and ship-ped the whole lot of them to the Pool," Aunt Emily says. "Where will it end?"

I have seen my Nakane grandparents only once since Christmas. Obasan told me Grandma and Grandpa went to visit friends and their old boat shop on Saltspring Island as they do every year. They have still not come back to their house in New Westminster. When Mother was with us we used to visit Grandma and Grandpa Nakane often and go to see Aya Obasan and Uncle Isamu who lived not far from them. I haven't seen Uncle for a long time either.

Aunt Emily treads back and forth across the wine-coloured carpet, her black pointed shoes with the single strap coming straight towards me then abruptly away. The round black fastener wobbles with every step.

"Your mother won't survive it either, Mark. We really have to get them out. We'll go together to the Security Commission tomorrow. I've met the woman there."

"You think she can help? In all this mess would there be time to listen to one story?"

"They'll have to. Oh, if Grandma and Grandpa had only stayed at home this year. We'll have to explain that your parents don't live in Saltspring. No one else from Vancouver or New Westminster has been shoved into that place."

"Is it so bad there?" Father speaks so softly I can barely hear.

Aunt Emily sits down on the bed and the wire slats suddenly form a rounded bulge above my head. I push back farther under the bed and my leg brushes against a red, white and blue ball that Uncle Dan gave me. It's covered in a layer of fine dust.

"It's a nightmare," Aunt Emily whispers.

The black coils at the ends of the slats squeal as Aunt Emily shifts restlessly. "All those little kids. And the old women like Grandma— totally bewildered. Fumi and Eiko can't take any more. They're so thin." Aunt Emily's voice is shaking.

Fumi and Eiko are Aunt Emily's closest friends. I have seen them often at Aunt Emily's place laughing and talking and teasing each other.

Father's fist thuds against his knees for a long time. Then, in a halting voice I've never heard him use before, he says, "I have to leave it all in your hands, Emily. My time is up."

There is a jump from the bed and the round bulge disappears in-stantly as the smooth metal slats lie straight and flat again.

"Mark, it can't be. Listen to your cough. You're not well enough. We'll get an extension—for health reasons."

"No—no. It's my turn. Others have been filling the quota and going in my place."

All this talk is puzzling and frightening. I cradle the rubber ball against my cheek and stare up at the white tufts like tiny rabbit tails stuck all over the bottom of the mattress.

I am thinking of Peter Rabbit hopping through the lettuce patch when I hear Stephen's lopsided hop as he comes galloping down the stairs.

"The curfew, Auntie!" he is calling. "Look how dark it is. Hurry! The police!"

There is a sudden jump and Aunt Emily runs to the door. "Damn this mess," she says in a panicky voice. "I'll have to go down the back alleys." She pauses at the doorway briefly, then she is gone. I can hear her feet running through the playroom and out the open door. In a few seconds I hear the click of the latch at the back gate.

The ball I found under the cot that day was never lost again. Obasan still keeps it in a box with Stephen's toy cars on the bottom shelf in the bathroom. The rubber is cracked and scored with a black lacy design, and the colours are dull, but it still bounces a little.

Sick Bay, I learned eventually, was not a beach at all. And the place they called the Pool was not a pool of water, but a prison at the exhibition grounds called Hastings Park in Vancouver. Men, women, and children outside Vancouver, from the "protected area"—a hundred-mile strip along the coast—were herded into the grounds and kept there like animals until they were shipped off to road-work camps and concentration camps in the interior of the province. From our family, it was only Grandma and Grandpa Nakane who were imprisoned at the Pool.

Some families were able to leave on their own and found homes in British Columbia's interior and elsewhere in Canada. Ghost towns such as Slocan—those old mining settlements, sometimes abandoned, sometimes with a remnant community—were reopened, and row upon row of two-family wooden huts were erected. Eventually the whole coast was cleared and everyone of the Japanese race in Vancouver was sent away.

The tension everywhere was not clear to me then and is not much clearer today. Time has solved few mysteries. Wars and rumours of wars, racial hatreds and fears are with us still.

JOY NAKAYAMA KOGAWA was born in Vancouver in 1935. When she was seven years old her family, along with thousands of Japanese-Canadians living along the British Columbia coast, was forcibly evacuated, first to Slocan and later to Alberta. Out of this crucial personal and national experience she wrote Obasan (1981), *her prizewinning first novel from which "1941–1942" has been extracted. She has also lived in Saskatoon and Ottawa, and currently makes her home in Toronto. A poet before turning to fiction, Kogawa has published three volumes of poetry:* The Splintered Moon (1968), A Choice of Dreams (1974), *and* Jericho Road (1978).

WAS THAT
MALCOLM LOWRY?

FRANCES DUNCAN

When I was eight my father died and my mother bought a shack on the beach at Dollarton. It was green and had painted in a white horseshoe shape on the front door: DUCUMIN. The outhouse was also green and its door invited one to BIDEAWEE which, when I deciphered the curving unspaced words, delighted me with its scatalogical daring. It did not delight my mother however, and she threatened at least once a month for as long as we owned the shack to paint both doors, but she never did, and the shack passed out of our hands four years later still weatherbeaten green, still inviting one to DUCUMIN and BIDE-AWEE.

In spite of its having a name we never called it anything but "the shack," never beach house or cottage or summer camp; my mother was a respecter of connotations and our shack would have had to be larger, neater, or more decorated to qualify for another noun. It was one of the long line of squatters' shacks stretching west from Roche Point light along Burrard Inlet and north from the light up Indian Arm to Dollarton and Cove Cliff. Ours was the third shack west of Roche Point directly across the Inlet from the railroad tracks and the oil refinery's stack of constant fire.

It was possible to drive halfway from the highway to the shack down a rutted double track so narrow the thimbleberry, salmonberry and cedar branches whipped in the open windows of our '49 Prefect and left scratches on its paint. We parked in a clearing so small that only a Prefect could turn and then loaded our food, clothes, toys, cat, bathing suits and gumboots into a battered black baby buggy my mother had procured at a secondhand shop to solve this final transportation prob-lem. Past my favourite climbing tree and down the trail which, in fall, the maples littered with leaves like giants' splayed footprints, winding

132   *This story was originally published in* Room of One's Own *in 1981.*

down and down, the buggy forcing back the bushes which gained revenge on our faces, the incline gradually lessening until suddenly we stood, always newly delighted, on the narrow grassy bank between the forest and the beach.

One of the marvels of the shack was that it stood right there as well, from its back windows appearing rooted to the forest, permanent and safely anchored, yet from the front we saw nothing but water and hills across the Inlet, and the shack became a houseboat; one flip of a moor-ing line and it could drift forever. There was a short boardwalk from the grassy verge to the veranda and if we had arrived at highest tide when the water tried to reach the grass and missed by only inches, the boards became a gangplank and we could see crabs scuttling among the newly washed and sparkling pebbles.

I see us now on the bank, the buggy stuck on some unseen rock, my mother jiggling the handle, my holding down a struggling cat while try-ing to lift up the front end. The cat scratches and leaps away, the buggy bounces over the rock and onto the boards and what I remember of this, even more than how I licked the small beads of blood from the scratch, what I remember are the smells. They are still stored pure and strong in some area of my brain, recorded by an olfactory nerve not jaded with smoke and drink and aging: the tangy hot and coolness of a forest, sun on cedar, on stones, on small wild strawberries, rotting, growing earth and roots, bleeding hearts and huckleberries, all damp and acrid and warm; and then on the narrow bank exchanging this pomander of rain forest for that of the beach: shock of hotter sun on me, on pebbles, on barnacled rocks, on the sea, salt, salt, do not breathe deep at first but test with gentle whiffs, rotting crabs and fish, a dead gull perhaps, seaweed dry and peppery-crackley jilted on the beach, slimy kelp strands the tide still plays with, lush and foam-collecting, wood smoke from some shack, oil and gas from a passing boat, a piece of rusted boom chain smelling like the city; then back to us, my mother's lavender, the buggy's cracked and tangy warming leather, and, if we stand here too long, the smells of cake and apples and red-running juicy beef.

Up onto the veranda then, unlock the large padlock always stiff and unyielding with its unquenchable thirst for oil; it had come with the shack and is loathe to admit us. That time for me, while my mother turns the key and pulls the lock, squeaks back the hasp, pushes hard on the moisture-swollen door, is as long and jiggly-footed as Christmas Eve, but the door grudgingly opens and I dash in to check all three rooms and relief stills my impatience, allows the curled-up ball of time to once again relax into the infinity of summer.

There is a special sort of mustiness in a closed up place by the sea that is not shared by lakefront cottages nor damp cellars in the city, an acrid salty sharpness, an awareness of fecund origins and destinies perhaps. It permeates the walls and floors and furniture, pricking nostrils as the brain sorts out and rediscovers: ashes in the stove, oil cloth, linoleum, sheets and blankets, old clam and oyster shells now used for pins and paper clips, lexicon, dominoes, comic books and popsicle sticks piled on shelves, last year's shorts and bathing suits, too-small sneakers, water-whitened; odours take on shape and solidity, becoming part of a child's primeval response to a wild and changeless place.

And now quickly outside to turn the stiffened, salt-caked clasps and remove the heavy shutters so light can help explore the shack. Four windows, one in each bedroom on the side, one at the back over the dishpan sink, one at the front looking over the veranda, all with smaller panes of glass, washed inside and out and again next day salt-sprayed, so even on sunny midsummer afternoons the shack inside was cool and dark.

The main room had a large black stove which insatiably emptied the woodbox and challenged my mother to bake cakes in its unpredictable oven, counter, table and untidy shelves all covered with worn, red-printed oil cloth, small pantry at the back which once the cat used for a bathroom, and everywhere unmatching chairs, wood-backed or wicker.

A double bed filled each bedroom, a foot perhaps of floor space on three sides, more bed closets than rooms, old sheets on rods for doors. My mother had one and I the other except when we had guests and then I shared her bed as I had done when my father was ill before he died. Or when we had a lot of company we children slept in blankets on the veranda, giggling, coming untucked, listening to the water lap the pebbles, to the thump and creak as the tide bunted a log into the pilings, mystified by grown-ups who preferred to sleep in beds.

Time at the shack stretched straight and sunny, marked by the coming and going of tides, the coming and going of friends, and each day when the water crept up the hot beach, we swam. The beach consisted of potato-sized rocks, barnacled sharp and slippery with lime-green algae. We wore old sneakers or special bathing shoes whose rubber soles whitened and cracked with the salt and the sun. Sometimes one came off in the undertow and I hobbled and paddled to shore, trying not to place my foot on barnacles or crabs or some hungry, tickley fish. Days later the tide might deposit the lost shoe, a curled-up cadaver in the line of jetsam, and I would retrieve it triumphantly, placing it to dry with others on the veranda railing.

At high tide we could swim in front of the shack, letting ourselves into the three feet of water from the railing in the space of time before the rotted screening was replaced, a biennial chore close to the ocean.

We helped the screen's disintegration, poking at tender spots with surgical precision, the fine metal giving way under our fingers, not thinking we were being destructive, but rather hastening the time a hole was big enough to scramble through onto the railing. There we crouched, turned around, dangled over the edge, feet scraping the shingles, escaping from pirates, knives between our teeth, or jumping noisily from the burning warship, white-knuckled until our numb fingers slid off the railing and we splashed into the sea, that cold, clear, salt water locating scraped knees and barnacle cuts with the unerring ability of a medieval torturer.

The beach sloped steeply so we did not have to go out very far at high tide to be up to our necks, but at low we could not go past our waists for fear of the sudden drop-off into the boating channel with its undertows and whirlpools. Frequently we went around the Point to swim where the beach was pebbly as if a philanthropist had raked away the rocks. We were cautioned to stay away from the line in the water which snaked directly from the lighthouse toward Ioco—it was a rip tide.

I certainly never went near it; RipTide could have been some Ogopogo relative who lurked just below the surface, his thrashing tail the line in the water, waiting to eat the legs of a child who went too close. Still, I learned to swim with my eyes open underwater hoping to catch sight of Rip Tide from a distance; I never did for he was canny, slipping away when his invisibility was threatened. I did not have a face mask or snorkel, had I, I would have seen all the fearful length of him like Leviathan or Nessie, would have felt the chill thrill of terror, kicked for my very life back to the beach certain the trailing kelp's tickle was his touch—or else I would not have seen him, would have discovered Rip Tide to be only the prosaic meeting of two swirls of water, and underneath that surface turbulence only the usual and unterrifying denizens: starfish, rock cod, anemones, mussels, and the omnipresent, irritating barnacle. Had I discovered this, I might not have been considered an obedient child, trusted after one warning to stay safely east of the Point.

My mother lay on a blanket against a log protected by a large, striped canvas beach umbrella, reading Agatha Christies, Mary Roberts Rineharts or Georgette Heyers while alone, talking to the other adults when we had company. After some time she would get up and advance slowly into the water, standing with the skirt of her bathing suit floating around her, glaring at my teasing attempts to splash her, then launch herself forward into a personal combination of dog paddle and sidestroke, carefully keeping her hair out of the water. I loved it when my mother swam. I'd swim beside her with my head above the surface but I always floundered in a stroke or two; my head belonged 135 in water as much as the rest of me. She was a good swimmer in spite of her idiosyncratic stroke, strong, steady, and enduring. She'd lived in English Bay and had swum each day before school, frequently across to Kitsilano and back. "In the winter too?" I'd ask, hoping to spur on these unbelievable reminiscences, but, "the water was warmer then," was all she would say, and laugh.

I was rarely given the opportunity to see my mother as endurance swimmer for as I swam alongside, moving my legs and arms twice for each of her strokes, she'd invariably announce, "you must be freezing, you lips are turning blue," and around she would turn and head for shore, ignoring my protestations, which were false bravado, for "blue lips" was nearly as terrifying a pronouncement as Rip Tide. How long would it take the rest of me to turn blue? Would I stay blue? If lips could turn blue and Anne's hair green, what other colours might the body break out in? And how could it happen without a person knowing it? Blue lips were associated with freezing as in "freezing to death"; could I freeze to death without knowing it? I obediently trailed out of the water, but waited a few seconds to show that "blue lips" didn't bother me.

Because we were not swimming directly in front of the shack, technically we had "gone to the beach" and that entailed a picnic. I stood shivering in a towel wondering how the air had cooled so much when the sun still shone, and watched my mother put out the food. It was packed in square glass containers with carved daisies on the sides and matching lids, potato salad, devilled eggs, lettuce and tomatoes, buttered raisin bread, and I remembered a time before my father went to hospital, before he was moved into my bedroom to die, a very long time before the shack, when the three of us had gone to sandy city beaches with these same containers. I knew my father had not liked sandwiches on a picnic; it was that sort of knowledge one has always had about one's family. I assumed my mother had told me. Or maybe, now I wonder, because of the way that sort of knowledge gets confused, if it was my mother who did not like sandwiches, for although she had given away my father's suits and sword and revolver from the war, she continued to use the glass containers.

As distinctly different as the times of high and low tide were the times of having company and the times of being alone. I couldn't have said which I preferred, no more than I could place a value on the tides. Both had good aspects and bad; at low tide clams and crabs and starfish were exposed for tormenting, but high transformed the pebbles into jewels and brought the phosphorescence up the beach. What I did not like, however, was the change from one state to another, from low to high tide, from companionship to solitude. No more does my daughter now; to get ready to go out or to leave to come home provokes an irritated outburst and I still do not like the transition between holidays and routine:

Then, at the shack, the arrival of company meant my solitary activities were interrupted by noisy, excited children who claimed the forest and beach in undisciplined forays, perhaps unwittingly trampling the seedling I was nurturing into a west coast beanstalk. But a week later, the exodus of this same company left the forest echoing with boredom and loneliness, left no pirates with whom to jump into the sea, no noisy, nightly games of snap or cheat, no cowboys and indians and so no reason to re-build the fort.

After I had grumpily waved good-bye I informed my mother so petulantly and continuously that there was nothing to do she lost patience and I could retaliate in anger. With her lips pressed together she stomped to the shack, already reclaimed by the cat, and her interrupted reading, and I stomped to my favourite tree, a cedar with bushy, low-growing branches which overhung the path. I climbed as high as my fear of heights allowed and sat in a green cave, peeling strips of bark off the trunk, crushing needles one at a time until my nostrils were filled with pungency, knowing the world to be a cruel and unfair place and my mother its inimical manifestation.

Slowly, as the branch turned my leg first frizzy-feeling and then numb, I remembered the hole I'd been going to dig, or the candies left in the box the company had brought, or that I'd not been able to climb my favourite rock or read my comics in peace, and maybe the fort would make a better hermit's cave than wild west outpost.

I opened the door and my mother looked up from her book. I studied her face; guilt prompted my apology. "Yes," she usually said, sounding impassive, but she held out a hand and I advanced and put my head on her shoulder, my face in the softness of her neck. "You have your father's temper, you must learn to control it, he did, he was a gentle person." I vowed I would learn, but then, with greater guilt for now he was dead, thought he could have left his daughter better gifts than red hair and temper, he could have left her height and slimness.

After the inevitable mention of controlling my temper, I could feel her neck muscles tighten into a smile. I stepped back and smiled at her and we shared the remaining candies, one for her and one for me, whether there were two or nine and if the number were uneven, I got a knife and divided the last, half for her and half for me. Still hungry, I offered to make her a sandwich as well but she usually declined, still smiling, and I got out the bread and peanut butter and the other most important ingredient, pickle or apple or lettuce or cucumber, whatever was my fancy of the week.

At home my mother made popsicles in flat, coffin-shaped aluminum containers, out of strawberry, lime or cherry kool-aid, and once, only 137 once, out of tomato juice. She never made popsicles at the shack; we had no electricity, no ice, no running water. We washed dishes, clothes and ourselves in the ocean with cakes of special salt water soap which never seemed to lather. Occasionally I and whatever children were visiting were made to take the soap with us on our swims. Those were the best baths, washing each other's hair, the soap bar skipping out of our hands, rinsing our hair by diving for the soap, sometimes finding it before the undertow dragged it to the middle of the Inlet where I imagined some mother fish delighted, her babies not. It did not float. We lost a lot of soap.

We brushed our teeth in the sea as well, the company children try-ing to use their Colgate or Ipana, spitting white blobs among the phosphorescence we stirred up with our toothbrushes until either the taste or my mother convinced them salt water was a better cleanser than their commercial products.

My mother must have had some deep alliance with the ocean—which she called salt chuck with west coast pioneer familiarity—for there was not an ailment it could not cure, not a mineral it did not contain, not a beneficence it could not bestow. Scraped legs, cut hands, gouged knees, all were sent into the chuck where the iodine, she said, was a better antiseptic than bottled mercurochrome. Head-aches, mild fevers were cured by brisk swims, although the sufferers were watched to ascertain that in their weakened state they avoided the clutches of both Rip Tide and "blue lips," and if the ailment were too severe—though I cannot imagine what that might have been—pneumonia perhaps?—a good dose of brisk salt air was next best.

My mother's trust in natural cures might have been consolidated by Rena. For the three years before his death my father had been in and out of hospital, which necessitated my mother's return to work and a succession of housekeepers who cooked and cleaned and looked after me. One was Kate from Switzerland whose idea of making toast was to cook only one side of the bread, but it was Rena, a short, fat, East European woman of indeterminate age but determined ideas, who might have influenced my mother's naturopathy.

I fell when I was seven, pretending I could ride a friend's two-wheeler, and exchanged half the gravel of the road for the skin on my arm. Rena's cure was plantain which she picked from the boulevard in front of our house and I attended school in utter mortification with green leaves peeking out of the gauze bandage. Every day when she changed the limp leaves for fresh ones she dragged me to my mother saying, "see Missus? Real good now, God gives us best," and my mother was so impressed by the cleanliness of the wound she ignored my pleas that Johnson & Johnson's cure, if not more efficacious was at least less obvious, and off to school I went to have my pride hurt worse from laughter than my arm had hurt from the fall. Definitely the cure over-shadowed the ailment and I finally understood my mother's expression, "adding insult to injury."

The salt chuck could not provide drinking water and it was my job to trek up the trail, up the rutted bumpy road and along the highway to a gas station, where I could also buy real popsicles, the most surprising of which were root beer and blueberry.

Years later at friends' cottages in Northern Ontario when we emerged from cool woods to hot, hot highway, my mind was unwillingly assailed by those early emergences from cool to hot, pails clanking against my legs, and then, on the return trip, from hot, tar-sticky macadam to the relief of the forest trail, pails now pulling my shoulder muscles, digging into my hands,slopping water on my sneakers. In Northern Ontario I squelched the unwanted memories, but sometimes wondered at their constant rise from the basement of my mind, for the birch and spruce and pine, lakes and rocks of Ontario were so unlike the cedar, maple, fir, gentle rotting humus and salt tang of Dollarton; only the contrast of hot and cool remained; was that enough, I wondered, to return me with phoenix-fullblown-ness to this earlier time?

Once, coming down the trail in the early morning, the water pails slipping and slopping from a stick across my shoulders, I surprised a deer. I stopped, but must already have made too much noise, pails rubbing bushes, feet clicking rocks, for it dashed away immediately. After that I stalked everywhere slowly and silently, a deerhunter, but although I was allowed within five feet of birds, the deer always eluded me. So did the raccoons and fortunately, the bears. I caught slow salamanders on the muddy path, and tried for a while to salt a crow's tail, followed our cat on mystery tours, short because I lost him or grew bored while he sat.

Once I found an injured squirrel and carried it to the shack rolled up in my tee shirt. It lay so still I was afraid it was dead but then it twitched and I knew I could save it, held it gently against the warmth of my chest, and showed my mother, whispering as one does near the ill. But she said it was dead, and I said, "no, it moved," and she said that happened—an after-twitch. I didn't believe her and wanted to say so, but the last time I had was on top of my memory. "Your father is dead, he died in the night." "I don't believe you, you're lying," and I'd run to my room. It was empty. "Where is he?" I'd asked and she'd told me they'd taken his body in the night. Now I wanted to ask if he'd twitched like the squirrel, if everything twitched when it died, but there are some things not safe to ask, some things one does not want to know.

The squirrel was stiffening and there was blood on my shirt so I found an empty candy box, dug a hole and had a funeral with a doll and 139 a Mortimer Snerd puppet for pallbearers. We sang *Onward Christian Soldiers* as we had at my father's funeral and then *Hark the Herald Angels*. I covered the box with earth and made a popsicle stick cross on which I carved *SQUIRREL R.I.P.* Later I dug up the box and poked the squirrel to make sure it was really dead.

Company at the shack consisted primarily of women and children, friends of my mother who came for a week, leaving their husbands at work in the city, or career women like her who had married late and been widowed early, who had only children about my age. These women, social workers and nurses, were the dominant decision-makers of my youth, the hewers of wood, wielders of machetes and hammers, and men were the background shadows, loved, enjoyed, considered and occasionally deferred to—as were the children. It was the natural order to me that King George would die and the Princess become ruler of Canada with all that televised pomp and ceremony. I doubt I had even heard of St. Laurent.

Both my parents had large families and I had many uncles who came to visit and whose questions my mother's frown made me answer politely before I was dismissed to play. Later I was summoned for leave-taking which consisted of a kiss and a quarter, but my uncles had military moustaches and moist lips and the latter gift barely compensated for the former. Once I ran away from an exiting uncle, trying to appear for my mother's sake, teasing and silly, but clearly aware that if left to me, I would not return to submit to the rape-like humiliation of that kiss. Just as clearly however, I was aware that a man's kiss was something women put up with, like dirty dishes and dust, soon disposed of and worthy of no further attention in the real business of running the world. I returned, I submitted.

Men might have seemed strange creatures with unpleasant demands but boys were my favourite company. Some of the girls who came to the shack were afraid of snakes, bothered by sandflies and crabs, preferred to stay inside reading my comics—although they complained there were too many Superboys and not enough Katy Keenes. The girls sometimes cried when scratched by bushes or barnacles, but the boys saved their tears for importances, fights usually initiated by me—with boys not only did I not have to control my temper, it gave me enough strength to push and kick them to the ground, in one instance to rip the shirt off my friend's back, buttons popping in Clark Kent fashion.

We played complicated games involving knives and sticks, forts and axes, that went on for days, then with sudden consensus switched to the beach where we constructed boats out of scrounged wood, nails, popsicle sticks and string for railings. Sometimes the warships were elaborated into houseboats with the addition of curtains attached so they really opened. The boys, away from their neighbourhoods, would play with my dolls, but here their imaginations flagged, and we usually switched to cars in the dirt at the edge of the forest.

I don't think I thought of myself as a boy, but neither particularly as a girl. I was fully aware of the anatomical differences which we had discussed and illustrated far away from the shack, but other than that minor and obvious difference, which I thought more a nuisance for a boy than a lack for a girl, I regarded us as the same, and whether I felt closer to boys or to girls depended on our activity: pirates or dolls, warships or houseboats. However, I must have wondered what it felt like to be a boy or thought that with practice I could compete in the forest, for once, early in our time at the shack. I walked into BIDEA-WEE, pulled down my pants, thrust my hips forward, and tried, as I had observed, to direct the stream forward. I then had to wipe the seat and floor and reach the shack unnoticed, there to change my shorts, pants, socks and shoes. Even the fact that no one knew my failure did not lessen the humiliation that there was something I would never master, no matter my desire or practice. It was after that I deliberately turned my back when boys had to pee in the woods, and told them they were disgusting.

Later, perhaps the following year, my mother introduced a further complication in my denial of sex differences by insisting I stop running around in public without a shirt. I stared hard at the boys' chests, cool and free in the sun; mine no longer looked the same. From then on I wore an undershirt as well as blouse or tee shirt, began to hunch my shoulders, continued to beat the boys in fights or races, continued to try to believe there were no differences, but when my conviction waned or reality impinged, I was, for a very long time, angry, that this was the way it was.

Although my remembered images of the shack are always bright with summer sun, we did spend Thanksgivings and winter weekends there as well, and then the grey waves beat up the beach, inexorably chewing at the rocks' thin snow cover until all lay nude and abject under the vanquisher's retreat. We walked along the beach at low tide, around the Point as far as Dollarton pier then back again, our feet growing numb in cold gumboots, but this discomfort ignored in the delights a winter sea threw up: seaweed of course, brown kelp, green sea lettuce, dark purplish dulse, and mixed with this glass floats from Japan, old fish net, corroded boom chain, rubber boots and summer sneakers, things from houses and wrecked boats—red and yellow chair backs, mugs, plates, shirts, unidentifiable metal pieces, rusting stoves and dishpans.

On these beachcombing expeditions we saw the permanent denizens of Dollarton, a private group of people who shunned the summer   141 residents. One man and woman we met quite regularly, at first only risking a smile above our acquisitions: a glass float, gnarled driftwood, or chairback; and then, later, stopping to talk. The man wore a red and black tartan mackinaw and the woman a faded green knit hat. They lived, we thought, in the shack with window box geraniums – the only window box on the beach. They were friendly; the woman and my mother talked, the man smiled at me, but I always walked away, continuing our search if we had just set out or heading home if we were done, for the man had a moustache like my uncles.

After that I seemed to see them everywhere, singly or together, as with the selective perception of learning a new word which then jumps into the air from every page or conversation.

As well as a favourite tree, I had a favourite rock, one of two left behind on the beach by a retreating glacier. It was about five feet high with handholds and a gentle upwards slope. The tide reached it first and I frequently sat until the rock was an island and water had inched up its barnacle skirt, sat looking across the Inlet until the water behind me had climbed as far up the beach as I could jump.

The other rock, farther to the west and from the water, was nearly seven feet high with steeper and smoother sides. A taller, older company child had claimed it as her rock and truly it was, for I could not scale it without help and that was only grudgingly and occasionally forthcoming.

Every few months when she was not around I attempted to climb the rock; one day, cold and raw in the fall or spring, the man was suddenly there. He said, "shall I give you a leg up?" and held out his hands cupped together. I must have been concentrating on my scrabbling failures for I had not heard him approach and I jumped with shock and fear. The rock hid both of us from sight of the shack and there was no one else on the beach. I wanted to run away but I would have had to dash by him and risk his grabbing me; more than that, I would have had to manifest my fear and I knew somehow, as with my uncles' kisses, that to let the enemy know my fear would increase its power over me. Still, I could neither let him touch me nor accept his help, and silently I shook my head and with a gargantuan struggle made easier from the force of fear, I gained a previously unnoticed toehold and threw myself on top of the rock.

From there I could see the green shack, smoke from the chimney, a corner of BIDEAWEE behind, could look down on my old favourite rock and the man. He still stood there, smiling. He said, "good for you," as if he understood, and I smiled back, embarrassed in case he understood it all.

FRANCES DUNCAN was born in 1942 in Vancouver, her home for most of her life. After receiving her M.A. from the University of British Columbia in 1963 she worked for ten years as a clinical psychologist. She began writing in 1973, and has published three juvenile novels: Cariboo Runaway *(1976),* Kap-Sung Ferris *(1977), and* The Toothpaste Genie *(1981). Her adult fiction includes the novels* Dragonhunt *(1981) and* Finding Home *(1982) and many short stories in* Room of One's Own, the Canadian Fiction Magazine, *and other periodicals. Duncan has described the genesis of "Was That Malcolm Lowry?" as "a conversation with some local writers. The topic, Malcolm Lowry's influence on the West Coast literary scene, soon degenerated into 'who had known Lowry,' and except for one writer who took pride in never having met the man, it seemed everyone else had had some personal contact with him — in short, had a Lowry story. At first I joined the writer who'd never met Lowry, but as the talk centered more and more on Dollarton in the forties and early fifties my memories were triggered.... This story is the result of that conversation. The result of this story is that I will never again trust a fiction writer's autobiography. I remain convinced that the man who wanted to help me on to the rock was Lowry"* (Room of One's Own 6, no. 3 [1981], pp. 80–81).

BROKEN TEETH

SKY LEE

It was kind of spring. I stepped off the bus on my way home. I mean my mother's house on east first avenue, just off the freeway. Actually I don't live there. I don't feel a part of it anymore. I didn't grow up in the cold composure that lives there now. I had other memories, sold off and left behind in a pulp mill town.

I have qualms about going home to my mother's house. My mother and a confrontation still lingers there behind a huge wood burning stove of long ago. Though nowadays, she stuffs a shiny new electric range with aluminum foil, and she covers the oventimer with clear saran-wrap.

But my mother could intimidate me. "Cock! Day after day. What do you do all the time that you can't even come home, eh?"

How could I even begin to tell my mother about my other life outside of her house. In fact, I always marched up those shaky pink backstairs too quickly, with the secret hope that maybe my mother would not be home. Thus, my token home visit would be duly recorded and in turn, reported to her. But by then, I would be sure to be gone. I know she would repeat the same lines over again, but not in my face.

When I reached the top of the stairs I banged and clattered on the screen door. It was locked securely. I peered through the netting and the glass, searching beyond the lace curtains for a responsive shadow within. I saw movement and immediately backed away. My eyes dropped to the welcome mat under my feet. Beside the mat, I saw the burnt ends of red incense sticks stuck in the smaller half of a small potato. Some ashes dusted the puddle of rain water that it sat in. The lace curtains lifted and I felt my mother's eyes stare at me. I wondered what special occasion I had missed. All Souls' Day? A Moon Celebration? Maybe the Flower Festival or an Ancestral Birthday. Who knows—maybe even Chinese New Year. I listened to each lock unfasten. The door opened, letting out the cat and her words, "So it's you. After so long, you finally decide to come home." She wanted con-

This story was published in the West Coast Review *in 1981.*

frontation. "Cock! Day after day, what have you been up to that you don't even come home, huh?"

"Ah Ma." I was never my mother's match. Already sagging I repeated dully, "Nothing much." Her eyes bore in. Mine lingered over my task of neatly placing my shoes on the pieces of cardboard boxes she had neatly cut up with a dull breadknife, to protect the linoleum.

"Any letters come for me?"

"None."

She kept a penetrating glare on me. Suddenly she accused, "Your grandfather died last week."

I was still at the door. But I had never met my grandfather – her father. He lived in Hong Kong. And I was born here. So why accuse me, mother? Yet, her guilt-ridden blow struck with the desired effect. This man died. This man was supposed to mean something to me. And I didn't even know. I didn't know because I was local born. Because I had moved out. Because I didn't come home to see her. In fact, I still didn't know. But I knew all the implications behind my mother's blunt remark. They flew through the air and imbedded themselves deep in my skin. I knew these all my life.

Yet I claimed innocence, "Is that so?"

Looking up at her I noticed a little crocheted flower and a little green ferntip bobby-pinned to black hair. Ornate reading glasses perched on her nose at an acute angle. She softened. I relaxed. My mother was used to my aloofness by now. And that was all the response she would see from me.

"Drink tea?"

"Sure." I sat down at the bright yellow dinette, on a matching chair. There were tiny gold flecks in the arborite surface.

My mother put a thick ceramic cup in front of me, coloured like creamed coffee, and it had the word "Stafford" stamped diagonally across its face. Because I was left-handed, the Stafford sign always faced me instead of out when I drank. Years ago, these Stafford stamped dishes were all the western dishes my parents owned besides the Chinese rice-bowls and soup spoons painted with wobbly gold fringes and awkward figures. I probably learnt to read with the Stafford stamp. My mother said that my father brought them home from the Arlington Hotel where he worked when it changed ownership and name. However, my father said he stole them – one piece at a time, each night when the boss was counting money at the cash register.

"Yep. The old fogey's dead, I guess." My mother was resteaming some home-made buns in a warped aluminum pot with a burnt black bottom. It danced loudly on the burner as the water inside boiled. I told her I didn't want any if they were filled with sugar and coconut. Pork was O.K. though.

"Ah. But he was my father after all. And your grandfather. How old 145 was he anyways?" She counted on her fingers. "Eighty-nine? He was eighty-nine last November. That's long enough. Your auntie wrote a letter and she said that he had sickened fast, then died fast."

"What did he die from?" I asked.

She threw me a look of disgust. "Eat it, I tell you! It's not the coconut and sugar kind."

"But it is so!" I complained.

"Well then, give it to me!" She prodded another steamy bun with her long fingers. "O.K. This one is pork."

But it wasn't. I ate it anyways. Across the kitchen, I noticed some plastic flowers which my mother had washed, clinging together and dripping on a rubber mat beside the sink. They looked cold and seemed to shiver in the vague grey light under the window. Splashed with colour, they tended to make me think that they were real. But I should have known better as my mother talked on and on about a sense of duty. A daughter's duty to her father; something that was foreign to my generation.

"Nothing is valued anymore. Nothing is cared for." she said. She softened. "Still, I am only just a daughter."

"Mother," I said, "why are you still buying those cheap plastic flowers?"

"What do you know . . . in the old days . . . the bullying. Back then, women were detested," she hissed, "like animals." Her hands tightened over the fine filigree border of roses around her teacup. "Do you know?"

I said, "They look so gaudy. And you've already got so many, mom."

"You think it was all stories back in those days, but it was very real. . . ."

"They don't look real to me at all." I was annoyed.

"I was eight years old. I was a little girl in the village then. And it was a bright sunny day when the air was fresh and full of wonderful scents. I was very happy. We were on our way to the market to shop—my family and I walked, my father and mother and little brother between them. He was clasping onto their hands, and sometimes they had to drag him. Such a hot day in spring. And the road became so dusty as we approached town.

Everytime we go to town, we always dropped in at third uncle's uncle's house. And who could have known after walking all that way, and climbing up all those steep stairs that they would not even stay to drink tea and gossip with the aunties.

As soon as we came in, my cousin ran up to me and offered to show me new kittens born last night. Excited, he said that the old mother cat had died in her labour. And now, more than likely, her wet little rats of children would not survive long after her. In fact, even as I peered into the dark corner of the back kitchen, there was already a limp, still bundle of fur in the quivering mass. Soon I left.

When I came back into the sitting room, it was deserted. They had gone on without me. Suddenly I heard my mother call shrilly at the top of her voice from the courtyard below. 'You crazy... come out here!' Her voice in the distance angry. 'We can't wait out here half a day for her while she sneaks off whenever she pleases.' My old man kept swearing softly to himself, staring at the hard ground. The thought of keeping him waiting out there on the street in the hot sun frightened me dearly. I thought to hurry.

From the top of the narrow shaky stairwell, I only had eyes for them outside. My father's red thunderous face sweating under the white glare of the street; and my mother with a flat expression, fanning him. Near the bottom of the stairs, my little brother was playing. And right in the middle of the second step down, my damned cousin had dropped an orange peel or something. Of course, I slipped on it and started falling headlong. What a giddy sensation that was! I jerked back but I still came face first, piling down onto my brother. I was knocked senseless. The jolt almost blackened me out; my head was reeling with pain and shock. I was so sick I retched when I picked myself out of the dust.

Then I saw my father – and he was a big man – roaring towards me in a tower of rage. Screaming, he was so furious I thought that his face was going to burst open like a melon. 'Damned bitch! Knock over my son, willya. I'll show you.' And my mother. She was shrieking all over the county. 'Sai-la! Sai-la! We're done for. She's killed my son.'

I knew my old man would beat me to death if he caught me in his fury. But I just sat there, crumpled. Well, he rushed up to me and stuck me such a blow across my cheek with his clenched fist. Even then, I was too much in pain to even feel it. He grabbed my blouse and dragged me onto my feet. I remember drops of blood soaking into the clean cotton, and spotting the dust. His hand raised to strike again.

This time, by instinct only, I tore myself away like a crazed cat and lunged into the store-room. I couldn't see through the tears and the turmoil; just threw myself behind the firewood and hid. I didn't know how long I hid there, but my nose and mouth was bleeding like a flood. There was blood all over me – hands, lap, smeared all over the water-vats I was sobbing on. Outside, my little brother was yelping loudly; everyone cooing and exclaiming all at the same time. My face was torn and so swollen I could hardly breathe. But worst of all, I had broken and chipped all my front teeth. Some of them just dangled off my shredded gums.

I had just finished growing them. And oh, the pain those broken teeth caused me, for years afterwards! And still my father cursed me. So I crept further into the wood pile. Later on, when my mother finally rummaged me out of there, her mouth dropped open to see me so bloodied. She said, 'My goodness, look at this thing. She's broken all of her teeth.' And to this day, the old bitch still recalls that incident. From time to time, she tells me about it. But I have never forgotten!"

The afternoon light had turned slaty and the leftover tea had grown cold. The re-steamed buns had shrivelled up and hardened again. I sat on my yellow chrome chair, completely dumbfounded. Yet something in my mother's eyes gleamed as she watched me for a response. So for her satisfaction, I wrinkled up my nose and blurted a polite "yech" out. And that was all the response she would see from me. Still, she seemed almost exulted when she whisked her rose teacup and my thick Stafford mug away.

"You know those teeth. They slowly rotted and abcessed. They didn't give me one moment's peace until I came to Canada and got them all pulled out by a dentist here. But I was thirty-four by then. In the old days, there weren't any real dentists in China, you know. Not like here now. People then, they used to carve a set of false teeth out of wood for their old people."

Standing at the sink, she shook out the last of the water from the eternal plastic blooms and stuck them one by one into a glass vase.

"Mom, didn't you say that you wanted me to cut your hair?" I asked.

"Hmm. It is beginning to look like a spider's web, isn't it?" She swung her head from side to side, peering into her reflection on the kettle. "Well, if you want to, may as well have it done now." Then she went on about having much to do to prepare a feast for my grandfather. And about burning some more incense. "Besides," she added, "if you don't do it now, who knows when you'll be back again."

My mother sat in the middle of the kitchen, wrapped in a gingham tent pinned around her neck with a clothes peg while I stood behind her and clipped and snipped. She counted on her fingers. "Let's see, your auntie's letter took about a week in coming.... Anyways, I guess it doesn't matter when we pay obeisance. And I'll have to go shopping down in Chinatown. How about Sunday then. A big dinner on Sunday. Mind you—you remember to come back on Sunday to eat and pay your respects then."

SKY LEE was born in Port Alberni in 1952 and since 1967, she has lived in Vancouver, where she now works as a nurse and as a volunteer with the Chinese Cultural Centre. A graphic artist as well as a writer, she holds a B.F.A. from the University of British Columbia. She worked with Makara, the now discontinued feminist magazine, as a layout artist, and illustrated Paul Yee's children's book, Teach Me to Fly, Skyfighter! *(1983). Her stories and graphics have appeared in various Canadian and American little magazines.*

A NICE COLD BEER

KEVIN ROBERTS

So how's the old dear, Pete? Wacker put Pete's bags down on the living-room floor. They were plastered with Quantas Kangaroos.

She's okay. Wonders why you never write. Pete walked over to the Marantz stereo, fiddled with the levers. Jeez, Wack, where'd you get the money for this?

Still into the bingo, is she? Wacker asked.

Yeah. Bangs on down the RSL Hall three nights a week. Jeez. This colour or black and white? Must be a 26-inch screen.

It's colour. How's the old dear's ticker? Wacker leaned his lanky form back in a chair.

Still got high blood pressure. Pete picked up a small black box. Why the hell haven't you written to her? Jeez. Does this change stations automatically?

Yeah. Wacker got up and pressed the buttons for Pete. The old man still trainer for the Ramblers?

Yeah. Jeez, you got 10 channels. He figures he's better than old Doc. Noble now. You know South went Premiers this year. Jeez, Wack, the old man still says you would have made league. How come you gave up on footy?

Ah. I dunno. Wacker shifted in his chair.

Knuckle leaned around the door. A big dragon tatoo writhed on his forearm. A shock of black hair hung about his eyes.

Some bird on the phone for you, Wack.

Nah. Tell her I'm out.

Knuckle disappeared.

Jeez. Where'd you meet up with those blokes? Pete asked, they give me the creeps. Especially the Dong. Where'd he get that bloody great cut? Pete drew his forefinger across his nose.

Ah. They grow on ya, Wacker said. The old dear still got the canaries?

 This story was first published in Flash Harry and the Daughters of Divine Light (1982).

A NICE COLD BEER

Oh yeah. She says to tell you they're breeding faster than rabbits. Wacker laughed.

How come you never wrote us? Pete asked. The oldies're really worried about you.

Wacker got up. Never had time. You old enough for a beer?

Is that a bar? Jeez. Look at this. Pete whistled. Whole thing just opens up, eh? Well, hell. A fridge and all.

Here, Wacker handed Pete a cold beer, the old man still working for Whippers?

Oh yeah, Pete laughed, they tried to get him to be foreman. Y'know what he said? Said he was too old to start screwing his mates, said he'd Kinghit young Whipper if he ever mentioned it again. Young Whipper, he backs off, says he never was game to tackle Wacker Junior, let alone Wacker Senior. The old man near pissed himself laughing.

Wacker shook his head slowly.

Sally Blair still around? Wacker asked.

No. She married young Bill Whipper. Lucky she was, they say. What with a kid and all.

Wacker got up. How's the kid?

She's okay.

Pete looked at his brother. Wacker's face was emotionless.

We don't see her much anymore now. With Sally married. I got a photo here, look. She's nearly six now. Hey, Wack. She's alright. This is a great place you got here. Hey, Wack. What're you looking at?

Just the lights.

Pete joined his brother at the window. So that's Vancouver. Jeez. It's pretty.

That's the big smoke Pete. Here's the photo.

No, Wack, you keep it. Wacker put the photo in his wallet.

The Dong poked his scarred face through the door.

Phone call for you, Wacker.

Tell 'em I'm not in.

It's Kenny.

Okay, Dong. Here, Pete. Have a look at these. Wacker handed him a pile of Hustler magazines. Have another beer. I'll be back in a sec. I'll keep this photo.

Okay. Jeez. Look at this one. We can't get these in W.A.

You like that beaver, eh Pete? smiled the Dong, lot of that in this town.

Yeah? Hey Dong? Did you ever play footy?

Hah, said the Dong. He held his beer can up high and let the last few drops of beer trickle into his open mouth. I never had time for outdoor sports.

You know old Wack there, he was the best junior full forward in the W.A. Country Carnival.

Yeah? The Dong walked to the bar. Want another beer, Pete?

Knuckle came in. Wacker says it's on tonight.

What's on? asked Pete, putting down the magazine.

Nothin much. Just gonna have a few beers, said the Dong, leaning on the bar.

Wacker came into the livingroom. Listen Pete. Something came up. We're going out for a bit. Why don't you watch T.V. and have a beer. I'll be back in a couple of shakes.

Jeez no. I don't want to stay home, Wack. Jeez, I've only seen you for a couple of hours. I'll come along.

Nah, said the Wacker, I'll take you out on the town tomorrer night. I gotta meet someone.

What's wrong with tonight?

Nah. You wouldn't want to go to this place. It's a dive.

That's alright. I'm in. Pete said flatly.

Jesus Christ. You always were a little pain in the arse.

They stared at each other for a second. Wacker turned away.

Ah. Let him come, said the Dong.

Yeah.... she'll be apples, Wack, added Knuckle.

Wacker turned to his young brother. Listen if we take you tonight, Wacker said, you'll have to do exactly what I tell you. I don't want you getting hurt.

Pete stood up.

Sit down, Pete, said Wacker, I'm not trying to push you around. It's a different world over here. It's just that you're straight off the boat. Canadian pubs are a lot different from Aussie pubs. They put the boots and knives in real quick. Okay?

Oh yeah. Pete sprawled on the chesterfield. If this new world of yours is so terrible why do you hang around in it?

I dunno, mused Wacker, I just fell into it. Y'know the big house here, and the bar. It's like you're not home and there aren't any of the old rules.

You said you were going around the world, Pete said, but you've been in Vancouver for five years! We were all waiting for you to come home.

Yeah, I know, Wacker shifted his big frame uncomfortably in the chair. It's like. When you make a break you feel free. For a while. Then you get trapped again. He did up a button on his red-checked shirt.

Ah, it's not so bad, said the Dong. Lotsa beer, lotsa nurses. Casual like! Don't have to work much.

Too right, said Knuckle. Broke me bloody back in bloody Adelaide. Bricklaying. Made stuff all. Here you just put in a coupla days slack arsing and you got it bloody made.

Sounds like bludging to me, said Pete.

Ah, said Wacker impatiently, you think you know it all.

No I don't, said Pete, but I've gotta get the plane to London in three days. I want to look around.

Look at you though, Wacker said, never could fight yer way out of a paper bag.

Pete was silent. Wacker's rawboned six-foot-four-inch form was topped by a sandy-haired, light-bearded face, the nose battered, big ears and deep set blue eyes. Pete was smaller, willowy, but with the same sandy hair and blue eyes.

We oughta leave the little bastard home, Wacker snorted, draining his beer can.

Nah. We'll be alright, said the Dong.

Yeah, let him come, said Knuckle, pulling the tab on a Molson as if it were a hand grenade. Let's have one for the ditch.

Ah, said Wacker in disgust, let's get going. He stormed out the back door.

Vancouver lay across the bay, sparkling lights and action. Pete felt very excited. That's the big smoke alright, Wack, he said loudly.

They all got into the Dong Special.

Jeez, said Pete, looking around from the back seat, what kind of car is this?

Dong Special! snorted Wacker.

Yeah. Modified Jensen Interceptor, said the Dong, wheeling onto the bridge.

Goes like hell, growled Knuckle, pulling the tab on a Molsons.

Wow! You guys are doing pretty well for wharfies, Pete said in admiration, I hear these canvas hoods leak, though.

What the stuff'd you know! snarled Wacker.

Nah, said the Dong slipping neatly between a semi and VW van, you gotta treat 'em with special stuff.

That's what I like, said Knuckle, special stuff.

Whoops! Ratbag Canuck! The Dong shouted at an orange Mazda trying to turn into his lane. He took a squealing illegal left turn onto East Hastings.

Doesn't look too impressive, said Pete, when they pulled up in the parking lot opposite the Grand Hotel.

Nah, said Knuckle, they got a stripper gets wild sometimes. That's all.

Y're not old enough, laughed Wacker, she'd squeeze you dry as a lemon.

The Dong and Knuckle cackled.

Good one, laughed the Dong.

Let's sit over here, said Wacker, close to the door.

No way, said Pete, we're too far away. Can't see anything.

Wacker and the others sat down in a corner next to the two big swing doors. Pete followed them, In the centre of the dim beer parlour was a plush red dias with ropes like a boxing ring. Huge heads of football and hockey players were painted on the walls.

Pretty gross, observed Pete. Christ, there's no windows!

Don't want nobody seeing what you're up to, said Knuckle.

Yeah. Canucks ain't in favour of booze, said Wacker.

Bit like being inside, added the Dong.

Except they don't have no beer there, said Knuckle.

Inside of what? asked Pete.

Inside your head, dopey, snapped Wacker.

Good one, laughed the Dong.

A group of bikers in leather jackets and shades drank with their black leather boots up on the tables.

What a bunch of no-hopers, said Wacker.

A big sway-bellied waiter with a florid, sweating face flopped four beers at their table.

When's the show? asked Pete.

The waiter pulled two dollars from a bunch hooked between his fingers and two quarters from his tin tray.

Ten minutes, he growled.

Thanks, said Pete, have a beer yourself.

The waiter picked up the two quarters and left without a word.

Not too friendly, is he, said Pete.

Nah. These places are real downers, said Wacker gloomily.

Well, said the Dong, here's looking up your kilt.

Yeah, added Knuckle, with a cold stethoscope.

Pete took a big gulp.

Jesus, Pete gasped, the beer's off!

Terrible horsepiss, isn't it, said Wacker.

Don't know why I bother, said the Dong.

Better than the waiter, said Knuckles. Hey Pete, hold your hand up like a man dying of thirst. Four fingers. You got it.

Hey Wacker, said the Dong, Pete gonna hang around for awhile?

Nah, said Wacker. He's gonna be a biologist. He's going to England Friday. Some fancy college. Commonwealth Scholarship. I'm proud of you Pete.

Don't know that I will, Pete retorted, maybe'll try longshoring with you blokes.

Ah, longshoring's boring bullshit, said Knuckle.

I don't know, said Pete, you fellows got a pretty good life. Big house. Fancy car.

Nah. Wacker's right, said the Dong. Yeah, we have lotsa parties, root a few birds, drink a lotta piss, but this longshoring's dead-head bullshit.

Drives a man to drink, added Knuckle as a fresh batch of four beers arrived.

Nah, serious, Pete. Wacker leaned forward and spoke quietly. The old man and me, we're just strong backs and big muscles, mainly in our heads. I get into trouble wherever I go, or hurt someone. Like Sally and the kid. But you got some brains. I never had. That scholarship. You could be someone.

You could've made league! exclaimed Pete.

Ah. That was... nothing. Don't you see? Hanging around here is all I can do. And it's trouble too. I done some stuff I'm not too proud of.

Like what? asked Pete.

Well, we got into dealing a bit, Wacker said.

Drugs you mean, Pete whispered excitedly.

Just for our friends. Just a bit of easy money. Coke and grass. Trouble is you can't back out that easy once you're in. Kinda sucks you into it. All the excitement.

Jesus, said Pete, that's where your money comes from

Keep your trap shut about it! Wacker turned to the others. Nothing much to show for five years in Canada. Eh, Knuckle?

A few notches on the old gun, said Knuckle.

Yeah. A few new wrinkles in the old trouser snake, added the Dong.

You two jokers are bad news, laughed Wacker, you're corrupting me baby brother. Nah, Pete's going to university.

Lotsa crack in them places, I'm told, said the Dong.

Ah forget it, said Wacker, disgusted, draining his beer glass.

Watch it, said Knuckle. One of them biker's coming over.

A skinny biker with a thin black beard and a shiny black leather waistcoat open on a hairy chest staggered up to their table.

G'day Kenny, said Wacker.

Kenny put out one tattooed arm and took Pete's beer, lifted it up, drained it, and slapped it down on the green cloth table.

He looked around at the four young men.

Just as well, said Knuckle.

Yeah, added the Dong, I wouldn't want to drink that.

Nah. Not after we all pissed in it, said Wacker.

The lights went out except for a spotlight on the red plush stage. The biker dropped a packet on the table. The Dong slipped it into his denim jacket.

You gonna stand there and block the view? Knuckle growled.

I hate bloody Aussies! yelled the biker. He turned and left.

Bit of a racist, ain't he? queried the Dong.

Christ. That was tense, said Pete, I didn't know what to do.

Nothing to it, Wacker said tiredly.

A blonde woman in a long red cape and silver lame dress climbed through the ropes. She held her hands above her head like a boxer and the audience whistled and yelled. She pranced on high heels to disco music, shedding clothes slowly.

She's older than me mother, said Knuckle.

Bragging again? said the Dong.

The stripper wiggled half-naked out of her black underwear.

The lights went off and a small spot roamed the tables. It stopped on Pete.

No way, said Pete, not for me.

G'wan, said Knuckle, she won't bite.

The light moved on, settled on the skinny black-bearded biker. He leapt up and ran towards the stage to cheers and hoots.

He's gone apeshit, observed the Dong.

In the dim light they saw the biker fall through the ropes and grab the stripper. She swore and kicked him in the head. Burly barmen ran to the stage. The bikers screamed and charged the barmen. Someone smashed the spotlight.

Let's go! said Wacker urgently.

Yeah, said the Dong.

They got up and felt their way towards the red exit lights. A yelling mob surged about them. The main lights went up and Pete stood transfixed. The whole beer parlour was one huge knot of tangled figures. A table flew through the air. Glasses crashed and voices cursed and yelled. Punches drove in the air, and men wrestled on the floor.

Wacker grabbed Pete's arm. C'mon, let's go! he said urgently.

Pete moved a few steps and stood by the door. His hand grasped a half-empty beer glass. He drank it. A high-pitched scream froze in the air. Pete walked outside. It was strangely quiet on the street. Pete stopped at the corner of the parking lot to urinate.

Wacker yelled from the Dong Special.

Hurry up, you stupid bugger!

Three figures ran past Pete. In the streetlight he saw one had a bloody gash on his head. They raced through the parking lot and into an alley beside it.

Pete walked, half-dazed, to the Dong Special, opened the front door and got in. At the same instant, a pair of boots came crashing through the canvas back and men hammered at the doors and windows.

Get the fucker with the knife! a voice yelled.

Drop it, Dong! roared Wacker, punching at the belly of the body poking through the back canvas.

The Dong Special took off, bodies flying and falling off and before it, the legs disappearing out the back window. The Dong Special skidded and swerved out of the lot onto the street and away.

Flatten 'er, Dong, yelled Wacker, looking back, they'll be after us.

I reckon some poor bastard got stabbed, said Knuckle tensely.

Reckon it was Kenny?

Dunno, said Wacker. You got the stuff?

Yeah.

Why'd they think it was us? asked Pete. His whole body was trembling slightly.

Don't be a stupid prick! spat the Dong, wheeling in and out of traffic.

Yeah, you dumb shit, growled Knuckle, you nearly got us all beaten to ratshit.

Pete was silent.

The Dong Special sped down Hastings and stopped at a red light.

Jeez, I think they're onto us, said Knuckle, there's a big black Ford trying to sneak up alongside.

Bugger the light! cried Wacker.

The Dong Special leaped across the intersection followed by the Ford.

Get down! yelled Knuckle.

Wacker shoved Pete's head down and fell back onto the floor. The Dong wheeled the car squealing, about and around, doused the lights and put his foot flat to the floor. The Dong Special sped in darkness down three blocks, doubled back, careened in and out of side streets and roared across the Bridge.

I think we're clear, said Knuckle. We got a few debts to pay back, though.

The Dong Special whipped about a few corners and was home.

Pete climbed out of the car.

Wacker heaved himself forward, out of the car, grabbed Pete, and belted him with a round arm swing up against the car.

Look! said Wacker, holding Pete by his collar. You want to play with the big boys. Look here! Right here. Put your stupid damn hand right here!

Pete put out his hand. There on the front passenger side of the windscreen, in a direct line from the torn canvas at the back, was a tiny bullet hole.

Pack your bag, said Wacker. Get out of here! Get out of my life.

Jeez, Wack. I'm sorry.

Get your bags.

Pete walked past him into the house. In the dark no one could see the expression on Wacker's face.

Who'd like a nice cold beer? asked Knuckle, squatting down to pull the tabs on four Molsons.

KEVIN ROBERTS was born in 1942 in Adelaide, South Australia, and came to Canada in 1965. After a brief stint of teaching in Dawson Creek and Quesnel, he lived in Vancouver while attending Simon Fraser University, receiving his M.A. in 1968. In 1969, he joined the faculty of the newly-opened Malaspina College in Nanaimo, where he continues to live and work. He has travelled extensively in Europe, and in 1984 spent five months as writer-in-residence at Wattle Park College in Adelaide. Roberts has published eight books of poetry, including Cariboo Fishing Notes *(1973),* S'Ney'Mos *(1980), and* Nanoose Bay Suite *(1984), several plays, and a book of stories,* Flash Harry and the Daughters of Divine Light *(1982), where "A Nice Cold Beer" first appeared.*

THE ANIMALS
IN THEIR ELEMENTS

CYNTHIA FLOOD

When Harry's parents "couldn't manage" their big house any more, put plumbing in an awkward closet off the front hall and a bed in the diningroom and never went upstairs again, Shirley had been contemptuous.

Thirty years later she cried in terror, "And I've come to that now, in my house! I won't live on one floor like a rat!" Harry was not sure that rats lived so; immediately he saw in mind his arcing birds; but his brother George, Shirley's husband, got out the Yellow Pages. Workmen came. Chairborne, Shirley rose in electrified stateliness from the first floor of her home to the second, descended.

The strong chair hummed for the twelve years till Shirley died.

The old brothers took to piling things on it that needed to go upstairs or down. Princess the cat liked snoozing there; perhaps the leather seat smelled good? But if a hand reached for the switch she jumped off. George got paler, less there, after Shirley died, and then he died too.

Harry did not use the chair at all now. The deep resonant thrumming felt too big in the silent house.

In time, in time a brief rest at the half-landing wasn't enough when Harry went upstairs. His heartbeat's volume made him shrink; would the creature beat right through the chestwall, pulse out into his hands? He stood on the stairs and waited for quiet. Sometimes the mice skittered and squeaked companionably under one particular tread, and Harry smiled. The veins at his wrists resembled the guywires of the phone pole in the backyard (the birds wound their claws round the strands so neatly), but surely his thin arms did not need so much support? Perhaps he was getting hollow-boned like the birds, for the bathroom scales George had bought forty years before had never given trouble and they said that there was, each Monday, a little less of him.

This story is published here for the first time.

Bird-bones. Thin as grass, they'd have to be. The radio once said that Indians used them as — flutes? Birds ate a lot. Harry ate as always. The green beans were frozen now, not canned, the cottage-roll shrink-wrapped in plastic, but cornflakes and baloney, fishsticks and ketchup, boiled eggs and canned peaches were the same. Sometimes when Harry rose from the table, sometimes when he was on the toilet, a blurry dizziness vibrated in his head. Number two was all right. It came only while he was upstairs, near the bathroom. Number one became more and more insistent during the day. When he finally could not struggle up the stairs more than once daily, he used the kitchen sink. Mother, Shirley would have been appalled. Princess patted curiously at the yellow stream. Harry scrubbed the sink hard after.

Cat and birds. No matter what hours Harry guarded the maple and old walnut and the swallows' place under the porch eaves, no matter that Princess's old legs were stiff and her eyes smeary, each spring at least one nestling died the death of the teeth. When Harry cast seeds and crumbs over the grass, Princess mewed so loudly behind the diningroom window that the birds would not come, and if Harry opened the door even a slit she leapt out hissing into the tall tangles of green. In the evenings Harry held her on his lap, while the radio talked and sang behind his shoulder, and he told her over and over that she didn't need to do that. Didn't he give her Puss'N'Boots, and milk, and cat-chow, every day? Didn't she even leave food uneaten sometimes, such a terrible waste? His fingers smoothed over and over the cats' aches; she rasped a purr, nosed his chill hand, put her paw on his veiny wrist. Next day, the same — but the crumbs and seeds were safely gone.

Sometimes slugs came overnight, or after rain. They came so fast that perhaps they grew right up through the wet dirt? Yet when Harry watched them journeying they hardly moved.

And Harry told Princess how beautiful the birds were, beautiful, beautiful, though the word didn't show how they darted, swooped, turned, spiralled down. The birds did their business in the air, on the wing. A little squirt and a splat on the window or porch rail — all done. Most of all Harry could not find how to tell Princess about when a bird landed nearby and looked at him. When that happened the rest of the day was different. Oh, their eyes. The pulsing feathers on the throat, the legs sheathed in tiny scales — but mostly the eyes.

Harry also worried about how Shirley and George had worked so much around the house. How had they found so much to do? After he had swept hall and kitchen, wiped counters, run the carpet sweeper, and used Dutch cleanser on the plumbing he could not think of anything more. He felt that the house did not look as it had. But perhaps Shirley had cleaned the rooms that were not used? Why? He had seldom entered Shirley and George's room, never since his brother's death; there was no reason to go into the spare room where Shirley had done the mending, none to struggle up the final staircase to the narrow black attic. Once he had gone downcellar with the man from Hydro to check the furnace. Beautiful moths there, giant spiders with markings all freckled like maple walnut icecream. Maybe Shirley had done things in those rooms. That was like how she and George used to talk about what they called old times. Jobs, visits, parents, occasions. Harry did not see why. His job had only been the place he was in when he was away from home, first Mother's and then Shirley and George's. Years in the basement stockroom, cartons and files; in forty-three years, not a day sick; she would have been proud, and liked the watch he got. And George had always been handy around the house, painted, contrived, right to the end. Harry loved birds.

Shirley had also made lists for George to take to the grocery, the laundry. Harry knew the Sunshine Market's layout by heart, and picked up his supplies weekly in the same orderly route round the store. Sometimes there was a confusing new product on the shelf. Then he went to the back and found old Mr. Gilbert, who gave sharp instructions to a child or grandchild. Mrs. Chang also had grandchildren, possibly greatgrandchildren, for with these people it was hard to tell age. As polite as she, they gave and received his laundry parcels with broad smiles he liked. Once he felt faint there. They sat him on a spindly chair and gave him strange tea. Mrs. Chang laughed and talked a great deal in Chinese when he took a second cup. He needed no list there either.

Time's altering puzzled Harry most. Waking just before the old Westclox went off at seven-thirty, he enjoyed Princess's warmth by his feet, or watched her crouching at the baseboards listening to the life within the walls; she lashed her tail and clicked her teeth, t-t-t-t. Harry lay in his high bed looking out over the back yard, and thought of the nests in the trees. Did birds have paths, roads in the air? There was a path worn on the downstairs hall carpeting, and threads stuck up like whiskers. Now somehow it was half-past eight.

Bath. He feared that someday he might not be able to get out. Not daily might be all right? or to sponge on the mat before the sink? But since childhood there had been bath, every morning, not wastefully deep of course, but under, and sometimes the thought was almost felt in Harry that certain parts of his body welcomed that immersion. Then get dressed, go downstairs, let Princess out ("She's coming, birds!" from the back porch), have cornflakes and toast. The last of Shirley's home-made jams was sadly gone. Harry missed her baking too. Once he opened the cupboard where she had kept her flours and grains and powders, and met a great soft flutter of minute papery wings, beige and brown. He closed the door. Tea steeped while he ate. Strong enough to trot a mouse as Mother always said. Ten-thirty. How? Clean up after himself, always, and then, his tasks completed, he could watch the birds, from the front porch or the diningroom windowseat, depending on the weather, but scarcely had he got comfortable before the noon *O Canada!* went off downtown. Sometimes Harry was breathless with speed.

So he no longer attempted two errands in one afternoon. Fridays became Bank, and Tuesday Laundry. Sometimes there was Drugstore. His parents hadn't had much truck with doctors, Shirley had despised people who went to them, but Absorbine Jr. made Harry's arms feel less stiff temporarily and the Neo-Citran the radio said about was nice before bed. Often though there were unknown new salesclerks. The tellers at the bank kept changing too. And the mailmen – the old fellow had stopped coming a while after George died and they couldn't seem to settle on someone new. Right now there was even a girl. She had curly red hair and wore shorts sometimes. Every morning she noisily thrust his meagre mail through the slot and jumped back down the steps two at a time, and by then Harry'd made it to the front door; every morning they waved and smiled at each other. Harry hoped that she would not be reassigned. She seemed a long way away, down there on the sidewalk. Commercial Drive, where all his errands were, also seemed further away than before, and a great many people now walked very fast there.

One day at the bank the vibration visited his head. He feared he might have to leave and try again next day, or ask for help – there wasn't a spindly chair. Neither of these dreadfulnesses happened. He did not even have to ask to move ahead in the line. Pride got him home. Next day he slept through the Westclox. At almost nine, worried, ashamed, Princess figure-eighting and mewing about his legs, Harry got himself downstairs unbathed to let the cat out. The hallway stretched before him like a bone's black tube, dark and curving-down and terrible, and he was sucked headfirst into it while birds squawked and hit the air around his head.

Harry did not feel like talking. That was nothing new, although he'd liked to hear George and Shirley's voices going on together. Homelike. Here was not home. These unknowns were nurses and doctors. He didn't have anything to say to them, and he must just work hard, very hard, to get better. That was all. One young doctor, Jewish he must be from the nose, had dark bright eyes, and Harry liked his visits. Then there was a sandbox in which he must feel for letters, to match them with letter-shaped holes in a container. The sand felt silky but got under his nails. Harry worked hard; he got pretty good at the matching. Now an exercise book. C dash T, put a letter in the middle to make a word. Impossible. No such. Then, as when a bird lands on a rainy branch and the drops frill off the leaves on to those below, there was an infinitely small touch in his head and the letter A arrived. He smiled. The young doctor smiled too. Then Harry wept, pointed to the word and wept. Some time later a nurse came saying, "Dr. Levin says to tell you Princess is all right." Belief and incredulity nested together in his mind. No speech. Birds flew distantly over the parking lot beyond his plateglass window.

Some of the food was surprisingly familiar. Shirley had made this jelly, with bits of fruit suspended in it. Harry wished he knew how, and how to make his left leg work. He thought he was doing his best; nothing happened. At first young girls helped him walk to the bathroom. Of course he could not go, and finally a man came. People got him to move his limbs in a way he saw, but did not yet feel was rhythmic. In time, in time the leg felt more, though it was ponderous, dragging, with dry skin shaling off like scales under an invisible knife. Once, perhaps a dream? Mrs. Chang was there, grinning at the end of his bed with a paper bag. Later, fat pale buns on his bedtray.

Mr. Gilbert strangely drove him home, and on the back seat Princess was angry in a cat-carrier. Her paw stuck out of a hole. At home she washed and washed, then slept so deeply he was fearful.

Harry could not get up the stairs. He tried for a long time. Then the doorbell rang and there was a woman.

Eventually, after tears, Harry saw that he would have to. He would have to use the chair. Princess got on to his lap and did not move even when he pressed the switch, and he cried and loved her. The woman walked beside him up the stairs, talking.

Harry was fussed, but he got to the bathroom all right (Number Two at mid-day, he was all disordered), and then came back downstairs again. The woman came beside him, talking, and she came into the kitchen with him, talking, and she opened the refrigerator and frowned.

This woman came in the mornings. She helped him dress and get breakfast. She worked about the house, did errands, got lunch, and left. Then for two days running she didn't come at all. He was relieved and upset. Things were difficult. Then she came again. While she cleaned, he watched birds clustering on the phone line, so still and yet a millisecond from full flight. "Weekend" arrived suddenly in his mind. He smiled at her, and she talked and laughed and gestured.

Since Harry did not get out anymore to see Mr. Gilbert or Mrs. Chang, or their grandchildren, or the unknowns at the bank and drugstore, he enjoyed having this woman to look at, to hear. The first time he saw the mailgirl that was nice too, for she ran right up the steps and talked and smiled, with the woman there. The smooth skin on her legs shone when she ran down again. There was no rhythm in Harry's walk, just slow thud thud thud, but once he got to the back 163 porch in the afternoon he could stay there now. He could stay, and watch, and watch. Crowds of birds all suddenly flew into a tree, so it was full of movement and sounds and leaves, and then they all flew away together like blown blossoms. The lilacs had birds'-eyes of rain shining all over their purple fragrant cylinders. The grass in the yard, uncut for years, was rich in small living things, and the land-birds dove into it like cormorants into green sea. When it got dark he must go in and check the oven and the fridge, because she left supper-foods there and if she found them untouched next day her face got wrinkly and her voice hurt his ears. And after supper he and Princess hummed upstairs together in the dark; Harry had trouble with light switches.

Several times the woman got him to the front door and pointed down to a blue car. Grasping the doorframe, he resisted. Her voice got loud but he wouldn't, he didn't care if tears came. Mr. Gilbert and the mail-girl arrived, talked; Harry looked away, where branches swayed under the landing weight of a bird.

The woman began to make him exercise each day as in the hospital only more vigorously. She also gave him new things to eat. There was a brown bread with hard bits in it, a cheese much stronger than Velveeta, a plastic cup filled with a sour junket. His mouth rejected the tastes. When it was quite dark Harry put these foods in the garbage, his heart beating fast as he buried them as deeply as he could.

Once after so doing he went still angry up to bed. Lying in the nest, he realized that he did not have to stay there; the chair would take him down and bring him up again, and she wouldn't even know. So Harry took a blanket and went, laboriously, out into the late summer night on the back porch. She had trained sweetpeas up the old trellis there, and trimmed off the sharp points on the old wicker chairs. Harry sat, and breathed fragrance. A spider's web veiled the moon. Princess, enraptured, vanished into the dark; Harry called her for a while and then let go. He lay back, and sleep took him. Some shivering time near dawn he woke, achingly rigid and with a swollen bladder. His left leg felt like a bag of cement. He urinated over the railing and watched the pool sink into the earth. There was a slug's silver trail on the pathway, heading for the house; he heard the very first curoo of the day from a pigeon under the eaves; he saw Princess come pad-padding through the dewed grass. He was days recovering. The woman's face and voice did that. He knew he could never repeat the act.

Harry looked about his house then, and saw that its aspect was different. This woman, like Shirley, knew what to do. Windows shone. The mealmoths were gone from the kitchen cupboards, which he regretted, but he knew their going was proper. He could clearly see the pattern on the diningroom carpet. Magazines lay on the coffee-table in the livingroom. Harry did not look at them, but he remembered George and Shirley doing so. Sometimes the woman read them while she drank mid-morning coffee, and he liked to see that.

There came a magazine with a front-cover picture of happy birds pecking at a big ball that hung from a ribbon. The birds' eyes gleamed on the shiny paper. Harry showed her. She riffled through the pages and found a series of drawings.

"It's how to make a feedingball," she said, "suet and peanut butter and seeds. Birds love them."

"Can we make it for them?" he asked. She dropped the magazine.

His mother's old yellow bowl stood on the counter. The mixture gave off a thick oily smell as the woman measured and ladled and poured. The liquids and solids began to coagulate. Suddenly she said, "You too, Mr. Eldridge," and put his startled fingers into the slithery dripping sticky grit-pocked sludge with hers. No, he could not bear it—but as he moved his hand the mass gave, pleasingly, beneath his pressure. He began to squeeze and squeeze, her hands were there too, and gradually between them the thing tooks its form. Still Harry could scarcely wait to wash and wash his hands.

The woman hung the seedball where Princess's greatest imaginable leap could never reach, and then came days, days, days of birds. Harry's eyes overflowed with the gloss and bloom of feathers, the speckles and stripes, the way one iridescence in a moment became another. He watched, he loved, for hours.

Deeply grateful, Harry felt his heart swell gradually with a disturbing awareness. There were some days of confused discomfort. Then he knew that he must do something for the woman in return and he knew, immersed at once in fear, that he must leave his house and his birds and Princess, and get into that blue car.

Once, years before, when Shirley was rising on her chair, the folds of her skirt had lain so that Harry had to see past her knees, and movement came between his legs. If only he could be on her as she rose, in her, fitting like a fish in dark water to nose and wriggle—and then came hours and days of shame, huddled in his room or thankfully at work where he did not have to see Shirley or George and could cover up his bad thought. As then, Harry skulked. He fought his knowledge, grew sullen, ate less, resisted the exercises.

Then, leaning out his bedroom window, he saw how the birds dropped and soared suddenly, and with screams and squawks encircled one of their number and attacked with a loud throbbing beat-beat-beat of wings. Harry saw. He wrenched himself down the stairs on foot, and got the woman to the front door. Pointing to the blue car, he nodded.

There was to be a special morning. Yes, there was to be a special morning; he was not clear about when, though, and so woke several times to agitation.

Then, "These are for you," she said on arriving, and when he got the parcel open there were dark blue undershorts, only of thicker cloth and with a string to tie. Without stopping she took him away then, down the steep steps to the distant sidewalk and into the openmouthed car.

Not a long drive. A low building. Old people in wheelchairs, younger people pushing. Harry could walk. Inside came a strong smell that scraped his lungs. Here was a big room with benches and padlocked metal cabinets, and beyond an arch lay a great piece of rocking blue that shone with bursts of light like a pigeon's neck-feathers.

He was naked. Then he had the blue shorts on over his dry scaly legs. The tiles were nubbly under his cold feet. Then came a ramp into the water, warm, surprisingly like bath, but deepness was coming at him; not bath, and she would not let up, she was making him go farther in, and farther. He glanced down and saw his shimmering body angle away from where he had thought it was, and the air and water about him were vast trembling territories. She made him wrap his fingers round a rail. Suddenly the translucent blue took him up and his legs were somewhere out behind, turning, sliding, and everything under his bathing-suit floated free.

Draw right back now and see old dried bone Harry, his skinny shrunken limbs fluttering down there in his corner of the tilting blue, with the lights and the Muzak pouring over him. His homecare worker is by him, a comfortable middle-aged woman in a modestly-cut bathing-suit. He turns to look into her eyes and says, "I am flying. What is your name?"

CYNTHIA FLOOD was born in Toronto in 1940 and has lived in Vancouver since 1969. She has been active in the women's movement and in Native Education programmes, and now works as an English instructor at Vancouver Community College (Langara Campus). Her stories have appeared in many periodicals and anthologies, including Queen's Quarterly, Room of One's Own, Atlantis, Common Ground *(1980)*, *and* New:West Coast Fiction *(1984)*.